7/02

Rouse Up
O Young Men of the New Age!

Also by Kenzaburo Oe:

Kenzaburo Oe

Rouse Up O Young Men of the New Age!

Translated by John Nathan

GROVE PRESS
New York

Published simultaneously in Canada
Printed in the United States of America

FIRST EDITION

Library of Congress Cataloging-in-Publication Data
Oe, Kenzaburo, 1935–
    [Atarashii hito yo mezameyo. English]
    Rouse up o young men of the new age! / Kenzaburo Oe.
    p. cm.
    ISBN 0-8021-1710-4
    I. Title.
PL858.E14 A9313 2002
895.6'35—dc21   2001051298

Design by Laura Hammond Hough

Grove Press
841 Broadway
New York, NY 10003

02 03 04 05   10 9 8 7 6 5 4 3 2 1

Rouse Up
O Young Men of the New Age!

1 : Songs of Innocence, Songs of Experience

When I travel out of the country for any length of time, including professional visits, I take one precaution against losing my presence of mind and emotional balance while I am a tumbleweed in an alien landscape: I make certain to take along the books I have been reading prior to my departure. Alone in a foreign country, as I am now, I have been able to encourage myself in the face of fear, aggravation, and despondency by reading on in the books I had been reading in Tokyo before I left.

This spring I traveled to Europe, perhaps I should say careened from Vienna to Berlin with a television crew, along a route that was bare of blossoms on the trees and, except for the forsythia that turn riotous yellow before their leaves appear and the crocus buds thrusting above the ground, without flowers. I had taken along four volumes of the Penguin Classics edition of Malcolm Lowry, whom I had been reading continually for several years. I say reading, but I had also written a series of short stories constructed around metaphors that Lowry had inspired in me. My purpose in rereading Lowry while I was traveling was to allow me to say to myself at the end of the trip, Enough! As far as I'm concerned, I'm done with Lowry! And, as part of that process, I would present each of my companions on the road with one of the Lowry volumes. When I was young, my impatience had prevented me from staying with a single author for very long. As I was leaving middle age, the group of writers I would read attentively in my last years and until I died became visible to me. And so from time to time I felt obliged to set out consciously to finish off one writer or another.

This time, in spite of the busiest schedule I have ever experienced, and managing even so to maintain a pleasant relationship with the TV crew, who moved according to the logic of their work, I read, on planes and trains and in my hotel rooms as we moved about, one after another of the Lowry novels I had underlined in red pencil at various times in the past. One day, just at sunset as our train was about to arrive in Frankfurt, I was reading *Forest Path to the Spring,* Lowry's most beautiful novella in my view, and felt myself being newly moved by the prayer the narrator had written down in search of encouragement for his work as a jazz musician.

I say "newly" because I had been moved by this passage before and had even quoted the first lines of the prayer in a novel of my own. This time, it was the continuation of the portion I had thought important previously, at the end of the prayer, that caught my eye. After a failed attempt to create a musical theme to convey the feeling of his own rebirth into a new world, the narrator calls out, "Dear Lord God!," and prays for help: "I, being full of sin, cannot escape false concepts, but let me be truly Thy servant in making this a great and beautiful thing, and if my motives are obscure, and the notes scattered and often meaningless, please help me to order it, *or I am lost. . . .*"

It was this final half line, which I had set down in its original English, that tugged at me with particular force, needless to say in the context of the entire passage. I felt as if I had received a signal, as if the voice of my patron were saying, "Come along now, it's time to leave Lowry's work and to enter another world where you should also plan to remain for a number of years," and gently pointing me in the direction of a certain poet and his work. It was a Sunday evening; the young draftees who had been home on leave since Friday were on their way back to army camp. Standing at the windows in the aisles of the sleeping cars, soldiers who looked like students were blasting a farewell to their city on little trumpets with compression valves; others, still on the platform, were being consoled by their girlish lovers and urged to board the train or, reluctant to take their leave, embracing them a final time. Stepping from the train into this particular crowd seemed to hone the sharpness of my own feelings of taking leave.

As we left the station and headed for the hotel, I had with me the Oxford University Press edition of the *Complete Works of William Blake* in one volume that I had found in the station bookstore while the crew was loading its cases of equipment. That night, I began devoting my attention to Blake for the first time in several years, no, in more than ten years. The first page I opened to was a verse that ends, "Or else I shall be lost":

> *Father, father, where are you going*
> *O do not walk so fast.*
> *Speak father, speak to your little boy*
> *Or else I shall be lost.*

I had attempted a translation of my own fourteen years ago—it was not until I wrote just now "in several years, no, in more than ten years" that I realized, looking back, that it was in fact much longer ago than that, an experience I frequently have when speaking of the past these days—at a time when I was writing a novella in an attempt to get through a critical period of transition between a handicapped eldest son and his father, myself. Now I found myself drawn once again to the world of a poet who had influenced me under such unusual circumstances, and I wondered if my return to his world had to do with my sense that my son and I were entering once again a critical period of transition. How, otherwise, would I be feeling that Lowry's "or I am lost" led so directly to Blake's "Or else I shall be lost"? That night, unable to sleep in my Frankfurt hotel room though I turned off the bedside lamp any number of times, I returned once again to Blake—on the red paper cover of my book the falling figure of a naked man was printed in India ink—and pondered this and other uneasy thoughts.

The second stanza of "The Little Boy Lost" from *Songs of Innocence* is as follows:

> *The night was dark no father was there*
> *The child was wet with dew.*
> *The mire was deep, & the child did weep*
> *And away the vapour flew.*

Nightfall was still bringing fog into the streets of Frankfurt—Blake might have said "vapour"—even though it was the end of March. Easter was only a week or two away; until now, the holiday had been just a concept to me, the origin of the braiding together of death and rebirth that underlay the grotesque realism of European folk culture, but now for the first time I felt I understood the eagerness with which it was awaited as a celebration. The giant horse chestnuts that lined the streets were bare of even the youngest buds; standing sleeplessly at the window I watched the fog, glowing with light from the streetlamps, wrap itself around their dark trunks.

When I arrived at Narita Airport, Japan was in full spring, and I could feel the brightness of the air relaxing my mind and my body, but my wife and my second son appeared to be at odds with my feelings. Even after we were in the car the television station had sent for me (normally we would have taken the airport bus to Hakozaki), neither of them said a word. They sat slumped against the seat, as if they had been forced to continue fighting a difficult battle even though they were exhausted. My daughter, in her last year of a private middle school, was overwhelmed by homework and preparations for high school entrance exams and I had not expected to see her, but neither my wife nor my second son had a word to say about why my eldest child had not accompanied them to meet me.

For a time I stared out the window, not searching for lingering flower blossoms so much as simply enjoying the vivacious budding of the shrubbery in the fading light, but soon enough I began to recall uneasily how many times I had been assaulted by the feeling while reading Blake during the last part of my trip, or losing myself between the lines of his poetry, that my eldest son and I, and my entire family along with us, were on our way into a period of critical transition. And I recognized, as I continued gazing out the window in silence at the buds on the trees, that I was preparing to defend myself against my exhausted wife's account of what was in store for me by putting off as long as possible the question "And how was Eeyore?" (as in some of my novels, I intend using the nickname "Eeyore" for my handicapped son).

But the journey from Narita to our house in Setagaya is a very long ride. At some point my wife had to break her silence. And once she began, she could not avoid speaking about the situation that seemed to have enveloped her spirit in pitch-darkness. And so, in barely audible despondency and a tone of voice that sounded helpless as an infant's, she finally reported, "Eeyore was bad! Very bad!" In a manner I could tell was carefully restrained, partly out of concern that the driver might be listening, she then related the following story. Five days after I had left for Europe, as though he had been seized by an idée fixe—fearing that it would strike others as bizarre, my wife would not describe it in the car or even at home until after she had diapered my son and put him to bed—Eeyore had become violent. It was spring break between his first and second year of high school at the facility for handicapped children, and there had been a gathering of former classmates who would now be separating. The students had assembled at Kinuta Family Park, near the school, and presently had begun a game of tag, with each child chasing his own mother. When my wife ran off with the other mothers, she apparently had been able to see even at a distance that my son had become furious. Terrified, she had stopped where she was, and my son had run up to her and kicked her feet out from under her with a judo move he had learned in gym class. My wife had fallen flat on her back and not only gashed her head but sustained a concussion and was unable to stand by herself. The teachers in charge and some other mothers had surrounded Eeyore with demands that he apologize, but he had remained fiercely silent, his legs spread wide and planted, glaring at the ground.

Beginning that day, my wife had observed Eeyore uneasily at home and saw that he was tormenting his younger brother, invading his room and pushing him around. But my second son was too proud to cry out loud or to tell on his older brother; even now, as he listened to what his mother was saying in the car, his body stiffened and he lowered his eyes as though he were ashamed in front of her, but he made no attempt to correct the substance of her story. My daughter looked after her handicapped elder brother in every imaginable way, including helping with his diapers, and her solicitude seemed to irritate him to the point where my wife had witnessed him punching her in the face. This kind of incident had accumulated until my son's intimidated, angry family was no longer troubling itself with him and he was spending his spring vacation at home playing records at an unbearable volume from morning till night.

Then, about three days ago, and this was something my wife waited until late at night my first day home to reveal, the family was gathered in one corner of the dining room eating dinner after my son had finished his dinnertime ritual of stuffing everything on his plate into his mouth at one time and gulping it down when he emerged from the kitchen with a butcher knife gripped in front of his chest with both hands, moved to the curtain in the corner opposite the family, and appeared to lose himself in thought as he gazed out at the darkness of the garden behind the house.

"I thought we might have to commit him! There's nothing we could do ourselves, he's as tall and as heavy as you are!"

My wife fell silent again. And together with my son, who had said nothing, we endured the long car ride that remained, withered as though we were in the shadow of something dark and looming. Although I was still to hear about the chilling episode with the knife, not to mention the bizarre fixation that had my son in its grip, I was already feeling overwhelmed by the accumulated fatigue of my trip to Europe. At moments like this, my first response tends to be avoidance: before I faced squarely what my wife had told me, I chose the detour afforded by consideration of another Blake poem (in deference to my wife, sitting there with my son between us, I refrained from pulling my copy of Blake's poems from the knapsack on my lap).

In *Songs of Experience,* there is a well-known poem, "A Little Boy Lost," with the indefinite article. Unlike the boy with the definite article in *Songs of Innocence,* this independent child protests to his father defiantly:

> *Nought loves another as itself*
> *Nor venerates another so.*
> *Nor is it possible to Thought*
> *A greater than itself to know.*
> *And Father, how can I love you,*
> *Or any of my brothers more?*
> *I love you like a little bird*
> *That picks up crumbs around the door.*

The priest who overhears this drags the boy off angrily and accuses him of being a devil:

> *And burn'd him in a holy place,*
> *Where many have been burn'd before:*
> *The weeping parents wept in vain*
> *Are such things done on Albion's shore.*

Our lugubrious car finally arrived at the house, and as I was carrying my suitcase into the dark entranceway my daughter appeared. As with her younger brother and my wife, there was unmistakable gloom in her expression, but the concern I had been unable to broach to my wife in the car—if Eeyore was on such bad terms with everyone in the family, was it all right to leave the two of them alone in the house together?—was dispelled. We greeted each other with as much cheer as we could manage, and went into the family room. Eeyore was on the sofa, his face buried in a sumo magazine, and he did not even look around. In the black, baggy trousers he wore to school and an old shirt of mine that looked to be too tight, he was kneeling on the couch facing the back, his rear in the air, and in that unnatural position he was poring over a photo roundup of the junior wrestlers who had just finished competing in the spring tournament. Looking at his back and legs, I thought I could see something *ambivalent*—myself, another self that had been present all the time I was away, and, in the same place, ready and steeled to reject that self of mine, my son. Since his height and weight were identical to my own and even the way he stood with his fleshy back and shoulders rounded reminded me of myself, it was if anything commonplace for me to perceive him as though he and I were superimposed as we lay there reading on that couch—in my case, on my back. Yet this time I could feel him (together with another son who was an identical version of myself) decisively at this exact moment rejecting his father, rejection that was no simple, spur-of-the-moment rebelliousness but determined and deliberate and part of a twisted process that was still winding on. So when I called out, "Eeyore, I'm home! How was sumo? Did Asashio win?" I felt I had been given to understand all over again the weight of the despondency that was oppressing the family. However, I had yet to look into my son's eyes. And it was his eyes that would force me that first night to face directly into the heart of the crisis that was already at hand.

While in Berlin I had bought my son a harmonica. When he didn't respond even when we called him, his younger brother, who had received a Swiss army knife, took it in to him where he lay sprawled on the couch, but he didn't even glance at it. After I had spoken to him a number of times at dinner he finally removed the harmonica from its paper wrapping; but instead of showing the interest any instrument normally evoked in him and trying to make it play, he merely fumbled with it unenthusiastically, as if it were a foreign object that was somehow threatening. Eventually, he did bring it to his lips at an angle and produced a single note like the sound of the wind by blowing into just one hole. It was as if he were afraid that instead of harmony an awful dissonance might sink its teeth into his nose if he blew into two or more holes at once.

I had been drinking the whisky I had purchased at the duty-free shop, but presently I stood up from the dining room table and set out across the room to where my son lay stretched out athwart the couch like a knife thrust into it. Without changing his position, he grasped the harmonica by one edge in both hands, overlapping them, lifted it on end in front of his face like a scepter, and looked up at me from either side of it. His eyes made me shudder. They were bloodshot as though with fever, burning with a yellowish luster as of resin, raw. A beast in rut, having expended itself on impulse in a frenzy of sexual excess, is still rocked by aftershocks of desire. The period of wild activity is meant to give way at once to inaction and lethargy, but deep inside the body something continues to rage. From the look in my son's eyes he was being devoured from the inside by a beast in the grip of that wildness and could do nothing about it, and the rest of his face, his dark eyebrows and finely arched nose and bright-red lips, was slack and blank.

Looking down into those eyes that smote my chest, I couldn't speak. My wife came over from the table to tell my son that it was time for bed, and he obediently took his diapers for that night upstairs. But first he dropped the harmonica beside him as if it were something he just happened to be holding that meant nothing to him. As he passed me he flicked his eyes in my direction and I saw once again the eyes of a beast, of a dog, laughing and laughing in a place absent of people until its eyes had gone red.

"Eeyore gripped that butcher knife the same way he was holding the harmonica just now, staring into the back garden with his head pressed against the wall where the curtain is. The entire time we were eating he didn't move a muscle, it was terrifying!"

When she came downstairs from having put my son to bed, my wife related the episode with the butcher knife and added a report of his bizarre remarks. Now that I was actually home, he was not defying his mother, and all she had had to do was tell him she was on the way to meet me at the airport and he had stayed at home and maintained a policy of nonintervention toward his sister. It was therefore only natural that she should have said to him when he began to act up that she would report his misbehavior to his father when he came home. At the time Eeyore had been listening to a Bruckner symphony on FM radio with the volume turned way up as usual, and he had shouted, in a voice easily heard above the blaring music, "*No, no, Papa is dead!*"

My wife was stunned, but managed to get hold of herself and tried to correct my son's mistake. Father wasn't dead; he had been away before for other long periods of time, but he had been alive in foreign countries, not dead. And just as he had always come home in the past when his trip was over, he would be home this time, too; in the loud voice that must have been required to vie with the Bruckner—as I listened despondently I opened the FM radio guide on the table to see which Bruckner had been playing and ascertained that it had been the Eighth Symphony in C Minor—my wife had tried to disabuse my son, but he had continued to protest stubbornly: "*No, Papa died! He really died!*"

In the context of his conversation with my wife, my son's responses, while bizarre, did have a certain logic of their own: "I'm sure you don't mean dead? Don't you mean away on a trip? You know he's coming back next Sunday!"

"Is that right? Is he coming back on Sunday? Even if he is, right now he's dead. Papa is really dead!"

The Bruckner Eighth continued endlessly, and as my wife shouted back and forth with my son she sensed that fresh blood was beginning to ooze from the cut on the back of her head and felt sick with exhaustion. Imagining a situation that might easily occur in the future, when her husband had really died, and she was attempting to coax her son into believing he was still alive in order to control him, she was further disheartened.

Nevertheless, the morning after I returned, I discovered a route to communication with my son that enabled the whole family to make up with him. Although I had been unable to sleep until nearly dawn, I sat at the table with the children while they were having breakfast. Eeyore sat obliquely to the table, apart from everyone, and ate slowly, using his chopsticks as though weights were attached to his arms (since he had begun taking the antiepileptic drug Hidantol, his movements were sluggish until midmorning, and he gave no indication of hearing anything we said to him). When we had finished and the children had returned to their rooms—it was still spring break—I went to sleep again on the sofa that my son had monopolized until the day before.

Presently a memory from my youth, or rather the re-creation of an actual incident from a specific time and place when I was young, filled me with a feeling of nostalgia so powerful and undiluted it was palpable and woke me, trembling, from my sleep. I was on the verge of tears. Seated on the floor next to the skirt of the sofa, my son was stroking my bare foot that protruded from the blanket with the fingers of his cupped right hand, gently, as if it were constructed of something soft and fragile. And he was whispering words of concern in a soft, calm voice. These were the words, alive with familiarity and nostalgia and shivering like a living jelly that I had heard on the way out of my dream: "*Foot, are you all right? Good foot, nice foot! Gout, are you all right? Nice foot! Nice foot!*"

"Eeyore," I whispered back, "foot is fine. There's no gout, so foot is fine."

My son looked up at me, squinting into the light, with eyes that had returned to looking as they had before my departure, and said, "*So it's all right? What a nice foot! What a really very excellent foot!*"

After a while, my son moved away from my foot and, taking up the harmonica that lay where he had tossed it down, played some chords. Before long the chords were accompanying a melody. He played a simple, beautiful tune that I knew only as one of Bach's sicilianas, in several keys, and seemed to have understood that he could play a chromatic scale by using the holes on both sides of the harmonica. I made spaghetti carbonara for lunch and surprised myself at how much pleasure it gave me. When my younger son and daughter were seated at the table, I called out to my eldest son, and he replied in a voice so clear and beautiful and extraordinarily calm that my wife gave a little laugh.

"I'd given Eeyore a definition of foot," I told her. That's what opened a passage between us and gave us a handhold on the day. The trouble is, I promised I'd define everything in this world for him. But so far "foot" is the clearest definition I've come up with and that wasn't even my own invention; it was gout that made that possible.

Definitions. A book of definitions of everything in the world. By way of demonstrating that the presentiment I described above had already come to pass, that I was moving back toward Blake or perhaps approaching him from a new direction, I want to begin by saying that when I was still formulating a book of definitions that was to begin with a retelling of Japan's constitution in simple language, a good ten years ago in other words, I was calling it, after Blake, "Songs of Innocence, Songs of Experience." And though I attempted to create this book in the form of children's stories with illustrations, I had a terrible time making it happen. Seven or eight years ago, in a public talk I gave on children and imagination, I said the following. By that time I had already made frequent attempts to begin in earnest and had been forced to acknowledge that the project I had in mind would not be accomplished easily. But I must have been hoping, and I believe I can read this feeling behind my words, that by speaking about it in public I could lever myself into moving forward.

> I began thinking about writing a primer to help children like my son and his classmates at the special school for handicapped children live their lives as adults. I wanted to convey to them in words they could understand what the world, society, and mankind were all about, and to say to them, "Go out and live your lives fully now but pay attention to these particular points." For example, what is life, a short, easy description. I wouldn't have to do it all myself; a variety of friends would help. The composer, T, for example, could be counted on to write something about music for my son. These were my thoughts as I sat down to work, but I found the project to be dizzyingly difficult. The difficulty in attempting to write about the clearest and simplest things in vibrant language that will stimulate the imagination is that in virtually every case the reality that must be conveyed does not permit that kind of description.

As I copy the above passage I notice that I was being dishonest in my speech. According to what I was saying there, I am at work on a book of definitions of the world, society, and mankind for my own son and his comrades in the special class for handicapped children. The constitution will be central to my theme. But the current reality under the constitution makes writing about it in concise, accurate, evocative language impossible. I am not suggesting even now that this is altogether contrary to the truth. Nevertheless, to be honest about it, the crux of the problem was not so much on the outside as internal to me. To put it more courageously, it was my laziness. To be sure, lurking behind my laziness was a sense of futility tinged with fear that had its own source in my misgivings about my talent. I had conceived this idea even before my son entered school. I began writing it for a child who had scarcely been out of his house, and as my son went to elementary school and then entered the special section for handicapped students at the middle school, gradually adjusting my style I created drafts for each stage of his life. Now I was writing for a young man about to enter the second year of the high school program at the special school, and the only solid definition I had provided him with so far was for foot, "nice foot," and I had only managed that thanks to an attack of gout.

When I came down with gout I was ruled entirely by the fiery red swelling at the base of my left big toe: as even the weight of a sheet was unbearably painful I lay in bed at night uncovered—sleeping only a little without the help of whisky—and sprawled on the sofa in the same state during the day, crawling to the bathroom with one leg in the air. At the time, Eeyore had just entered the special class at middle school, and, watching his father, who dwarfed him in height and weight, reduced to helplessness for days on end, made a deep impression. He did his very best to be useful to me. As I crawled down the hall obliged to learn how painful a shin bone could be, he would scamper after me like a sheep dog in pursuit of a stray sheep and more than once, tripping over his own chubby, clumsy body, would fall on my gout-ridden foot. I couldn't help screaming aloud, but the way he withered right before my eyes at my suffering was enough to fill me with a phantom doubt that perhaps I was a savage father who beat his son. And that thought incised itself into me like a wound. As the attacks gradually subsided, my son would stroke the rose-colored swelling at the base of my toe with slightly bent fingers—supporting himself with his other hand to keep from leaning his weight on me—and would speak aloud, addressing my foot, "*Nice foot, are you all right, what a very nice foot you are!*"

"There's no question that Eeyore was very bad, that he behaved badly, but I think that what was really going on was that he was understanding for the first time that his father would die," I said to my wife after some reflection. "The part that's hard to understand is that he seems to be thinking that people who have died will return, but if we observe carefully I have a feeling we'll come to see what's behind that notion, too. Because Eeyore doesn't say things off the top of his head. Besides, when I was a child I think I had the same thought. At any rate, when I go away on a trip and stay away for what seems like forever isn't it natural that his thoughts should jump ahead to after my death? His father goes away to some distant place and the feelings he experiences are the same as if he had died, and on top of that, his mother attempts to run off and leave him behind—no wonder he was frantic. It was just a game, but to a child, games are models of reality. I thought about the knife, too, and I think the way he was holding it was meant to be defensive; maybe that's also why he was peering out into the garden. I wonder if he wasn't standing guard against an enemy in order to protect the family in my place now that I was dead?"

I continued, silently, not to my wife but to myself, as follows: Since my son had begun to ponder with his own kind of urgency what would happen following my death, was I not obliged as his father to prepare him, unflinchingly and without falling into idleness, for his relationship to the world, society, and mankind after that inevitable moment had arrived? As to whether I was capable of actually writing a complete guide to the world, society, and mankind in language he could easily understand that would keep my son from losing his way along the road of life following my death, I had the feeling it had already been made clear to me that this was in fact not possible. Nevertheless, somehow or other I must do what I can to attempt a book of definitions intended for him. Let me think of it not so much as being for him as for myself, a book of definitions that would cleanse and encourage me. My experience with gout provided my son with a precise definition of "foot," and through his understanding I had been made aware of what constituted "nice foot." Carried along by the momentum I had achieved on my trip, I was continuing to read Blake intensively—why couldn't I overlap my reading of the English poet with the writing of a book of definitions? And why not write it as a novel, this time without worrying about using language my son and his comrades could understand, about the experiences that had provided me with the definitions that were critical to my sense of self and about my longing to pass them on to innocent souls?

I had a fantasy once, and wrote about it, that on the day of my death the total accumulation of my experience would flow out of me into my son's innocent spirit. And if my fantasy should come to pass, when he had buried the handful of bone and ash that his father had become, my son would read the book of definitions I had yet to write. With this childish fantasy as something to cling to, in hopes of finding shelter from myriad thoughts about the difficulties my son would encounter in the outside

world after my death, it seemed possible that I might sit down
to work on this book of definitions.

River—the experience that gave me the definition is etched in
my memory as vividly as the discovery of "nice foot" that I had
shared with my son. It was a definition so precise and clear that
the man who provided it scarcely needed words. At least ten
years ago, I was on an airplane traveling east from New Delhi
with the veteran writer, H. He had appeared to be asleep when
suddenly, catching my attention with a brisk movement that
made it clear that he was not, he pointed out the pressurized
window at the river cutting a deep arc like a surgical scar across
the clay-colored plain below. An instant later, he had sat back
in his reclined seat and had closed his eyes again and I was leaning across his lap to survey the view through the window. (Before we boarded the plane there had been what I took to be a
confrontation between us, and, though we had resolved it, his
words and attitude just now had further heartened me.) As it
happened, the plane was just banking into a turn as it began its
descent: my field of vision was filled entirely by what could only
be called the quintessential river in India, the true river among
rivers. Until then, my archetype had always been the limpid river
that ran through the valley in the forest in Shikoku where I grew
up, but from that moment on I retained a second image of the
essential river: clay-colored, just a shade paler than the color
of the ground, doubtless flowing toward what must be a clay-
colored sea but imperceptibly, in what direction, it was impossible to know. From the slightest movement of Mr. H's wrist and
finger a minute before, and from the fluttering of his lip as he
spoke as though it were a continuation of his silence or perhaps
did not speak, I received and retain in memory to this day, together with the incidents that occurred before we boarded the

plane, what I still consider to be the best possible definition of "river."

On the day we traversed the Indian continent in a plane, Mr. H and I had spent a good ten hours waiting for our flight, the only Japanese among the Indians. In that entire time, other than the word "river" that may have been just the fluttering of his lips, and an invitation to read an article in the *International Herald Tribune*—"You might be interested in this"—and, before that, in the taxi on the way to the airport, an episode about dirty eyeglasses, he had not spoken a word to me. And until just before our flight to Calcutta finally departed, I had been feeling that his silence was due to anger at me for my compulsiveness about time and my ignorance of how things were done in India. The truth was, if it hadn't been for my jumpiness, Mr. H might have spent the ten hours relaxing in our hotel instead of waiting around on an autumn day with nothing to do in an airport as drab and deserted as a warehouse.

In what I took to be his indignation, Mr. H was unapproachable as a fortress. Born into a merchant family that had been shipping agents on the Sea of Japan for generations (the only one of his brothers who had turned his back on the world of commerce, he had been the one to inherit what might be called the essence of his family's accumulated humanity), he had set out just after the war for the chaos that was China, as though in search of hardship, and had found what he was looking for. On his return, he had become an author and an intellectual with a style of his own, though very much in the postwar school. But there was something about him that had nothing to do with his family background or his lifetime experiences, an inherent personality that included stubbornness about his feelings that made it impossible for anyone to divert him once he had set his course. Particularly not the person responsible for his anger.

Before it had become plain that he was fuming, Mr. H had removed his *International Herald Tribune* from its paper cover and shown me an article whose contents I can convey vividly: it was about the cellist Mstislav Rostropovich's attack on the suppression of free speech in the Soviet Union. Still in Russia at the time, Rostropovich was dedicating himself to defending his comrade Solzhenitsyn, and I had copied his remarks in the flyleaf of the book I was reading that day: "Every human being must have the right to express without fear his own thoughts and his opinions about what he knows and has experienced. I am not talking about simply regurgitating with minor modifications opinions that have been fed to us . . ."

As Mr. H's anger gradually revealed itself, I sensed that it was not only directed at my blunder and at the airline but also related to censorship and civil rights violations in Russia. I was led to this by the anecdote he told me about eyeglasses. We were in New Delhi at the time to attend a conference of Asian and African authors, but there were also a large number of Soviet writers present, including a woman poet who was an old friend of Mr. H's. The previous night, he and the poet, whom I shall call Madame Nefedovna, a smallish woman his age, in her mid-fifties, whose utter lack of intellectual restraint and cosmopolitan, Jewish-looking features made her appear ten years younger, had sat up arguing until late. As Mr. H was a veteran of too many international battles to be careless or indiscreet in a conversation with political overtones, I refrained from asking questions, but I judged that the argument had reference to the declaration by Rostropovich in the paper and was about the current civil rights issue in Russia. While Mr. H was on familiar terms with the cultural bureaucracy, he had always been clear about identifying emotionally with the artists and scientists whom Rostropovich was defending. The criticism he continued to voice at the African-Asian writers' conference, tenaciously but with great tact and strategy, addressing the Russian representatives in the calmly delivered English that suited him, was on their behalf. If, however, it was the case that Madame Nefedovna was overdoing her actual involvement in the civil rights movement in Moscow, she would have been well advised to reconsider, for if this was noticed, she would find herself as a Jew not only unable to make trips abroad like this one but also prevented from pursuing her activities at home—apparently Mr. H had tried hard to persuade his friend that he was correct. But "that unrepentently stubborn Russian female intellectual," as he called Madame Nefedovna, had rejected his admonition out of hand, with the familiar ease that came from having met him at writers' conferences for fifteen years. Mr. H had been wearing glasses since his youth, but Madame Nefedovna had only recently begun using reading glasses, which she carried in her handbag. She needed them for the fine print in the volumes she pored over in her research—a distinguished poet, she was also a recognized Sanskrit scholar—and, like many people who do not wear their glasses all the time, she rarely cleaned them. Mr. H was in some respects a fastidious man, and it was accordingly his custom to clean them for her, but that night he had instead pinched some lint from his pocket and dusted it on her lenses.

Such was the story Mr. H had told me in the taxi on the way to the airport. When we arrived, he installed himself at the counter of a newly opened bar and began drinking beer or something stronger, ignoring me entirely. Our flight had been scheduled to leave at 7 A.M., and in my uneasiness about separating from the Japanese writers' group and setting out alone on a journey with Mr. H, there was no question that I had overdone my insistence on the accuracy of the timetable. Moving back and forth down the hotel's roofless corridor that faced a courtyard garden like a small forest, I had gone to awaken him repeatedly—I recall an unbearably desolate tree, the giant black trunk and fallen leaves of golden brown more like minerals than plants, a tree impossible to imagine outside India, which remains on my mind because I do not know its name—and later, when it appeared that he had no intention of getting up, I had tipped a bellboy to drag him from his room. What I had neglected to do was phone the airport to inquire whether the flight was on time. We had finally raced to the airport in a taxi, arriving just before scheduled departure time, and found that the flight had been delayed, and the delay had been extended hour after hour with no explanation, and then it was the afternoon and still there had been no announcement that the flight would be departing.

It occurred to me that Mr. H, who understood how India worked and had even written a book based on his experiences in the country, might have known all along that an on-time departure was out of the question, and that his anger at me was therefore more than justified. While he sat at the bar drinking by himself, I waited near the electronic board on which departures were posted, listening for an announcement about our flight, and read a book about wild animals in India that I had purchased at the gift shop in our hotel. A memoir in dead earnest by a plantation owner named E. P. Guy, the book was written in a prose style that mirrored the rectitude of its author's character and life, yet was filled with details that were bizarrely amusing and made for perfect reading on the road. I have this book with me even now as I write, with Rostropovich's remarks copied on the inside cover. Based on eyewitness accounts from friends in the region of Kashmir, Guy described the following bizarre phenomenon at the time of the partition of Pakistan in 1947. As Hindus, who viewed cows as sacred animals, crossed the new border into India from Pakistan, and Muslims, who eat no pork, moved in the opposite direction, the wild animals in the region instinctively sought their own route to survival. Whole herds of wild oxen in Pakistan migrated to India, and wild pigs in similar numbers crossed into Pakistan in search of a safe environment.

It was now late in the afternoon. We had been waiting that long and, even so, thinking I might make Mr. H laugh with the animal episode, I sat down on the bar stool next to his and ordered a beer. The bartender's attitude seemed, for want of a better word, Indian: with a dusky disagreeableness that might have been directed more at life in general than at his customers, and an expression on his face that seemed to say "So now we have a second Japanese alcoholic," he passed me a lukewarm bottle of beer. When I told my animal story after drinking the beer, Mr. H listened without the slightest show of interest, his gaze never moving from the sorry shelf of bottles and the large map of India on the wall across from him. This left me helpless, with nothing to do but order another beer and stare at the same shelf of bottles and map on the wall. As I sat there, drinking one beer after the other, I felt the onset of an impulse that was by no means unfamiliar to me.

When I first became aware of this impulse at age seventeen or eighteen—as I think of it, my son's current age—I named it "leap," using the English word, a name that I continue to use though clearly it was a youthful invention; and when I feel a leap approaching I do what I can to distance myself so as to avoid being taken over. But there are times when I have behaved in odd ways that have carried me forward as though to welcome the leap. If I include drunken behavior, leaps of one degree or another possess me about once a year, and it may be that their accumulated impact has twisted and bent the course of my life. Or, possibly, leaps have made me the man I am today.

In this particular instance at the New Delhi airport, the leap I took, not so much rude or nasty or anything I can think of other than dangerous, was to ridicule an author I had admired for years by writing a poem that portrayed him in a ridiculous way as a man past middle age who was suffering the pain of an unhappy love, and to show it to him as he sat drinking at my side with his anger on display.

I began by copying the map of India on the wall onto the back of a coaster. When I had marked various points on the map with asterisks, I then composed a poem in English, incorporating the place names I had starred. The title was "An Indian Gazetteer." The only thing I remember clearly about my pseudo-English poem was a man getting on in years brooding over his sake cup about his similarly aging lover going off to the provincial city of Mysore. This part has stayed with me because the point of my scheme was to use a pun on Mysore as the basis for an insinuation. That very day, Madame Nefedovna had in fact departed, in her case by train, for a conference on linguistics being held in Mysore.

My sore: in the small dictionary on my desk as I write, I find the following definitions for "sore": 1) a place that is tender or raw, a wound, an inflammation; 2) inflictions or hardships of a mental or emotional nature (including sorrow or anger), unpleasant memories. To be honest, it had never occurred to me that the friendship Mr. H and Madame N had sustained across years of meeting at international conferences had anything to do with love. Those of us who had been influenced by Mr. H and his generation of postwar writers during our college years sometimes indulged in carrying on like naughty children in his presence; O, for example, another young member of our Japan writers' group, had frequently teased him by treating Madame Nefedovna as though she were his lover. But O shared my respect for Mr. H and Madame N as veteran intellectuals who had always insisted on their own individuality, and had no more

intention of pigeonholing them as lovers than did I. Nevertheless, I slid the coaster inscribed with my doggerel innuendo into
Mr. H's field of vision as he stared down at the bar (he had removed his glasses and hung his head, the shape of which put me
in mind of a distinguished warrior from a powerful clan in the
Middle Ages). If you think you're angry now, I thought to myself in the grip of a leap I could not control, have a look at this!
If you can indulge your feelings for hours on end, why should I
pussyfoot around you!

Without changing his position, Mr. H appeared to read the
coaster, his eyes narrowing with the effort. Then he put his
glasses back on and I could tell from the tightening between his
temples and his eyes that he was slowly rereading my brief verse
a second time, and then a third. I had begun to feel regret at once,
as though the world were going dark, and then he slowly turned
his face in my direction and the look in his eyes struck a blow
that took my breath away.

I described my son's eyes the first time I looked directly into
them on returning from Europe as the eyes of a rutting beast
still rocked by aftershocks of desire following sexual frenzy, as
unbearable eyes that looked as though he were being devoured
from within by a ravening beast. What I failed to note and wish
to add here was the bottomless grief that was revealed above all
else in the yellowish resin luster of those eyes. Reports of my son's
unmanageable behavior while I was away and his response to
the harmonica I had brought him, not to mention my own travel
fatigue, had frayed my nerves and deprived me of the emotional
leeway I needed to read and register his grief.

Writing this now it is hard to imagine how as a father I
could have failed to see that massive grief in the desolation of
my son's eyes. And I can't help feeling that, healing the rift
with my son, I became aware of his grief through the agency

of a Blake poem, "On Another's Sorrow," which includes this stanza:

Can I see a falling tear,
And not feel my sorrows share,
Can a father see his child,
Weep, nor be with sorrow fill'd.

One of the "Songs of Innocence," the poem concludes with the following verse:

O! he gives to us his joy,
That our grief he may destroy
Till our grief is fled & gone
He doth sit by us and moan.

I was able to read the grief in my son's eyes even more directly, as though it were in my own experience, because I was equipped with a definition of grief that had appeared for just an instant in Mr. H's eyes that day at the bar in the New Delhi airport.

2: A Cold Babe Stands in the Furious Air

"Innocence dwells with Wisdom, but never with Ignorance," Blake wrote. This aphoristic note is appended to one of his epic poems, together with the following, to me not entirely clear but nonetheless appealing, phrase: "Unorganized Innocence, an Impossibility." I have returned to the poem in question repeatedly at various times but have always skimmed my way through it. Given the nature of Blake's epic poetry, it might be said that anything less attentive than poring over the details is not reading it at all; nevertheless, in my own way I have discovered verses that have inscribed themselves on me. Consider, for example, in the heroic poem usually called *The Four Zoas,* properly speaking, with "Zoa" signifying "living thing" as in the Greek version of Revelations, "The Four Zoas, or, The Torments of Love & Jealousy in the Death and Judgement of Albion the Ancient Man," the unforgettable prospect of the dead, at the time of the final judgment, revealing themselves as they were in life, wounds and all, as they stand to accuse:

> *They shew their wounds they accuse they seize the oppressor*
>   *howlings began*
> *On the golden palace Songs & joy on the desart the Cold babe*
> *Stands in the furious air he cries the children of six thousand*
>   *years*
> *Who died in infancy rage furious a mighty multitude rage*
>   *furious*
> *Naked & pale standing on the expecting air to be delivered.*

When I wrote just now that I "skimmed" these lines, I didn't mean to imply that I could read Blake fluently. On the contrary, it remains difficult for me no matter how often I read and reread the original year after year. In particular, the voluminous poems known as the "Prophecies," from Blake's middle period, are knotty with passages that impede the foreigner's understanding. Even so, I always imagined that even I could have made my way close to the full meaning of a poem had I taken the time to move carefully through it with the help of a commentary. And I did make it a point to acquire whatever Blake studies and commentaries I found in Western bookstores. I still do. At the same time, since my student days I have had a kind of fear that once I began reading Blake line by line I would come to feel that no amount of time was adequate, no matter how much time I spent. Besides, I wanted to taste whatever I felt moved to read, for example the entire *Four Zoas,* which is 855 lines long, and so, with a sense of urgency as my guide, I have made a practice of finding my way along the stepping stones of what I am able to understand unaided.

If I were to quote another passage from *The Four Zoas* that has stayed with me vividly, without reference to the complex narrative of the work or, for that matter, to the premise of God or the godlike person at the center of Blake's unique view of the universe, it would be the following:

> *That Man should Labour & sorrow & learn & forget, & return*
> *To the dark valley whence he came to begin his labours anew.*

The first time I read these lines, quite out of context, I was a student in the department of general education in my first year at college. I recall the circumstances clearly, and even my posture as I read, my head thrust forward. I can't have been at college for more than a few weeks. I was sitting in the library that had been there since the days of the Imperial Upper School, on the campus that was apparently of botanical interest for its variety of azaleas (on the way to the library, the azaleas were in full bloom, and I remember having remarked about each and every flower that it couldn't compare to the real azaleas that blossomed on the mountain slopes that rose out of the valley where I was born, not to mention the fact that my azaleas protected the loam on the cliffs with their roots).

I discovered the verse in a folio-sized book that was lying open on the table next to where I was sitting. A number of other Western volumes were bundled in a partially untied silk cloth alongside the book, but there was no one seated in the chair in front of them. Lifting myself out of the chair I had just settled in, I peered over at the opened book and began to read, distracted by the direct and indirect quotation marks at the beginning of each line, the nearer, lower half of the right page. When I came to the lines quoted above, I sensed that I had been handed a decisive prophecy about my own life, only now entering a new phase—in truth, I sat there stunned. Just then, the owner of the book that had been left open—as I think about it, he must have been younger than I am now—a person who appeared despite his youth to be a professor or an assistant professor, returned to his seat. He stared at me unblinkingly, his eyes fastening themselves to me as though with glue, and as the thought flickered across my dazed brain that this was perhaps an area of the library that was reserved for the use of faculty, I left my seat as though to flee. The professor or assistant professor never took his eyes off me, and I wondered uneasily if he might be thinking that I had been trying to steal the Western books that belonged to him (in those days, imported texts were not readily available to students).

As for the verse which had caught my eye, I had not even asked the book's owner to confirm for me whose poetry it was or the work it came from—it had seemed to me to be a dramatic poem—but I was not about to forget lines which had shaken me in this way, and it was my thought that I would certainly be able to track them down again on my own. In those days, I tended to rely on the power of my memory; besides, the lines in question had lodged themselves firmly inside me. I had been sitting near a corner where a large Webster's dictionary had been installed on a high stand, another reason for supposing that I had chosen an area for use by researchers and scholars with special privileges, and had stood up reflexively; cutting diagonally across the vast hall of a reading room, I sat down in the opposite corner, and, without taking out the Gide novel I had been struggling my way through with the help of a dictionary, I cradled my head in my hands and lost myself in thought.

... & return / To the dark valley whence he came—I remember thinking first of all that I had never consciously considered the valley in the forest where I was born and raised a "dark valley." The area in our village along the main road that included our place was known as "the Naru-ya"; and since the word we used to denote flatness in our dialect was *naru-i*, I had taken the name to mean "flat." But the children of the Korean laborers who had been brought to the village under coercion to haul lumber out of the forest said that *naru* was the word for sun, and ever after I had conceived of our valley as a sunny place.

Now, having left the valley for this great city, it occurred to me abruptly as I sat there in that large, impersonal building, holding my head in my hands next to a lamp attached to an even more impersonal cubicle, that my valley was in its way also a dark valley, although it was not only in the negative sense that I was thinking of the word "dark."

That Man should Labour & sorrow & learn & forget—the notion that "labour" and "sorrow" were not opposites but two adjacent aspects of life was not unpersuasive; it put me in mind of my mother's labor after my father's death when I was in my late teens. The words that followed struck me as a frighteningly accurate prophecy about my own future.

I had entered Tokyo University and was just beginning to study French. I had chosen the field after a year of deliberation following my graduation from high school, and I felt no hesitation about continuing it. Even so, I was aware of an undercurrent of incongruity. Now, through the agency of Blake's verse, I sensed I would be able to bring this uneasiness to the surface by thinking about its connection to having left my valley behind me. I had set out from a poignantly familiar place to live a marginal life in a corner of a giant city whose very topography was a mystery to me. I was studying French, but other than that, except for some part-time work, I was being spared from having to "labour" at anything. Which meant that, for the time being, I was also being spared "sorrow"; I was living a life on a plane apart from *Labour*

& sorrow, but only temporarily. To be sure, I was learning French, but before long I would forget it, I felt certain of that.

... *& learn & forget*—it was as if, in my case, I was learning only in order to forget. I had left the valley as though I were being chased away only to begin a life of seclusion in the giant city and this was the entirety of that life. In the end I would return to the valley. Whereupon the "labour" and "sorrow" I was being spared temporarily in my life in the city would begin in earnest.... *& return / To the dark valley whence he came to begin his labours anew.*

Slumped heavily in the chair, I sat without moving, my head in my hands. When it was time for lunch, I bought bread and a croquette at the stand at the entrance to the dorm and made a sandwich like everyone else, dousing the croquette with sauce—the student association had posted a notice at the stand that was a sign of how miserably poor the times were: "If you have not purchased croquettes, please refrain from pouring sauce on your bread!" I ate my sandwich standing among the crowd around the drinking fountain: I didn't have the money to buy milk. I surveyed the prospect of my life and had the feeling I was just now accepting the dismal view for what it was; the students all around me appeared naive as children.

As I had expected when I read those lines on the page opened next to me, I did after all discover on my own that the poet in question was Blake. To be sure, it was nearly ten years after my experience in the library at the Komaba campus, about a year before the birth of my eldest son. While I was a student of French literature, and for four or five years after I graduated, whatever reading in a foreign language I did was exclusively in French—I continued to feel that I was "learning in order to forget"—and always while sitting at a desk so that I could use a dictionary and make notes in the margins. Somewhere along the way, perceiving that I was not going to be a scholar of French literature—confirming an early sign of where *& learn & forget* was heading—I began including books in English in my reading once again; and, feeling free to lie sprawled on a couch, I made my way through a wide variety of English literature consulting the dictionary infrequently and writing nothing down. The change was due in part to a new lifestyle that came from being married.

And so it happened that I was reading an anthology of English poetry, which included Blake. As I read a stanza from one of Blake's Prophecies, I felt certain that the style, the shape, and the sentiments of the language were identical to the lines that had struck me so forcibly that day in the past as I was moving from boyhood to youth. I felt so certain that I went to Maruzen bookstore that same day and purchased Blake's complete poems in one volume. Moving from line to line with only a glance at the first few words, I began a search for that verse which was in my memory yet not literally memorized. By the following day, I had succeeded in identifying the lines in the long poem I have mentioned, *The Four Zoas*.

It was already the middle of the night, but I telephoned my friend Y, a classmate at Komaba who had gone on to graduate school in English literature and was now a lecturer at a women's college. I asked if he could think of a scholar who might have had a book open to Blake in the library and would have been a middle-aged professor or assistant professor in the days when we were students. If the scholar in question had published anything on Blake, perhaps there was a commentary on this section in *The Four Zoas*.

"Professors with some connection to Blake at Komaba in 1953 or '54, or on loan there from the main campus, right? That would be Professor S or Professor T, but the age doesn't fit. They would both have been over fifty in those days." As long as I had known him, Y would always cite the objective facts before he was willing to speculate, which he now did as follows: "I suppose it's possible, and this is only conjecture, that it might have been a famous character who was known to people in English lit in our years as the 'autodidact.' The story was that he got sick and had to drop out of the old Imperial Upper School. About the time we were there, he recovered and was trying to talk the university into readmitting him. There was no chance of it happening, the system was entirely different, and he had a history of mental instability, but apparently the Dean's Office was letting him hang around in the library. He'd show up with a volume of poetry, usually John Donne, and he'd ask a student to open to any page and then predict the student's destiny from the metaphors and symbols he found. I never met him in person." I had received an unmistakable signal that it was precisely my own destiny that was foretold in the verse, in this case not from Donne but Blake, on the page opened on the desk next to me. I had retained this impression for close to ten years, and I had just now gone so far as to track down the lines.

"The nickname 'autodidact' came from Sartre, your specialty, I think from *Nausea*." My friend sounded uncomfortable, but he also seemed to enjoy the revelation. "Apparently he proposed things, you know, in the nature of homosexual acts to the students he got to know when he predicted their destinies."

"I wasn't good-looking enough to get into that kind of trouble. But I am thinking the man who opened his book to Blake next to me must have been this 'autodidact.' Which would mean the book must have been his own and not the library's, so there's probably no point in going there to look for it now—unless of course he still shows up with the same book—"

"He's dead. He got blatant about that behavior I mentioned and, just like the Sartre character, he was thrown out of the library—in *Nausea* I think he was arrested, wasn't he?—anyway, he wasn't permitted on the campus anymore and apparently that triggered his depression. Someone at the Dean's Office got worried and went to his apartment. He'd been dead two or three days when they found him. It was in the papers."

The lines I had seen and remembered are a description of the "caverns of the grave" spoken by one of the wives of the divine figure who is a character unique to Blake's epic poems. At the time of my first encounter, if I had possessed the city-boy poise to question "autodidact" about the verse when he returned to his seat, perhaps he would have touched on my own destiny in the course of his explanation. If his words had overlapped the augury of my future that I had read in the poetry myself, I might have believed his prediction—I have no idea how the other young men he encountered had reacted—and become his disciple. Sooner or later, of course, his homosexual advances in my direction would have put an end to the relationship.

. . . & return / To the dark valley whence he came. The *dark valley* in this line, despite the negative adjective "dark," filled me with powerful longing. After the birth of my eldest son, which seemed to make definite all over again the impossibility that I would return to my valley—what purpose could French possibly serve there?—I found myself unable to say *my* valley except in the domain of my imagination; nevertheless, there were times when I dreamed of returning with my son. I want to emphasize that I was not dreaming while asleep; these were reveries that had the curious quality of occurring in the brightness of consciousness while I was awake. I say this to readers who might otherwise be tempted to divine my fortune in these dreams as though they were of a variety familiar to them.

My mother and other members of the family were assembled in the main room in what appeared to be the shadows of a dim light that gave their skin an inky look—this was literally a *dark valley*. I recall that my father, who had died when I was a child, was also sitting there somberly in formal Japanese robes and family crest. I had just returned to the *dark valley* with my son, his head still bandaged where the lump had been cut away (even in the reverie, my wife never appeared). The entire family, my mother included, viewed my handicapped son as the one and only asset I had managed to wrest from my life of *Labour & sorrow* in the great city. Under the circumstances, no one was cheering, but their expressions were saying "Congratulations!" and "Well done!" Over time, I returned to this scene frequently. As my son grew up, the pair of us appeared to alter, but my mother and the rest of the family in the *dark valley* never seemed to change. Thinking about it now, I see clearly that the image I created in the form of a daydream was connected to thoughts of death. That would explain why my father, who had died at about my current age, was the only one in the room wearing an old-fashioned formal kimono.

A definition of death. To me, this was connected to multiple layers of experience from my early childhood in that valley in the forest on the island of Shikoku, and to the topography of the valley which, without reference to those experiences, I am unable to recapture in my mind. Naturally, in the more than thirty years that have passed since I left the valley I have accumulated other experiences having to do with death, but I realize, looking back, that these were secondary. It was in the valley that I encountered death as an equitable visitor to both my grandmother and my father, whom she had influenced so powerfully. And it was in this valley that I first saw a man who had hanged himself. In the latter case particularly, "in this valley" is a crucial signifier of the experience. When I recall the scene that day, centered around the corpse hanging by the neck, this becomes clear.

The body was discovered behind the stone Jizo altar, in an enclosed area that was slightly lower than but abutted the woods around the Shinto shrine. The little man who was considered beneath notice even by the children when they ran into him along the main road had hung himself. My kid brother went to touch the body—"It was swinging like crazy," he reported. I observed from behind the crowd that had gathered from the village and beyond. We were standing in an area used for airing sake barrels, in the only brewery in the village, already out of business by that time, an area the children were not normally allowed to enter. Looking past the stone Jizo and the Shinto shrine to the deeper green that lay beyond, surveying the forest, which was not a place where people lived, with the hanging corpse at the center of my field of vision, I was filled with admiration. Ah! A man picks a spot like this to hang himself! With the corpse as focal point, the significance of the valley's topography became clear to me (when I used this way of seeing things as the basis of an explanation of how our village was structured, the teacher at the Imperial public school, who was not from our region and required a context I couldn't create, laughed at me as though in pity).

A definition of death. I want to begin with another incident from my experience in the valley. This one left me with an actual scar on my body, and the scar allows me to feel as though the incident continues inside me even now.

It was already late in the war and I was a fourth-grader at the public school. Around the back of our house and down the narrow slope that separated us from the neighbor's, you came to the Oda River. To my mind, the river was an alternative to the main road that ran past the front of the house: when you put together a raft and floated downstream, meanings normally hidden became clear. One morning early in the summer, when the air and the water were still chilly and my friends had stayed

away from the river, I waded in alone armed with a spear gun
for fishing. Although it wasn't a distinct motive, I recall now
that I was clearly being influenced, my pale, scrawny child's
body-and-soul together, by the story of an accident that had
occurred upriver two or three days earlier in the vicinity of Oda
Miyama.

The particulars had made their way downriver to our village as idle conversation here and there along the roadside: a
child had drowned in a pool of the upper reaches of the Oda
River. The boy had dived deep with his spear gun; he was after
the fish that schooled in the caves beyond the crevice in the rocks.
Where the crevice opened, you tilted your head to one side and
slipped through the first narrow barrier. From there, though
your shoulders wouldn't clear, it was possible, if you shifted
slightly to the side, to straighten your head and survey the cave
and even to extend your arms into it. When you had your fish
speared, if you reversed direction and backed through the barrier by tilting your head to the side again, you could float back
to the surface. The boy had completed the better part of this
process handily when he neglected to tilt his head at the last
barrier. With his jaw and the top of his head clamped between
the rocks above and below him, they had had a time of it raising his drowned body to the surface, so it was told. Even a grown
man might forget a small thing like turning his head aside when
he was out of air and fighting to reach the surface—the account
of the accident came with a lesson. Alongside the adults, I was
listening.

The next morning, wiping my goggles with a handful of
punkweed, my useless spear gun in my right hand—the rubber bands of the sling were rotten—I kicked boldly across the
sun-flooded surface of the water. I made my way upriver, to
where the swift current created a deep pool at the base of the
two rocks known as "the Couple," one large, the other smaller.

We children seemed to know the name of every rock on the Oda River, and of every pool and every rapids. It was in that way, by putting it all in words, that we grasped the topography of the valley.

On this morning, although I had stayed away until now because I was not certain I had the lung power to sustain me to the necessary depth, I intended to dive all alone to a place I knew only from hearsay—the adults called it Carp Cave. I planned to have a look inside the crevice in the rocks; if you got deep enough, I had heard, you could squeeze through the barrier by that same tilting of the head to one side. I dived. As if I had tried this before, as if, just two or three days ago, I had tried it in this same water upriver, my dive carried me down to the rock barrier and I worked my head through by turning it and then shifted my position sideways, holding my body horizontal against the upward current. I straightened my head: in front of my nose, in a pristine space brimming with the faint light of the dawn, was a school of carp beyond counting. Unmoving carp, a still life. Of course they appeared still only in relation to the mass of the school; each fish was swimming ceaselessly upstream against the current, which moved even here at the bottom of the pool. Their pale, green flesh was lit from within and embedded with tiny silver points, which also gleamed. And the small, round, watery black eyes of each carp in that school of fish were returning my gaze. I extended my right arm and fired, but the cave was deeper than I thought, and the spear propelled by rotting rubber didn't even carry to the school. I wasn't disappointed; I even felt it was appropriate that the fish had not been disturbed. I would enter this cave smack in the middle of the river in the valley, this egg no matter how you looked at it, just as I was, and go on living here, breathing through gills.

I have the feeling I did in fact stay underwater for a very long time. I even feel that I'm still there, it's as though my whole life until now were summed up in what I read in the ceaselessly shifting pattern created by the carp as they adjusted their positions. Nevertheless, at a certain moment I moved backward from the direction I had taken through the rocks and suddenly my jaws and head were clamped tight in the narrow passageway. What remains in memory after that is flailing around in terrible fear and choking on the water I had swallowed. Then I remember powerful arms thrusting me forward deep inside the cave, in the direction opposite my struggle to extricate myself, then hauling me out with my legs in a tangle. Blood spreading like smoke from the cut in the back of my head. I had been released from the rocks and the grip of hands, and now the current dragged me, still underwater, toward a shallow rapids. As I write, I stroke the back of my head with the fleshy pad of my left thumb and locate the scar from that gash on the rocks. If I had remained there in the cave I would have no wound in my head, I would have stayed on as I was in the valley, naked as the day I was born like a fiend hid in a cloud, without tasting labor and sorrow, not learning and not forgetting—in the grip of these often repeated and familiar sentiments, I trace the line of the scar with my thumb. . . .

The phrase I just quoted as it came to mind, "like a fiend hid in a cloud," also happens to be Blake. The association is rooted in having recalled while reading Blake later the boldness and bravery of that experience, the feeling I had had of thumbing my nose at the world and everything in it with a grin on my face. The poem is a well-known work titled "Infant Sorrow" (I translate *piping loud* as "screaming in a high voice" rather than the more conventional "crying with voice raised"):

> *My mother groand! my father wept*
> *Into the dangerous world I leapt:*
> *Helpless, naked, piping loud;*
> *Like a fiend hid in a cloud.*

When I read these lines about the birth of a child, they evoked for me the ruinous exuberance of that morning. Churning the light of the river's surface with joy, I had set out for the pool at the Couple in a direction that was exactly opposite that of a newborn baby's cry (as though I had affixed a minus sign to it). Symbolically, I was trying to return to my mother's womb along a road in the opposite direction of birth (by advancing in the direction of the minus sign I had installed). But the groaning occasioned by the pain of birth, related neither to grief nor to joy, is neutral; there should be no need to convert it with a minus sign. Dead already and therefore on the other side, my father would welcome his son's return. From the dangerous world, I was returning to the place of safety where I had begun. *Helpless, naked, piping loud; / Like a fiend hid in a cloud.*

That is what I took away from the experience, brought to clarity through the mediation of Blake; and implicit in it was yet another definition of death that was dear and familiar to me. That morning, it was my mother who had discovered me, awash in the shallows like a wounded fish, bleeding, my body thrust up at an angle to the river's surface, and who had taken me to the hospital. Apparently, suspicious of her son's odd agitation that morning, she had followed me from the moment I descended the slope to the river. Which seemed to mean that it must also have been my mother who had pulled me up from the depths of the pool at the Couple after first pushing me, as though in punishment, back into the cave. Through the water clouded with blood (like amniotic fluid!) I have the feeling I may have seen a woman in her late thirties with dark eyebrows arched in an inverted V like a cat's back, her narrowed, angry eyes glaring at me. But could a woman underwater have been capable of that tremendous strength? From the beginning, I had been aware in a child's way that there were elements of this experience that were difficult to talk about. As a result, I said nothing about the incident even to my mother, who, for her part, told me only that she had discovered me bobbing up and down in the shallows, and, to this day, has said nothing more. If it was my mother who came to my rescue at the bottom of the river, it was also my mother who gave me the wound in the back of the head, which remains as a scar even now. What I remember about that wound is that I became feverish and unable to move, and that my mother cradled my upper body in her lap and repeated, as she changed my bandages, "It's too cruel, too cruel . . ." Even for a child, it was not possible to interpret this exclamation as being limited to the wound in plain sight; as I turned the experience of that day over in my mind, it became increasingly difficult to ask my mother about it.

As time passed, I became convinced that the image of my mother's angry face in the water was merely an echo from a dream I had had later while feverish, a conclusion that was part of a process that released me from my mother. The dream was recurrent, but, for precisely that reason, I was able to conclude to myself every time I awoke that it was in fact a dream and not reality.

However, when I married and my first child was born impaired, the image in my dream was exposed to a new light of reality. This was due partly to my mother's attitude and her habit of consciously alluding to things in fragments, and partly to memories she called up in me with her insinuations.

When my son was born with a bright-red lump the size of a second head attached to the back of his skull, I found myself unable to reveal the true situation to either my wife or my mother, and, having installed the baby in critical care for infants at Nihon University Hospital, I wandered around in a daze. Meanwhile, not only the actual head but also the lump appeared to be well nourished and growing; the lump in particular was beginning to radiate vitality that was obvious at a glance even through the glass partition around the critical-care ward. Two and a half months later, I asked Doctor M, who had been caring for my son—and looking after me as I struggled unavailingly to recover from the shock of his birth—to perform surgery.

My mother had arrived in Tokyo the night before the operation intending to help and, having decided before lifting a hand that her presence would be if anything a burden to my wife, was preparing to return to the valley in the forest in Shikoku the following morning after accompanying us as far as the hospital in Itabashi. She was terrified, and my wife, who was no less afraid, was trying to comfort her. Still in her twenties and yet to recover from her debilitation at the time of the birth, I recall that my wife was like a baby chick being blown in the wind. I sat there, in our combination living and dining room, banging my rattan rocking chair against a glass cupboard and feeling out of place as I watched the women. They were sitting on the synthetic rug on the wooden floor of the adjoining room, facing each other across a small trunk, their heads nearly touching as they spoke. Strangely, for two people with such a difference in age and no blood ties, they looked very much alike.

My wife spoke absently, her voice thin and frail. "Eeyore doesn't respond to his parents' voice like a normal baby. If there's a moment during the surgery when life and death separate, we won't be able to call him back to the side of life, it worries me sick . . ." My wife had been saying the same thing for days, and my response had been that a normal child wasn't going to be much better off if that happened, all we could do was leave it to the surgeon and hope for the best.

My mother's agitation was resonating with my wife's anxiety and amplifying it. With emphatic nods more like a furious shaking of her skinny neck, she said, "That's exactly the way it is! In our area, there were lots of times when a life that was bound to die heard the voice of its relative and came right back to life!" Inhaling sharply, she seemed to bite down on her tongue.

On an impulse, selfish when I think about it, to find someone who would commiserate with me about my son's abnormality, I had gone to see my mentor, Professor W, at the private college where he had moved to create a new department of French literature. I had written elsewhere that I watched him flush bright red from his brow to his neck, and now I was recalling what he had said in that state, in a tone of voice he might have used to tell a joke with grief in it. Sitting in his bright new office, his eyes averted from everyone, he had whispered: "In these times, it's not clear that it's better to have been born than not to have been born."

"If the body incorporates elements aimed at both life and death," I said now, "and if a baby exists at the border between the two, maybe we should honor the baby's freedom, the baby's body's freedom! In times like these, it's not clear that it's better to have been born than not to have been born!" These words, spoken diffidently as I banged my chair against the wall in the cramped room, my wife and my mother both ignored, but I saw the profile of my mother's face turn pale and stiffen. Ah, I thought to myself, regretting the imprudence of my remark, this face with eyebrows like inverted V's isn't simply tense, it's very angry!

"You heard him, that's who we're dealing with, so we can't count on him, we're obliged to use your *strength* to help our Eeyore." My mother spoke in a whisper, and my wife, her hair in pin curlers and her face seeming even smaller, nodded fecklessly.

It wasn't until later that night, when I sprawled alone on the bed in my study, that I came to the conclusion that I had misheard my mother, or rather, misunderstood her. It was clear to everyone that *strength,* mine or my wife's, would have nothing to do with the operation in the morning. All we could do was rely on Doctor M. That had been implicit in my wife's apprehensive conversation with my mother about the difficulty of ascertaining the baby's own will toward life. Then I realized that my mother must have meant blood, from the blood—*chi-kara,* rather than strength, *chikara.* Two kinds of blood flowed in the infant's body, mine and my wife's. Having decided that blood from her side of the family could not be counted on where the body's inclination toward life or death was concerned, my mother must have been suggesting to my wife that *her blood* would have to encourage Eeyore in the direction of life.

Having realized this much, I felt certain that the face I had seen in the depths of the pool at the Couple, with the inverted V's for eyebrows, had indeed been my mother's face, and I felt I understood as well that she had angrily written me off at the moment of the accident as a person capable of stepping off the road to life intentionally. Looking back, I could identify a number of instances between my son's birth and his first operation when she had revealed this judgment about me.

Thanks to Dr. M and his assistants, the long operation was a success, my son was liberated from the glistening lump that was like a second head, and my wife and both our mothers were understandably overjoyed. As the young father, I was also very happy, but I recalled the conversation the night before the operation and felt constrained and embarrassed about demonstrating my joy.

A definition of death. I am not able to say that I have provided my handicapped son with a definition of death that is at once accurate, uncomplicated, and capable of encouraging him. What is worse, my wife and I have used the word carelessly in his presence. Looking back, I realized that this had been going on for more than two years until the crisis that made us aware of it, repeatedly. I am clear about how much time had passed because it was late in the spring two years ago—my experience has taught me to believe in the hidden link between the changing seasons, that is, the cycle of the universe, and events that occur deep inside our bodies—that my son experienced an epileptic seizure, an incident that was an unmistakable turning point in our daily life with Eeyore at its center. As we didn't consult a specialist at the time, it wasn't exactly the case that the seizure was diagnosed as epilepsy. Even so, when we informed Doctor M of what had happened, he did not object to my insistence on describing it as an epileptic seizure.

From the onset, my wife and I were of different minds about this. We weren't necessarily opposed—where my son was concerned we often faced in the same direction but took different views. There were times when my son lost his sight briefly and froze where he stood in the street. If this had happened at a railroad crossing or in a crosswalk it would have been dangerous. These events had been occurring intermittently for five or six years, and Dr. M had been controlling them with Hidantol, a drug that caused Eeyore's gums to swell to rosy redness until they protruded from the spaces between his teeth like kernels of red rice but had no other apparent side effect. Hidantol was an antiepileptic, and as such provided me with a basis for diagnosing my son's new seizure.

My wife had heard from her friends in the PTA at our son's special school that epilepsy was a different animal, and that if this were indeed epilepsy it was a very mild case. The term used on the report after the medical exam for middle school was "brain separation syndrome," and although these words were more than adequate to strike terror into the hearts of our nonmedical family, the word "epilepsy," as my wife insisted, did not appear. I searched a number of encyclopedias, looking under "epilepsy" for a subentry on "brain separation syndrome," and failed to find it.

As it happened, my wife wasn't even home when my son had the first of these major new seizures. It began with an unusual atmosphere that felt like the concave underside of protruberant symptoms like screaming or spasms. We were in the living room; I lay reading on the couch as always, and my son was sprawled on the rug on the floor listening to a Mozart record at low volume. Presently, instead of putting on a new record, he pushed away from himself with both elbows, like an infant with no appetite weakly rejecting his food, the pile of records he had selected. This registered in my consciousness like a small thorn. But I continued to read. Before long, an impression of interruption reached me from where my son lay. I looked up. He was propped up on his elbows, all expression gone from his face and his open eyes like stones. Saliva was drooling from between his slightly parted lips.

"Eeyore! Eeyore! What's wrong?" I called out to him. But Eeyore was engaged completely with the difficulty inside himself; as if to say this was no time to be responding to the exterior, not even to the voice of his father, he remained motionless, his head propped heavily in his hands, his face a void.

I jumped up, and, in the brief moment it took to move to his side, he began slapping the floor with his left palm and arm, not wildly but with deliberate force. *Slap, slap,* he struck the floor, and now his eyes rolled up and showed white.

"Eeyore! Eeyore! Are you all right? Does it hurt?" As I shouted meaningless questions I wrapped the handkerchief I took from my pants pocket around my left thumb and forced it between my son's teeth. He bit grindingly down on the joint and I moaned as though to express the pain he was enduring in silence. A minute or two later, he stopped slapping the floor and relaxed his clenched teeth. I lifted him as he rolled over on his back, and when I laid him on the couch he fell into a deep sleep and began to snore at a menacing volume.

It was this physical display by my son's body that I chose to interpret as epilepsy symptoms. Partly because he was home on spring break, my son had apparently neglected to take his medicine for several days. But was this really epilepsy? I needed a definition, and though I consulted a number of encyclopedias in search of one, my wife and I did not go back to Dr. M for a detailed explanation. Over the course of more than ten years we had come to understand that, where our son's illness was concerned, the doctor would make sure to inform us about anything it would avail us to know, and that asking about the rest was an exercise in futility for laymen like ourselves. Admittedly, our custom of not asking may have had to do with deep-seated fear.

Since that first episode, I find myself constantly on the lookout for information that I can feed into my definition of epilepsy. For example, a recent article by the cultural anthropologist Y, in which he analyzed the Greek director Theo Angelopoulos's film *Alexander the Great*. Apparently the chieftain of Greece's peasant guerrillas is portrayed as an epileptic. When the troops descend to the banks of a river to replenish their water, Alexander has a seizure as he gazes at the river's surface. Instantly, to shield him from the gaze of his men while he is in spasm, his next-in-command shouts "About face!" On the march, Alexander baptizes the young men they encounter along the way and christens each one of them Alexander. In an attack by government forces, one of the young men is wounded in the head but is lifted onto a horse and manages to escape from a same battle in which the chieftain is killed and the army decimated. Later, in the scene where the youth enters Athens, the narrator intones: "Thus did Alexander enter the city." The almost too obvious significance of the line was to establish a connection between this scene and the episode when Alexander the chieftain appears in the village as a young man with a wound in his head.

In my biased reading of Y's analysis, I paid particular attention to the above references to epilepsy. Superimposing the wounded youth who was entering Athens now onto the chieftain Alexander in the past led me to the following conclusions: leaders were epileptics because of wounds to the head sustained when they were young; the youth who had just now received his head wound and who was destined to lead the resistance as the next Alexander would just as certainly develop epilepsy. In this manner I created a mythological logic that connected head wounds, epilepsy, and leaders.

I was reinforced in this by the fact that the articles on epilepsy I had found in encyclopedias cited head wounds sustained in infancy or childhood as one of its causes. I concluded that my son's epilepsy was the result of his head surgery when he was two and a half months old. During the operation, the lump on his head was found to contain something like a Ping-Pong ball. When my wife and I had visited Dr. M's office to learn the results of the operation, he had asked if I would like to see it and at first I had declined.

It had never occurred to me for an instant that my son's brain may have been injured during the operation. And yet how could surgery that removed so large a lump and closed the default in his skull have failed to affect an infant's brain? In fact, he had done well to survive the surgery, and I had come to feel respect for his symptoms, as though the recent appearance of epilepsy were a medal for his vitality. Further, and I realize this is hardly more than a mystical reverie, I felt at times as though my son were standing in for me, taking on the epilepsy that might have been produced by the head wound I received at the time of my narrow escape at Carp Cave. At those moments, as

I fingered the scar that was in the same place on my head as was the fault on my son's skull, it seemed to me that the huge power that had manifested underwater at Carp Cave was connected directly to whatever it was that had caused my son's abnormal birth.

Eeyore was lying on the couch watching the news on television—for several days after his first seizure, as though the twisting inside his body had yet to untangle, he had been withdrawn, doleful, and silent—when suddenly, as the newscaster reported the death of a certain elderly master in the world of Japanese classical music, he sat up with surprising agility and shouted, emotionally, "*Oh! He died! He's dead, he's completely dead!*"

The poignancy of my son's lament was a shock to me. It came from somewhere so unexpected and took me so completely by surprise that it was also comical.

"What's wrong, Eeyore, what happened? Did he die? Did you like him that much?" As I questioned him, I felt I might burst out laughing. I'm sure I was smiling.

But Eeyore didn't respond; he fell back on the couch and covered his face with both hands and went rigid. Halfway to the couch I could only keep moving, though I did lose the smile from my face, and continued, "C'mon, Eeyore. You don't have to be so upset." Kneeling at his side, I shook him by the shoulders, but he went even more rigid. For no reason, I tried pulling his hands away from his face, but they were locked into place like a steel lid—I recall that it was around this time that his strength was developing to a point that was beyond our ability to manage—and I could only kneel there staring at his fingers, sentient and refined in a way that seemed to set them apart from the rest of his body.

The comprehensive impossibility of approaching my son. I had experienced the same feeling after his epileptic seizure. He had been used up, as though his entire body had been involved in frantic exercise. Just before he had fallen asleep and begun to snore, and again afterward, when he had awakened, I had repeatedly asked, "Eeyore! Were you in pain? Was it hard to breathe? Were you nauseous? Were you in pain?" but he had remained locked away inside himself, disgruntled and feeble and refusing to respond to my inquiries. Then and now, on two occasions since his seizure, I had experienced my son as an individual whose interior world was closed to me.

In the past, I had always assumed I knew everything that was happening inside him. But I had been unable to discover a single thing about the panorama that must have unfurled as he lay there slapping the floor with his eyes rolled up. (When he had fallen asleep and begun to snore it was as if he were exhausted from having worked on a great project that included beholding a momentous vision. I even fantasized, as when I had peered into Carp Cave long ago, that his vision had included a glimpse into eternity.) And now I was similarly lost, with no basis for even guessing at the thoughts about death that could have produced that heartrending cry of grief and loss. Where had such strong feelings about death come from?

I was to be given an answer soon enough. That same spring break, still wrapped in the gloominess that was an aftereffect of his seizure, my son was listening to an FM broadcast with the volume turned way up. This had continued for hours until everyone in the family was out of patience. Finally, Eeyore's sister, half his size, had requested him to turn the volume down a little and he had made her cower with a menacing gesture.

"Eeyore! You know better than that!" my wife said. "After Papa and I are dead, your brother and sister will have to look after you. If you behave this way no one will like you. What will you do then? How are you going to get along after we're dead?"

So that was it, I acknowledged to myself with a feeling of regret. In this way, repeatedly, we had been introducing my son to the issue of death. But this time his response to our refrain was something new. *"It's all right! Because I'll die. I'll be dying soon, so it's all right!"*

For an instant there was a pause like an intake of breath— my wife had been thrown by this subdued assertion no less than it had dazed me—and then she continued, speaking now in a tone of voice that was more soothing than reproachful:

"Of course you're not going to die, Eeyore. What makes you think you're going to die? Who told you that?"

"I'll be dying right away, because I had a seizure! It's all right, because I'll be dying!"

I moved to my wife's side where she stood at the couch and looked down at my son: he was covering his face resolutely with both hands, his dark eyebrows and the sharply raised bridge of his nose, which resembled his movie-actor uncle's, visible between his fingers. New words to say seemed to stick in our throats, as if we both felt how futile they would be. His voice had been so forceful just now, yet already he was perfectly still, not a muscle moving.

Thirty minutes later, as my wife and I sat in silence and for some reason facing each other across the table in our dining room, my son shuffled past us on his way to the bathroom. He was still covering his face with both hands. His sister, feeling responsible for the situation before, was at his side, clinging to him as she spoke: "Eeyore, be careful! If you cover your face while you walk, you'll bump into stuff. You could trip and hit your head!" Probably, this was also intended as a criticism of her mother's approach to scolding earlier. Eeyore's younger brother fell into step and moved off with him to the bathroom. Through the unclosed door came the sound of copious urinating. Finished, Eeyore seemed to go straight into his mother's bedroom across the hall.

"I think it's bad to talk like that," my daughter said when she returned. "It makes Eeyore feel lonely when he thinks of the future." Her face seemed pinched and small, as though covered in goose pimples.

Standing side by side with his sister, her younger brother spoke, revealing that he, too, had evolved a position that was independent of his parents': "Eeyore was wiping his tears with his forefinger straight out and horizontal, like he was slicing across his eye with a knife. That's the proper way of wiping tears. Even though nobody else does it that way."

Forlornly, ashamed of ourselves, my wife and I were recalling the words we had repeated endlessly until now—"After we die, Eeyore! What will become of you? What will you do!" For my own part, I was also realizing that, inasmuch as I had never considered carefully how these crucial words might echo deep in my son's heart, I had not yet arrived at a definition of death, not even at a definition of what it meant to *me* let alone to him!

Like an earthquake, the epileptic seizure had produced tremors beneath the surface of Eeyore's body and emotions. As he recovered from its aftereffects and, when spring break ended, returned to special class at middle school, he also seemed to regain his psychological well-being. Following the seizure, there was a time when even the way he listened to music had seemed abnormally off balance, but now his rapt attention conveyed once again an impression of unclouded pleasure.

Nevertheless, there was no room for doubt that a concept of death, whatever its nature, had taken root in him. Every morning, when he finished dressing himself properly to go to school, Eeyore sat down on the rug in the living room. Spreading his plump thighs and dropping his rear heavily to the floor, he hunkered down and opened the morning paper. To read the obituaries. Encountering the name of a new illness, he would hold his breath as he deciphered the Chinese characters he had learned by showing them to my wife and me, and would then recite with feeling: *"Ah, there was lots of dying again this morning! Pernicious pneumonia, age eighty-nine, coronary infarction, age sixty-nine, bronchial pneumonia, aged eighty-three. Ah! This gentleman was the founder of fugu-fish poisoning research, venal thrombosis, age seventy-four, lung cancer, age eighty-six. Ah! There was plenty of dying again!"*

"People are always dying, Eeyore, but many more new people are born every day! Now off to school you go and don't worry! Be careful at the railroad crossing, otherwise—"

Otherwise, you might die yourself—my wife had choked back the second half of her warning with a shudder.

Eeyore became sensitive to reports of food poisoning on the evening news. Beginning in early June in the rainy season and into summer, there were a number of incidents. Each time, he would rush to the television set and parrot the newscaster at the top of his lungs, for example: *"Ah! An entire party at the Nippori outdoor market got food poisoning from their box lunches, the lunches were the tea-shop variety!"*

A week or two later, summer vacation having begun, we took a train to Gumma prefecture where we have a cabin in the mountains, and Eeyore wouldn't touch the box lunch they sold at the station that he looked forward to eagerly in a normal year. We repeatedly urged him to eat. Before long his eyes became severely crossed, and covering his mouth with one hand he thrust the other out in front of him defensively. This rejection was so emphatic that strangers turned to eye us suspiciously, as if we were imposing a cruel punishment on our child. That summer, my son also stopped eating sushi, one of his favorites until then. Basically, he refused to put any raw fish in his mouth. Pigs' feet, which he had always liked, became another of the dishes he declined to touch after overeating gave him diarrhea. The result was that he lost twenty-two pounds in just under a year. It seemed this was also a reaction to having been told by the school doctor that he would develop problems if he became obese.

Because he has learned to take his medicine religiously, Eeyore hasn't suffered another major seizure like the one that terrified me, but there have been a number of episodes during the past two years that were like harbingers of a seizure. Whenever this happened and he had to stay home from school and spend the day on the couch, my son would mournfully announce a new abnormality in some organ of his body: "*Ah! There's not a sound coming from my heart! I think I'm dying! My heart isn't making a sound!*"

My wife and I would fashion a stethoscope from a rubber tube and hold it to my son's chest and ear. Or provide an amateur consultation about coronary seizure, choosing words my son could handle, struggling somehow to ease his concern about death. At the same time, I would probe to discover, using the pain or the anxiety he was experiencing now as a bridge, the form in which he had been aware of these same feelings at the time of his first seizure. But in the end, I was never able to uncover any substantial information.

I did manage in the process, indirectly, to extract Eeyore's assessment of certain behavior of his own that had baffled me until then. If I were to re-create the conversation that took place between us—actually, I made numerous inquiries over time, but if I were to summarize—our dialogue was as follows. My son's reply, obscure as it was, had about it a strange ring that did put me and my wife in mind of something.

"Eeyore, a while before you had your seizure you remember pulling out your hair? You pulled out the hair above the plastic flap in your head, little by little, remember, and you made a round bald spot? You kept it up every day. Was that because it was itchy? Was the skin on top of the flap pulling? Did it hurt? Did it feel so bad inside your head you couldn't stand it if you didn't pull your hair out? You must remember? What was going on?"

"*That was an interesting time! The old days were interesting!*" My son's smile was absent as he spoke, as though he had sent his thoughts to a distant place.

As the rainy season ended and summer began in earnest, we took my son to Nihon University Hospital. I have described his violence while I was away in Europe, and assuming this had a physical cause he would have to be examined by a specialist. My wife went to the reception desk at brain surgery to present the usual card requesting an examination by Dr. M, and when she returned to the couch in one corner of the waiting room where I sat with my son she seemed dejected. "Dr. M turned sixty-five and had to retire. He's still here a few times a week and apparently he'll see patients who request a special appointment."

My son was in high spirits at the prospect of meeting Dr. M for the first time in a long while. Grasping right away that for some reason the doctor was not waiting in the examination room beyond the curtain—he was always swift to comprehend matters concerning himself—his vitality ebbed. My wife and I were stymied; it was as if we had never doubted that, so long as we showed up at the hospital, Dr. M would be there— eternally!—to give us reliable instructions about our son. Now we realized, looking back over those nineteen years, that while Dr. M's examination room and white smock, and his decisiveness and the well-bred humor beneath it, had never changed, his posture and appearance had been moving year by year toward old age. Images of the doctor played across our minds like flashbacks as we sat there in silence. But I was the most disheartened. When my son's name came over the speaker and my wife took him in to see the new doctor, I stayed behind on the pretext of looking after our belongings.

Ten minutes later, he emerged from the examination room with his bright mood restored. My wife also seemed encouraged, but beneath her excitement I could sense that her mind was still wheeling, and her interior agitation prompted me to steel myself for the next revelation of difficulty. She reported that Eeyore had to have a number of tests; we were to do blood and urine first and then go to radiology.

On our way to the lab, my wife told me that the new doctor had been assisting Dr. M ever since he had first operated on Eeyore nineteen years ago. And he had expressed doubt that the symptoms of recent years were related to epilepsy. As far as he could remember, Eeyore had been born with two brains separated by the defect in his skull. Having determined that the external brain was not functioning, Dr. M had excised it, but the portion of the living brain nearest the site of the surgery controlled the optic nerve. If the brain had been traumatized there, Eeyore might well suffer a loss of sight for brief periods of time, and the symptoms we had interpreted as epilepsy could be related to the same problem—

I interrupted: "Two brains? They cut away the brain on the outside that wasn't working?"

"The doctor said you definitely knew about it—and I finally understood what they meant when they put down 'brain separation syndrome.'"

Two brains: that would make clear beyond any possibility of misunderstanding the meaning of the deformity my son had brought into the world with him, of that glistening, flesh-colored lump large enough to be mistaken for a second head—but it was impossible that I could have learned this from Dr. M at the time of the operation and concealed it from my wife.

"You know that pen drawing of a brain on the wall above the desk in your study?" my wife said. "There's a single eye in the middle of it, and judging from the size of that eye, the brain seems a little smaller than normal. I wonder if that isn't a sketch of the other brain?"

I did prize that sketch of a brain. It had been used as the frontispiece in a collection of essays that Professor W had published just after the war, *On Madness and Other Matters*. But, as far as I was consciously aware, I had placed the illustration in a wooden frame and hung it on the wall because I had been profoundly influenced by the following passage in that book: "There are those who say that great achievements are impossible in the absence of madness. That is untrue! Achievements enabled by madness are invariably accompanied by desolation and sacrifice. Truly great achievements are attained by humanistic individuals laboring honestly, tirelessly, humbly while acutely conscious, far more so than others, that they are susceptible to madness."

After the operation, when Dr. M had told me about the object like a Ping-Pong ball, I had pictured it, because of the association with a defect in the skull, as a sort of bone; now my wife seemed to suspect that my description to her, of a lump that contained bonelike material, had been intentionally misleading. As though I were under the influence of my wife's suspicion, I was having second thoughts of my own. Perhaps Dr. M had informed me about the two brains right away and I had prevented myself protectively from registering the information. And perhaps it had been my subconscious understanding that had drawn me so powerfully to Professor W's ink drawing of a brain that, based on the proportion of the single eye, was clearly smaller than normal.

With a word of thanks spoken in the tone of a radio announcement, Eeyore emerged from the X-ray room into the corridor. Tests were a major undertaking for him: though he worked hard at following the doctor's instructions, his clumsiness was so extreme it made me wonder whether his bone structure might be abnormal. The X rays had been the last test, and as we climbed into a taxi my son said earnestly but with elation in his voice, "*It was extremely painful, but I did my best!*"

Something was troubling me. "That condition you mentioned," I said to my wife. "Did the doctor explain it in a way that Eeyore could understand?"

"I think so—he seemed very interested. He said, 'Oh boy! Two of them, two brains!' Something like that."

"*Exactly! I had two brains! But now I have one. Mama, I wonder where in the world my other brain went?*"

A laugh burst from the cabdriver, who had been listening; he flushed from his cheeks to his ears and seemed angry at himself for his gaffe. Some drivers who make hospitals the hub of their business have what might be called a mission to make a show of sympathy for patients and their families. Our driver's solicitude had backfired, and he seemed to be punishing himself. But when my son was in a good mood he enjoyed punning and word play, even now he had been mimicking a television commercial, so if anything the driver's laugh would have flattered him. Riding the wave of the moment, I said, "Eeyore, your other brain died. But there's a fine, living brain doing its very best inside your head! But you had two brains, that's really something!"

"*You bet it is—really something!*"

How to handle this new information, that there had been a pair of brains? I sat vacantly, unable to resolve my feelings, and Eeyore's cheerful surprise at learning the truth, his exultation, provided me with a hint. What reason did I have not to be as encouraged as he was by this new knowledge? My son had come into the world burdened with two brains, but he had survived surgery and the aftereffects—doing his best though it was extremely painful—and he was standing on his own two feet.

"Eeyore, you're alive because that other brain died. You need to take good care of the brain you have and do your best to live to a ripe old age!"

"Exactly! Let's do our best and live to a ripe old age! Sibelius was ninety-two, Scarlatti was ninety-nine, Eduardo Di Capua lived until he was one hundred and twelve! Oh boy, that was really something!"

"Does the young gentleman like music?" the cabbie asked in an attempt to recover lost ground, his eyes on the road ahead. "What kind of a musician was that Mr. Eduardo?"

"He wrote 'O Sole Mio'!"

"You don't say! Isn't that something! You take good care of yourself!"

"Thank you very kindly, I'm going to do my best!"

I was picturing a desert landscape. A cold babe—a babe who was only a small-sized brain with a single eye opened in it—stands in the furious air. It screams, the kind of scream a babe who is only brain matter can scream: . . . *the children of six thousand years / Who died in infancy rage furious a mighty multitude rage furious / Naked & pale standing on the expecting air to be delivered.*

3: Down, Down thro' the Immense, with Outcry

About two years ago, when my son was still in the special class at middle school, there was a period when I was trying to teach him to swim. For several months in the autumn and winter of that year, I took him with me to my swimming club at least once and sometimes three times a week. I was prompted by a remark the physical education teacher made to my wife at Parents' Day, about how difficult Eeyore was to handle during swimming drills. Apparently, the teacher had expressed his view that my son lacked the will to float, even the body's instinctive will to float—"It was a little like training a cup." These thoughts were disturbing to my wife, but when she reported them to me I knew immediately what the teacher was talking about. And when I took my son to the pool, the nature of the poor fellow's distress became so clear to me that I had to laugh out loud. There was no question that this was going to be harder than teaching a cup to swim.

If you put a cup down on the water's surface, it will fill and sink. But if a cup had ears you might at least say, "C'mon! Let's try to stay afloat!" In my son's case, while it was clear that he did not float, it wasn't so easy to say with any finality that he sank. Standing in the pool I would give him instructions, and it appeared that he was doing his best to follow them obediently; at the same time he also appeared oblivious. Gradually, I stopped imagining the part-time phys ed teacher's irritation and began feeling my own.

"Again, Eeyore! Head in the water, arms out in front, and let's kick those feet as hard as we can!"

My son wasn't afraid of the water. He didn't hesitate for an instant. And he moved just as I told him to. It was just that he moved at a pace that had nothing to do with the standard I was vaguely expecting. Slowly. Like a viscous liquid sinking into a blotter, or a bivalve burrowing into the sand.

Lowering his head peacefully to the water and extending both arms in front of him, he lifts his feet from the bottom. He moves his arms in a manner that suggests he is picturing himself not only floating but swimming the crawl, but the motion is so thoroughgoingly gentle that his arms seem to encounter no resistance from the water. Meanwhile, his body gradually descends toward the depths. And at a certain point in the process, in an entirely natural move, Eeyore stands on the bottom again. He doesn't panic on the way down, there is no writhing or swallowing lungfuls of water. Since in the course of this series of actions he has advanced two or three feet, repeating the series will carry him, very slowly to be sure, from one end of the pool to the other. It appears he may even be thinking secretly that this is his way of swimming in the pool.

I called out to him constantly, "Dig your hands into the water" or "Try pushing forward with your feet," and each time he responded in the same amiable way, *"That's an excellent idea!"*

But the minute he lowered his head to the water he began to move like a swimmer in a dream or an image in a slow-motion film and showed no sign of improving. Sometimes I put my goggles on and swam alongside to coach him along: underwater, his movements were calm, so very calm that I could see his deep-set, oval eyes wide open in an expression of quiet wonder and could see each bubble from his nose and mouth as it rose glintingly toward the surface. I found myself wondering whether this might not be the manner in which nature intended a person to behave underwater.

Though I took my son with me to the pool twice a week and sometimes more, there was no indication that his swimming style was changing. Since the swimmer himself appeared to be having a good time, there was nothing wrong with that; but on days when the pool was crowded, we had a problem. The club had two pools for competitive swimming and three deeper pools for diving and scuba training, but Eeyore could use only the twenty-five-meter main pool when a lane had been reserved for "leisure swimming." When the main pool was occupied by swimmers from the swimming school or those practicing in the training lanes, the only other place available for him to swim was the twenty-meter pool reserved for club members.

But since mid-autumn, there had been times when the doors in the glass partition around the Members Pool had all been locked. It had been reserved, in other words, by a special group. Since they were never there for more than two hours, I would let Eeyore swim in a training lane in the twenty-five-meter pool when one happened to be open, or, failing that, we would wait for the group in the Members Pool to finish. Once Eeyore had put on his bathing suit and gone downstairs to the pools, there was no point in even mentioning that swimming might not be possible that day. On the other hand, if it came to waiting, my son would sit on the bench at poolside for as long as necessary without saying a word.

The group that had chartered the Members Pool was unique to the club, and had its own unique pattern of activity. It consisted of fifteen young men in their late twenties. I can be definite about their number because we could hear them counting off before and after practice on the other side of the glass partition. For reasons I shall explain, the counting was in Spanish—*uno, dos, tres, cuatro*—and always ended with *quince*.

The young men were of course Japanese, and everything about them, from their bodies to the expressions on their faces to their most trivial movements, made it appear that they were being trained in the manner of our former military. Their roll call in Spanish was unmistakably military in style. Some time ago, I spent several months in Mexico City; and I remember waking on a Sunday or holiday morning to children outside the apartment shouting back and forth in a Spanish round with vowels that was so familiar it took me back in a flash to the Shikoku village of my boyhood and churned my dreams as I awakened—the Spanish of this roll call had nothing in common with the language of my youth; there was a growling coarseness to it that was the sound of a Japanese soldier.

There were other things about these young men that smacked of the military: their short crew cuts, the khaki bathing suits like short pants they wore when they came downstairs to the pool—when I ran into them as they were getting off the midsize bus like a patrol wagon that brought them to and from the club, they were wearing dark- and light-green-striped camouflage suits—and the identical look of their bodies. The swimmers from the university swimming club who worked out in the weight room on the third floor had skin and muscles that were the product of bringing excessive nourishment under control in the course of a pampered life of luxury. Theirs were privileged bodies, supple and abundant to a degree that was almost wanton. When they weren't exercising, their spoiled, juvenile faces had a way of looking slack and foolish. The military young men, partly because they were ten years older as a group, were another physical type entirely. Their bodies were also developed, but there was something hungry and reckless about them, as if they had earned their muscles doing hard labor like digging ditches. When they trained in the pool, they swam like amateurs, flailing the water powerfully but ineffectively with their hands and feet; and their leader, a man named Shumuta who had a national reputation as a swimming coach, seemed disinclined to correct them.

When the young men arrived in their lockup of a bus with its windows narrowed by wooden frames, they filed into the club through the employees' entrance and changed in a corner of the swimming-school locker room that was reserved for their exclusive use when they were in the building. While they were swimming in the Members Pool, the glass partition was kept locked, and when they were finished they showered and drove away in the bus without ever using the steam room or the sauna. In other words, the sphere of their activity isolated them from the rest of the club, but some of the women members were openly resentful nevertheless: "It's like they come here to swim from prison. They don't even talk to each other, and those grim faces! Those guys aren't living in the same age as we are!"

I remembered this last remark in particular because I had received the same impression; it felt to me as if the golden years of Japan's postwar resurgence would fit nicely into the gap in time that separated the college swimmers and the young men's group. Their leader, on the other hand, Mr. Shumuta, was a sunny, vivacious individual who seemed very much in the present, and while the young men were in the pool he would sit in the steam room or soak in the hot tub and strike up cheerful conversations with anyone in earshot. In fact, the contrast between Mr. Shumuta and the young men he led was so extreme it pointed in the direction of something almost grotesque about their relationship.

Although I didn't ask about details—Mr. Shumuta's background was apparently common knowledge among the regulars at the club and making outright inquiries felt awkward—there was no question that he had been an Olympic-class athlete in track and field. At the height of his career, several of his toes had been severed in an accident. The pink stubs seemed raw even now; when he sat soaking in the cold-water tub with his meaty but firm legs thrown out carelessly in front of him, it was impossible not to notice them. After the accident, he had apparently given up competition and built a successful career as a personal trainer to athletes, traveling as a regular member of the Japanese team to one Olympics after another. Until recently, he had also taught physical education at Keio University. The director of the athletic club at Keio had been his prize student during his college days, and as a result of that connection it seemed that Mr. Shumuta had been an adviser to our swimming club ever since it had been founded. Undoubtedly, it was this history that had persuaded the club, in a radical departure from its own policies, to allow private use of the Members Pool, albeit for limited periods of time.

His high, jutting forehead and two cheeks like three opposing hillocks in the face of a huge baby, Mr. Shumuta would

install his large body in the sauna or the hot tub and fill the room
with hearty laughter that echoed off the tile wall, yet when you
actually spoke with him it was immediately clear that this was
not a man who was characterized by youthful innocence. Not-
withstanding that glistening face of a happy giant baby, the
narrow eyes like wrinkles beneath wispy eyebrows made you
wonder if a smile had ever crinkled them before.

"*Sensei*"—on his lips the word didn't sound like the standard
salutation used among faculty colleagues to address each other;
there was contempt in his emphasis, as though he were a day la-
borer with something gnawing at him speaking down to a man
who earned his living in his study. When I went into the steam
room alone, having left my son soaking in the tepid hot tub, Mr.
Shumuta had called out as though he had been waiting for me.

"I heard about you from a friend in Mexico City. I've been
going down there since the Mexico Olympics. Someone else I
know, a Japanese, he owns a pretty big truck farm and I'll be
taking some young fellas down there and moving in. The Mexi-
cans are making a fuss about importing labor into the country
but I expect that'll go away—as soon as I get them trained a little
on the farm we'll take off for the wilderness. Anyways, *Sensei,* I
was hoping you'd give my boys a talk about Mexico—it would
be great if you could do it in Spanish!"

"I can't help you there! I only picked up a few words and
phrases—"

"C'mon now, let's not be modest! A man of your background, I'll bet you speak like a native if you're in the country
for half a year!"

"I did stay in Mexico City, but I didn't concentrate on learning Spanish."

"You can say that till you're blue in the face, but I know
how easy it is for a *sensei* like you to pick up a language. You
take my boys, now that's a different story! As long as they're at

training camp they're only allowed to use Spanish. It's a solid
year with no furloughs and no Japanese books allowed in the
dormitory. No newspapers or television either. Not even radios.
There's a few of them have taken to speaking Spanish in their
sleep. The trouble is, they wake up, you get my meaning? By
now they must be starved for Japanese; someone got hold of a
cartoon magazine one of the kids in swimming school had
brought with him and the whole gang was all over it like sharks,
tearing it out of each other's hands until pages went flying. I
caught them in the act and threw the whole lot into the changing
room and made them run the gauntlet buck naked. I was careful to make sure that none of the children were peeking in—the
director here is pretty fussy about discipline. If you ask me, you
can't do better than a little whomping on the buttocks, you get
my meaning? Anyways, I'd really like you to speak to them in
Spanish. About half this gang used to be right-wing fanatics, and
the other half were Commie agitators. All of them would love to
have a discussion with you, I'm not sure why. The ones who studied with M *Sensei* "—Mr. Shumuta abruptly mentioned the name
of the famous novelist who had committed suicide a number of
years ago—"are the keenest—"

"I really can't speak Spanish—I have enough trouble with
English if I don't prepare in advance."

"There you go again! You don't have to be so cautious. My
boys are *former* radicals; now they've seen the light and they're
off to Mexico in search of a new world, they're not into violence.
It's debate they want, just debate, you get my meaning? Think it
over—how about sometime around the tenth anniversary of M
Sensei's suicide? Wouldn't that be something! I'd appreciate it!"

I noticed Eeyore's eyes peering anxiously in at us through
the heat-resistant glass, as though disturbed by Mr. Shumuta's
explosive laughter, and I stood up and left the sauna. I was feeling curiously guilty about the invitation he had offered me in a

voice that was both amused and a challenge. The truth was, I did speak Spanish—I wondered whether it wasn't simple cowardice that was making me so cautious about these *former* rightists and leftists who were said to be interested in me?

Following my conversation with Mr. Shumuta, I couldn't help thinking about his young men, and my interest in them led directly to personal issues of my own. As it happened, the tenth anniversary of M's suicide was approaching, and posters for commemorative events to be sponsored by various groups on that day began appearing on street corners.

Meanwhile, one of the club's members had come to his own conclusions about Mr. Shumuta's group that cast them in a different light than their leader. He seemed to place particular importance on the tenth anniversary of M's death. This member's name was Minami, and while there were those who felt that his critique was based on negative rumors that were motivated by resentment of the group for monopolizing the Members Pool at designated times and locking others out, he was, after all, an assistant professor studying the physical and psychological dimensions of sports medicine at Keio University, where Mr. Shumuta had formerly taught, and this gave him a degree of credibility. On the other hand, he and the other regular members of the exercise club retained a certain happy-go-lucky quality from their student days and teased one another in a manner that appeared jocular but concealed malice. All the while he spoke, sitting in the sauna—Mr. Shumuta happened not to be there—a smile had played around his gentle, feminine eyes in counterpoint to the murky darkness of his subject.

Minami held that it was not quite the case, as Mr. Shumuta had represented, that some of the young men in the group had studied with M. In fact, while it was true that the group was split between extreme positions on the Left and the Right politically, the bond that united all its members was their adherence to M's philosophy and M's action. Not all of them had belonged to his private army, but most of them in their individual loneliness had read and admired his writing, and had felt abandoned when he committed suicide. It wasn't until after his death that they had formed a group to study his thinking and his action. At some point, a student who had been a member of Mr. Shumuta's athletic club had served as the middleman in bringing his former coach and the group together. Mr. Shumuta had become friendly with M at the gym where he lifted weights.

Mr. Shumuta had been advising the group for ten years; but they had been training at a camp with their numbers reduced only since the end of the year before last. A majority of voices had called for culminating their activities on the tenth anniversary of M's suicide, and when they had dissociated themselves from those who demurred, the remaining number had built a training camp in the woods along the Odakyu train line with funds that Mr. Shumuta had raised from a powerful figure on the Right with whom he was also said to be friendly. Land in Mexico was indeed being held for them, and they were currently in training to immigrate there, which explained the emphasis on Spanish. As it happened, one of Minami's young colleagues was teaching Spanish at the camp. It was apparently true that only Spanish was allowed at the training site, but the instructor had reported that the young men were most zealous about weapons training with converted sheath knives and other gear. "I don't know what Shumuta is plotting, but I don't believe those young braves are intending to start all over in Mexico because things have gone from bad to worse in the ten years since M died—how do you know they're not thinking now is the time to rise up and use those knives they've been honing for ten years! When M was alive, he said more than once that he hated your politics, right? And after the incident you criticized his suicide. You show up to give a talk, what's to stop them from taking you down as first blood on their way to battle in the streets? They could even be planning to use their Spanish as code when they storm the Tokyo Garrison in Ichigaya to avenge M. . . ."

New posters about the tenth anniversary of M's death were appearing in the streets every day. And one day a few of Mr. Shumuta's students deserted while they were at the club. This gave rise to new thoughts about the group. Although I wasn't there at the time, I happened to be present at a conversation about the incident between Mr. Minami and Mr. Shumuta and learned some of the details.

One afternoon early in November when I arrived at the club with Eeyore and we went downstairs, no one was swimming in the Members Pool. As we were on our way there after taking a shower, a student who was working at the club part-time came running over to let us know that it was closed. There had been an accident that morning, he said, and the wall of glass brick facing on the street had been broken. Peering through the glass on this side, I could see that the far corner of the exterior wall across the pool was caved in as though it had been tunneled. Three men in coveralls seemed to be inspecting the hole; they were probably estimating the cost of repair. Meanwhile, Mr. Shumuta was moving his hard, inflated-rubber-tire body busily back and forth, talking volubly in what appeared to be high spirits.

With no idea of what had happened, I took Eeyore to the main pool and waited for the break between swimming-school classes to let him practice his slow-motion underwater approach to swimming. Then I sat him down on a bench alongside the pool and swam some laps myself, kicking hard to save time.

When we went upstairs to the sauna, Mr. Minami and Mr. Shumuta were in the middle of a conversation they appeared to be enjoying. I sat down apart from them and began lathering Eeyore's body with soap to avoid having to say hello.

"Glass brick has gone way down! I thought we'd be looking at ten thousand but it's only a fraction of that and they're not even charging for the repair—I started feeling guilty . . ." As he spoke, Mr. Shumuta's head moved back and forth on a neck that was thick as a bull's and soaking wet with what was clearly sweat and not hot water from the tub.

"The important thing is that no one was injured," Minami said woodenly, as though he were trying to distance himself from Mr. Shumuta.

"That's because they've been tempered! It would take a lot more than that to hurt them. Even if they couldn't avoid injury they wouldn't get into that much trouble. Light stuff, nothing major! Those bodies have been tempered! Now they're like me—an ordinary person would have lost a foot in that accident I had!"

"They say that two of them lifted the bench and the third guided it from the back and they slammed it into that wall to open an exit for themselves. Then apparently they used the bench as a bridge to the outside over the broken glass. They had a perfect plan, like pros!"

"Pros at running away are no use to anyone."

"So what now? Did you inform the police?"

"*Sensei,* this is none of the police's business! Whoever wants to run away should do it. Boys like that would be of no use to us even if we brought them back. At my place, we have strict rules about how we live but nobody's watching to see that people don't run away."

"Then why did they wait until they got to the pool to escape? I mean, shattering a glass wall with a bench and fleeing in a bathing suit is a dangerous stunt; one false move and they could have been seriously injured—"

"Those bodies don't make false moves." Mr. Shumuta laughed his hearty laugh again. "I'm not sure why they didn't have the good sense to change clothes. Were they afraid of running into me upstairs? Or did that wild hair they caught when they were down at the pool feel like it just couldn't wait?"

"Probably both." In Minami's curiously clipped reply there was no trace of the young girl's bashfulness that normally played around his eyes when he spoke.

"But look here, most of them stayed right where they were even though that wall was breached and I wasn't around—"

Without responding, Minami rose and headed for the locker room. Mr. Shumuta turned in my direction, his enigmatic eyes like deep wrinkles in a face that was otherwise illuminated by a meaningless smile, but I had no desire to take over the role of listener and kept my concentration focused on scrubbing Eeyore's hair.

"That's a big mistake, *Sensei,* that kind of coddling is no good for a retarded child! I bet he still wets his bed at night. You've got to give him a sense of independence, and that means you've got to temper him!" Mr. Shumuta knit his skimpy eyebrows in a scowl, but his face retained the look of a cheerful giant baby and the effect was merely grotesque. At that moment, Minami returned for his goggles and bathing suit and began to talk and, though I felt a little sorry for Mr. Shumuta, I took the opportunity to hurry out of the sauna with Eeyore in tow.

"Shumuta *Sensei,* shouldn't you be getting back to your students right away? How do you know the fugitives aren't plotting to sneak back and dragoon the others? There's a group that's using the photograph of M's severed head for a rally poster, and there's a rumor going around at school that they're plotting something for the tenth anniversary of the Ichigaya coup d'état.

Your boys are cut off from news about the outside world, but what would happen if that poster were shoved in their faces? I wouldn't be surprised if the whole gang joined in!"

M had chosen to die by his own hand on November 25, the anniversary of the patriot Shoin Yoshida's death. The day arrived, and there were special programs about the incident on radio and television from morning till night. I had been out of the country at the time, but there were images and sound bites that brought back the moment with a vividness that made me feel I had witnessed it in person. I did observe that the horrific photograph of M's severed head did not appear on the television screen or in the newspapers, and that coverage of the student rally that had used the photo as a poster was also suppressed.

Early that afternoon, Eeyore returned from special school with a note from the physical education teacher. According to Eeyore's own report, which he delivered as though he were reciting it, he had been asked how his swimming was progressing and had replied only that he didn't remember. The teacher was recommending that we should resume swimming lessons, and when I suggested we might go to the pool that day, Eeyore was enthusiastic.

When we arrived at the club, as if Mr. Shumuta had accepted a challenge to bring his young men to a pool in the middle of the city on M's anniversary, his group (whose roll call must now have ended with *doce*) had already occupied the Members Pool and was thrashing around in the water. The swimming school was also in full session, and for the moment I was unable to find a lane that Eeyore and I could use. We sat down on a bench on the exit side of the showers to wait for the next recess in classes; winter weather had arrived, and it felt awkward and out of place to be sitting there naked without even going into the water while people outside in the street were in their over-coats against the cold. The bench was positioned above the pools: from where we sat we could survey the expanse of the twenty-five-meter pool on the left and the locked glass partition around the Members Pool. The deep, narrow pool reserved for diving and scuba diving was immediately in front of us.

At the far end, an instructor from the university who was also well known in the swimming world—I had used his book to correct my stroke in the crawl—was coaching a schoolgirl the club was grooming to be a competitive diver. Standing at the long edge of the pool, which put his back to the glass partition, the instructor had the girl dive repeatedly from a board that was adjustable with a round handle; but the basis of the judgments that caused him to nod or shake his head in the brief moment when the girl was in the air between the board and the water's surface was imperceptible to the eyes of a novice. Even so, there was something enthralling about watching her young body tense for an instant, contract, explode, and finally release into a state that appeared utterly relaxed.

Before long, Mr. Shumuta appeared at the instructor's side dressed in a training suit. In the same position as the coach, with his back to the young men in his charge, he observed the diving practice intently. Bringing the men to the club on the day of the rallies at all had been a courageous move, but it appeared he wasn't comfortable about taking his time in the hot tub and the sauna while they practiced, as he normally did. On the other hand, he must have felt that standing guard at the Members Pool would have amounted to a loss of face and therefore had chosen instead to observe the diving practice in the neighboring pool.

Abruptly, a silent commotion broke out on the other side of the glass partition. A jostling throng of young men in khaki shorts gathered at the glass wall and appeared to be gesturing frantically. As I rose from the bench I saw Mr. Shumuta turn as though in panic to confront the disturbance on the other side of the glass. What had happened? At that moment I was in the grip of an urgency of my own that was entirely out of context; if M's severed head had incited those young men to riot I would neither cower nor step aside nor flee; I would take my own stand against the power of that severed head, however helpless I might be to oppose this robust private army, even if it meant taking a beating in front of Eeyore.

The next instant, one of the young men in the crowd cracked the glass with a resolute blow of his fist. Thrusting an arm now bloodied to the elbow through the opening, he gestured in this direction. Through the same break in the splintered glass the muffled voices of the young men in chorus struck at me like a blow to the stomach.

El niño, el muchacho, la piscina, difícil, enfermo . . . peligroso, anegarse!

In other words: the child, the young man, pool, difficulty, illness, dangerous, to drown—they were shouting whatever Spanish words they had at their command. With a move so very slow it felt contemptible even to myself, I turned around and verified that Eeyore was not sitting on the bench. As I stood there Mr. Shumuta sailed past me with astonishing agility for a body that bulged all over with muscles and I perceived for the first time, feeling released from a question that had been troubling me: So that's it! He looks like the Michelin tire man!

On the other side of the showers against a pillar was a tank six feet across but forty-five feet deep that was used for underwater practice. Normally it was covered with a net, but I had a feeling I might have seen it open on my way in this morning. I hurried after Mr. Shumuta; he was planted in front of the tank, peering down into it, and then I saw him strip off his training suit in two motions. He eased himself gingerly into the water, feet first. Before the ripples had spread across the surface, I glimpsed Eeyore, his mouth wide open, slowly sinking as though he were swimming in space. "Down, down thro' the immense, with outcry, fury & despair"—the line occurred to me out of context as I leaned over the tank with both hands on the rim. In front of my nose, Mr. Shumuta's large, red foot with the missing toes was thrust above the water as he spiraled perpendicularly down toward the bottom of the tank.

On our way home that day, Eeyore and I sat side by side on the train as forlornly as two children who had almost drowned. My own gloom was partly due to something Mr. Shumuta had said to me when he had finished helping Eeyore cough up the water he had swallowed.

"Taking care of the children is sure a major pain in the rear! But it's not as though we can leave off in the middle once we've started!" There was nothing high-handed about his tone of voice this time, as when he had scolded me for coddling a retarded child, but his words still struck me like a coup de grâce—in that moment of emergency, the only thing I had been able to do was recall a line of Blake!

At times like this, there was only one person in the world who could encourage me, and he was sitting at my side. I was aware of Eeyore stealing looks at me, as if he were trying to measure in his own way whether it would be appropriate for him to speak up uninvited. Pulling myself together, I asked, in a hoarse voice that sounded too dispirited even to my own ears, "Eeyore, what's wrong? Are you still feeling bad?"

"*No! I'm all better,*" he replied emphatically. "*I sank. From now on I'm going to swim. I'm ready to swim now!*"

4: The Ghost of a Flea

This July, a young American came to see me. A graduate student at the University of Virginia, she was writing her master's thesis on two Japanese authors, M and me, and so our conversations were a kind of fieldwork for her research. At a public seminar at the university where she had enrolled, she had spoken about researching the Japanese approach to the themes of sex and violence, and late that same night, probably because she was delicate, with the sort of build and features that appealed to the Japanese, she had received a phone call from a man with a creepy voice who inquired if she were Ms. Martha Crowley and explained that he shared her interest in sex and violence and wondered if they could meet alone for a conversation?

Martha inquired about me and about my work, but she also questioned me closely about my impressions of M based on having known him while he was alive. At some point, I observed that while he was famous for having built himself up with weight lifting, M had actually been short even for a Japanese.

"Now that you mention it, I always had trouble picturing his aesthetics of death and violence as the writing of a big man with bulging muscles."

This indication from Martha that M's stature made sense to her was abruptly interrupted by my son in a voice so loud that he startled the American student:

"*He was really very short! He was about this size.*" Extending his arm palm down, Eeyore held it about ten inches above the floor and peered beneath it as if he were observing something tangible.

"Eeyore! I didn't think you remembered M! You've never said a word about him until now! I'm really surprised."

In fact, I had realized right away what my son had been indicating just now by his remark and gestures. Invading the Eastern Division Headquarters of the National Self Defense Forces in Ichigaya, M had committed *hara-kiri*—Eeyore was picturing in his mind the severed head that had been propped on the floor in the newspaper photo of the scene. In what form had the memory of that photograph been preserved, for more than ten years, inside my son's damaged mind? Until now I had never once spoken a word about M, yet Eeyore appeared to be firmly in touch with the actual presence of that severed head beneath his palm. I noticed that Martha must also have figured out what his gestures represented; the expression on her face, deeply terrified, made me wonder whether this was how she had looked when she had received the phone call from that stranger.

Two years earlier at my swimming club, in a forty-five-foot-deep tank of water—I learned from a notice that was posted after the accident warning of danger that it was called the "dark pool"—my son had nearly drowned. I have already described how the young man who had thrust his arm through a glass wall to alert me, and his companions, and their leader, who had actually brought Eeyore up to the surface from a depth of thirty feet, had all had something to do with M's thought and action while he was still alive. But even then it had not occurred to me that my son would remember the name associated with that newspaper photograph of a suicide by hara-kiri, an incident that had occurred when he was a little boy just entering the special class at elementary school.

"Professor, your essay on M and Malcolm Lowry never quite made sense to me," Martha said calmly, as if to explain the internal circumstances of the surprise she had revealed—though I was the object of her research and not her teacher, she used the English word "professor" as a convenient term of respect toward older Japanese—"but now I understand. M's severed head must have brutalized the spirit of children like Eeyore. And when they grow up, that severed head might influence their lives like a shadow they have to live in, something they can't conceptualize. . . ."

"I don't think so in Eeyore's case," I objected. But my chest was pounding in the darkness inside me, in this son of mine in particular with a mind that would always be a child's and a body on its way to becoming an adult's with the bone structure of a large man; the power of that image of the severed head could manifest itself gigantically. I glanced down helplessly at the corpulent figure with his outstretched hand still leveled just above the floor.

The essay Martha mentioned, my thoughts on the M incident and on the explicit violence of M's self-expression, was a commentary I was writing for a collected edition, difficult to obtain for a student outside of Japan, which I had copied and sent to her. I had titled my piece "The Politics of a Severed Head and the Tree of Life," and although it's an unusual thing to do in a novel I want to quote a passage from it that bears directly to what Martha was saying.

I began, "M's performance, from agit-prop speech to suicide by hara-kiri, staged for a large audience of SDF troops and for the benefit of the television coverage he had anticipated, was the most beautifully elaborated political spectacle we have beheld since the end of the war. Even the photograph of his severed head standing erect on the floor, said to have been taken by chance, may well have been a part of his overall scheme. This, too, was a performance designed to tighten focus on the details of the human body itself against the background of a universe structured by Imperialism." I wrote "this, too" because I was contrasting M's actions with *Account of an Elegant Dream,* a work of fiction by another writer, a book that had been annihilated by political power and that, though it pointed to an interpretation in a direction entirely opposed to M's actions—it was here that we could see the bottomless polysemy of image and performance in a work of literature—had achieved an expression of the same thing. "However, this performance of M's, in which the details of the physical body as represented by a bloody, severed head propped on the floor were installed against the background of a universe structured by Imperialism, was taken seriously, at face value, by none of us, not by those who supported the demonstration based on M's suicide nor by those who rejected it. Upon reading the word M had chosen for the banner he displayed, 'manifesto,' a word with univalent significance only, we wrapped everything that was happening into a univalent package, the 'M Incident.' For better or for worse, this is what we did, whether we supported the demonstration or rejected it, at least insofar as what was communicated in the mass media. The fate of that photograph taken as though by accident provides a concrete example of this interpretation. When the photograph in question received a prize for journalistic photography, the newspaper and photographer involved declined to accept because they feared it would mean they would have to exhibit the photo again. And so the photo was consigned to darkness. . . . Why, after the furor that surrounded the Incident had quieted, did the mass media decline to bring to the foreground the minutiae of death as performed by M? Because the social repercussions created by *Account of an Elegant Dream* had already taught them a lesson: to cover comprehensively a performance that emphasized details of the human body against the background of a universe based on an Imperialistic system, conveying its multilevel significance with its full power of provocation intact, was to risk the danger, even under a constitution affirming the Imperial system, of real violence. And this, as he played out his exquisitely conscious performance unto death, was M's only miscalculation: expecting the power of his performance in a political space to express its manifold levels of meaning despite the limit imposed by a word like 'manifesto,' unique among literary expressions in its intractable univalence. But media coverage of M's suicide by hara-kiri deleted the multivalence of his performance and simplified it into an image of M haranguing the troops below him in his private army uniform, a fanatic's headband around his head, and continued to recess the image until even the sound of his voice was lost in the background and all that remained for us to see was an empty 'manifesto' dangling on a banner. . . . To those who affirmed M's suicide, this meant that a powerfully evocative physical reality generated by an Imperialist ethos had failed to materialize. In other words, the 'M Incident' had been deprived of the momentum required to trigger a chain reaction of explosions by superimposing the Imperialist ethos on contemporary society. Undoubtedly, there were those who regretted the stripping of power that caused the Incident to misfire. Conversely, those who decried the Incident, while they succeeded in exposing the manifesto's conceptual univalence and refuted its assertions, were not able to avenge the *Account of the Elegant Dream* incident by exposing and superseding the Imperialist ethos it once again evoked. This amounted to a failure to exploit the opportunity M presented to grasp firm hold of a new image of Japan's future. This process of failure was initiated by the removal from our sight of that bloodied head by the seasoned, cunning hand of a powerful figure. . . ."

At dinner that night, Martha drank impressively in her well-bred way, and with the help of the alcohol seemed to recover from the aftereffect of her earlier fright. She told stories about attempts to seduce her, directly and indirectly, beginning with the phone call from the man with an interest in sex and violence, during the half year she had just spent studying in Japan without her American husband, who was also an intellectual. Compared to her first stay ten years earlier, Japanese attitudes seemed to have changed, and she had frequently observed blatant examples of the changes. Apparently, her academic adviser had been among those who had propositioned her, but she described him jokingly as moving close to dangerous ground while playing the buffoon yet never exceeding his limits as an intellectual. Despite her amusing stories, Martha must have been preoccupied by Eeyore's own performance earlier: before long she narrowed the focus of her criticism of the Japanese in general to me personally.

"When I first read your analysis of M's severed head I thought it was exaggerated. But that really did imprint itself on Eeyore, didn't it! I can't imagine how terrified he must have been when he saw it!" When she began in this vein I had expected her to repeat herself drunkenly, but it turned out she was still capable of building an argument: "You wrote that a force controlling the media had recessed the image of M's severed head and blurred its power to provoke. But do you really think that the Japanese view of the cosmos based on the imperial system could have been uprooted and thrown away simply by acknowledging that severed head and debating about it? A view of the universe the Japanese have held for more than twenty-six hundred years? I can't imagine that disappearing any time soon. And if I'm right, then in effect you were expressing your desire that the power of 'M's severed head' would reunite the Japanese inside a universe based on the notion of an imperialist system! In effect, you and M were expressing the same desire— I actually tried establishing other sorts of connections between you in an essay I wrote—"

Nonsense! I thought to myself even as I recognized, in a brain that had absorbed a greater quantity of alcohol than Martha's, a certain logic to her argument. It also occurred to me that the weakness of my own essay was responsible for a misunderstanding for which I couldn't blame this American student, but before I could put this into words she continued, her terror written plainly in her face once again: "But what matters most is that the memory of M's severed head is engraved in Eeyore's mind! That's horrible! What are you going to do about erasing that terrifying dream from the mind of a handicapped child? Professor, isn't that more important than contemplating a universe based on the imperial system?"

Each time I think about this, I must acknowledge that Martha was correct. Although she returned to her own country some months ago, her words stick in my craw. Probably, the task ahead of me is more difficult than she imagined. Removing the nightmare that remains like a stain in Eeyore's somehow clouded mind. First, I would have to determine the nightmare's form and whereabouts. We happened to discover the existence of a nightmare about M's severed head propped on the floor. Now Eeyore and I would have to determine together whether it was still alive in his mind in the way that Martha had imagined.

When I wrote just now of the difficulty of locating and removing the nightmare threatening Eeyore I had something specific in mind. I refer to my son's apparent inability to understand what is meant by the word "dream." More accurately, I have not been able to ascertain whether he dreams but is unable to apply the word "dream" to his experience, or whether he has never dreamed and is therefore thrown into confusion when questioned about his dreams. I have probed this time and again, but it remains unclear.

Nonetheless, the issue Martha raised about Eeyore's nightmare does not disappear. And why shouldn't there be a wound of fear that never manifests in the form of a dream but lodges forever in a dark and indistinct place with no possibility of catharsis? The photograph of a severed head propped on the floor exists, and to Eeyore it appeared to be an individual human being in and of itself. Moreover, from his mother's response to the newspapers and television coverage at the time—I was traveling in India—Eeyore sensed that this must be an important human being and remembered the name M, and these impressions remained locked away without rising to his consciousness.

Yet again, who was to say that dreams had not begun flooding into Eeyore's mind for the first time as he entered adolescence? What sort of tumult might this new experience be provoking? The thought made me want to provide him with a definition of dreams. This had occurred to me before, and I had tried repeatedly in the past to engage him in conversation about it: "Eeyore, do you really not dream? You go to sleep at night and wake up in the morning, and sometime in between maybe you're at a concert listening to a piano—hasn't it ever seemed that way? You're asleep, you're sleeping, but you're playing with your sister or talking to your brother—haven't you ever remembered anything like that when you wake up in the morning?"

"My gosh, that's difficult! I forgot!"

"It happens but you forget? Or you don't remember because nothing like that ever happened? You take your medicine at night and get into bed and go to sleep, and nothing happens, and when you wake up it's morning and Mama is there to wake you up? Or while you're sleeping you have a feeling you're listening to music, you can even see shapes of the performers, anything like that? Eeyore, that's called having a dream!"

"Listening to music—Mozart wrote a song called 'Dream Pictures.' K-five-five-two. Gosh! I haven't heard it. I'm sorry!"

Fruitless as it was, this exchange is an example of my son participating willingly in a conversation about dreams. Where this subject was concerned, this was the rare exception. In the course of my repeated attempts to bring up the subject, Eeyore began sounding his refrain for the most adamant rejection:

"That's enough. I want to stop now!"

To my wife, listening in silence at his side, his resoluteness was terrifying. I suppose she feared the day would come when Eeyore would close the channel from his mind to all things in the world, our family foremost among them, with a final *"That's enough! I want to stop now!"*

She never gave voice to her fear, but I suspected she may have read a warning of this outcome in Eeyore's tantrums just before his nineteenth birthday when I was away in Europe.

Thinking back, I recall discussing with my wife while Eeyore was still a child, or more properly an infant—in his case, compared to other children, infancy seemed to extend itself interminably—his apparent inability to dream. This was in direct response to the discovery by the teacher in charge of Eeyore's special learning class, during a three-day and two-night trip to "wilderness school," that Eeyore didn't know what dreaming meant. Another child in the group woke up crying from a dream. At first, Eeyore listened with interest to the instructor's soothing words, but when the child persisted in crying Eeyore seemed ready to attack him. The instructor felt that his hostility was due to frustration at not understanding what it was to dream. My wife was lamenting what seemed to be the absence of the dream function in Eeyore's conscious and subconscious mental processes, and I tried to console her with the help of a Blake poem.

"There's no need to be so worried because a young child may not dream. A classmate is frightened by his dream and cries, and it seems that Eeyore is unable to understand his distress, but you shouldn't be upset about that! Blake wrote a beautiful poem called 'A Cradle Song.' It begins: 'Sleep sleep beauty bright / Dreaming o'er the joys of night / Sleep sleep: in thy sleep / Little sorrows sit and weep.' But listen to what happens next: 'O the cunning wiles that creep / In thy little heart asleep / When thy little heart does wake / Then the dreadful lightnings break.' In Blake's view, we humans have fallen to earth and therefore all of us, as adults, have 'cunning wiles'; if Eeyore doesn't have to install them in his heart while he's asleep what could be better than that? In Eeyore's life, cunning wiles are unnecessary. And if he can make it through life without needing them, wouldn't that be wonderful?"

I was speaking as a young husband—it was at least ten years ago—words to a wife who was still close enough to her girlhood to struggle against the pull of brooding thoughts inside her.

"Where can I find that Blake lullaby?" she began asking recently, out of the blue, reminding me of our earlier conversation. But this time I was the one who was fretting about Eeyore's inability to dream and persisted in questioning him about it. Possibly, my wife had recalled the Blake poem I had read to her and asked to see it in print in response to my talk about Eeyore's dream deficiency, not so much to refute me as to lure me back to my earlier way of thinking. And certainly her request had something to do with the rapidly increasing number of books about Blake strewn around the sofa where I lay reading since my return from Europe this spring. This directness about all things was how my wife lived her life. Which meant that she might ask me any day why I had turned away from my earlier thinking and was now insisting that the power to dream was essential to Eeyore. Late one night, sipping the whisky I needed to sleep, I tried rehearsing an answer in advance: "Because I happen to be Eeyore's father, and dreams have a role in my profession. So it's only natural for me to want my son to have at least some capacity to dream!"

So far words had worked well enough, albeit in a whisper, but there was an image lodged inside me, of dreams and fathers and sons, that made me feel inadequate to describe it with any fluency or ease. So I fell silent, and caused my mind to go silent, and strained to hear the image as though I were listening to the wind. This was not an image I had created; it had been revealed to me in words that were not my own. "So we gave him the good news of a boy ready to suffer and forbear. Then, when (the son) reached (the age of) following him about here and there [(serious) work with him], he said: 'O my son! I have beheld a dream in which I offer thee in sacrifice: Now see what is thy view!' (The son) said: 'O my father! Do as thou art commanded: Thou will find me, if Allah so wills, one practicing patience and constancy!' So when they had both submitted their wills (to Allah), and he had laid him on his forehead (for sacrifice), we called out to him, 'O Abrahim! Thy faithfulness to the dream has been seen! [Thou hast already fulfilled the vision!]' Thus indeed do we reward those who do right. For this was clearly—a trial. And we redeemed him with a gorgeous sacrifice. And we left (this blessing) for him among generations (to come) in later times."

I have copied this passage from the Koran, not from Genesis in the Old Testament. One reason is that the internal image I derived from this episode is based on the Iwanami paperback translation of the Koran by Toshihiko Izutsu; another reason may be that in the Koran, but not in Genesis, it is a dream upon which the episode turns. "Thy faithfulness to the dream has been seen. . . ."

The faithfulness in question is of course Abrahim's to Allah; but to me it represents the faithfulness, through the agency of a dream, of the relationship between Abrahim and his son. "O my son! I have beheld a dream in which I offer thee in sacrifice: Now see what is thy view!" "O my father! Do as thou art commanded: Thou will find me, if Allah so wills, one practicing patience and constancy!"

Calling to mind this glorious dialogue between father and son when I am alone in the middle of the night—buoyed by the power of alcohol—I am confronted by a thought which I can only let pass through me like a storm with my face red and my head bowed, a thought that will circle around me my entire life. For five weeks or so following my son's abnormal birth, I had longed for his death, in other words, to destroy him. My longing was not based on a revelation from Allah appearing in a dream, nor on the agreement of my son. It was merely my egotistical desire to protect a future for myself and my wife, who still knew nothing of her baby's abnormality, a longing of searing urgency like hot coals beneath my feet!

If, during those five weeks, I had found the accomplice I was searching for in the hospital where the baby was lodged, would I not have succeeded unscathed in eliminating my son and in extinguishing his brief memories of life?

But at the end of five weeks I managed to recover—sometimes I feel I can hear a voice whispering to me from just behind my ear that all I really accomplished was resigning myself to not murdering the infant, avoiding punishment under the law and deep depression—and agreed to an operation for my son. Since then, pushing away the calamity that has continued to assail us as a family, we have survived. And my son has made it past his nineteenth birthday. Even so, no powerful detergent has allowed me to wash out of my life those disgraceful five weeks, nor do I expect to succeed at this as long as I live. Based on this feeling I expected that, as my son developed the power of his intelligence step by deliberate step, the day would come, having reached a certain stage, when he would say the following (I imagine that his voice will be soft, as when, at age five or six, able to distinguish as many as one hundred different bird calls, he would murmur, for example, "*kingfisher, red kingfisher*"): "Father, to tell the truth, since I was very small I've been having the same dream. I'm even smaller in my dream, I've just been born, and you're trying hard to find a way to murder me."

I also thought about Eeyore's dysfunction as it relates to the more positive function of dreams. This was likely to be useful in preparing a reply to my wife when she asked why I had begun only now to lament Eeyore's inability to dream.

I dream. Sometimes my dreams reveal an escape tunnel leading to the brightness beyond the real world which constrains me. My son, constrained even more closely by the real world than I, also dreams. Perhaps his dreams are his escape tunnel; and perhaps, if something like the thin winter sunlight shines down that tunnel, then his tunnel and mine might connect. Down the tunnel of my dream I glimpse my son liberating himself inside his own dream. . . .

I had an actual dream that illuminated this formulation lucidly from beginning to end. I had just begun devoting my days to reading Blake's Prophecies with the help of David V.

Erdman's commentaries. Reading Blake was directly related to my dream. Perhaps I should say my dream was based on my amateurish, distorted reading of Blake.

The world of Blake's mythological poetry teems with demigods who manifest the power and function of the universe, well-known figures such as Urizen, Luvah, Tharmas, and Los. Then there are Ahania, Vala, and Enion, demigods who are also unique to Blake and who may be considered projections of the female principle. Next come the symbolic characters who serve to render manifest the structure of this world as part of the divinely ordered universe, a cast of many characters. Each time I encountered a new name I would underline it, make a note in the margin, and transfer the name to an index card, and in this way I gradually became familiar with Blake's Prophecies. His power to express his symbolism with such aliveness that it seemed empirical was also acting on my brain as I dreamed.

The scene of my dream was a broad meadow beyond that tunnel that led away from the constraints of the real world. In a spot that was not visible from inside the tunnel stands a young but robust holly tree. Ah, I realize, dreaming, so the place I have been imagining until now is this broad meadow. In that case, the tunnel from my son's dream must lead here too. Sure enough, as though endowed with the power to see for the first time by the very thought, I behold Eeyore having just emerged from his own tunnel, radiant in the nakedness with which he was born. He stood as in Blake's early painting *Glad Day,* bathed in sunlight with his arms flung wide and balancing on one leg. I not only accepted my son's nakedness as natural, I was persuaded that this powerfully muscled body was his true essence (a fear of food poisoning had caused him to cut down on his eating recently and he had lost weight but was still flabby in the chest and belly), that a man's body, in Blake's words, "does not exist distinct from his soul."

Eeyore's naked, quintessential body was a revelation to me. I described it, its whereabouts in my dream, in a note I scribbled on an index card at my bedside the minute I woke up: *My son presented to me the most beautiful body of his life. The tempered muscles of a youth ripple beneath the radiant skin of an infant. The sensitivity and spirit revealed in this body are unmistakably symbolic. They are the lucid expression of a certain spiritual essence. Dreaming, I understand perfectly that this essence, in the universe of my dream, defined by spiritual symbols only, is known as "Eeyore." My son has fallen to earth in order to reveal to me the spiritual essence "Eeyore." Had he not existed, I would certainly have perished without ever discovering the spiritual essence "Eeyore." Presently, I become aware that to my son in my dream, I, too, appear as a symbol manifesting a certain spiritual essence. I notice that I have assumed the form of the birds whose voices were the only sounds he took pleasure in hearing as an infant. "Wren" is the spiritual essence my life conveys. If I could see its shape, invisible to me, the meaning of my life, having been born into the universe to labor, sorrow, learn, and forget, would be revealed. With the quiet beating of wren's wings I fly toward my son's gleaming head, trying to see my own form reflected in his eyes.*

But a dark whirlpool drew me down, blissful at having touched the kernel of the universal meaning of my life and just as terrified, to awakeness on this side of the tunnel. But, even awake, as I described the dream on the index card, I felt that the spiritual essence "Eeyore" was still firmly in my grasp and that all I had to do to capture it was write it down.

The specifics of my dream made it clear that it was rooted in my memory of Blake's painting, *Glad Day*. In the world of Blake's mythological epics, the gorgeous young man who is the naked figure in the painting is called Orc and symbolizes the passion of fire. On another symbolic level, he also stands for the kinetic energy of the French Revolution, a subject of urgent interest to Blake. In the sense in which I used the expression in my dream as though it were familiar to me, Orc embodied in the world of man and in the universe of demigods which overarched that world the *spiritual essence* of the passion of fire. Twenty years after he had painted *Glad Day,* Blake attached a commentary to it which began, "Albion rose from where he labored at the mill with slaves." In Blake's mythological universe, Albion represents Everyman. The Albion who laments, in the poem in *Songs of Experience* in which a youth is burned to death, "Are such things done on Albion's shore?," is at the same time the old word for England, the country of "white land." As I studied a reproduction of *Glad Day,* it occurred to me that in my dream I had superimposed the figure of my son, the manifestation in the mythological universe of the *spiritual essence* "Eeyore," on the radiantly joyful figure of Albion, liberated from his labors everywhere on earth, that most good and beautiful form of humankind itself.

I had another dream, also influenced by a painting of Blake's but largely painful, in which the essence of body-and-spirit Eeyore revealed itself as baleful. In this dream, the opposite of the earlier, Eeyore laid bare a spirit so base and mean that I lowered my eyes when I came face-to-face with him the following morning. Once again he is naked, but this time his nakedness as he stands in a darkened kitchen is ugly and malevolent. Having come in through a rear door he stands with his legs spread, and I am squatting with my face against his lower belly as though rubbing it, the reptilian odor so strong it remained in my nostrils even after I awoke. I have bared his penis to examine it, it remains rigid even though he has ejaculated, and I recall that this is the condition the young men in our village called "fool's bone." Plainly, even in the darkness, Eeyore's penis, like a kneadable mass encased in a leather bag, was bloody. I was seized by the deepest despair, and by a bizarre jubilation entangled in it that threatened to burst from me in a hoarse scream. I sensed the agitated presence outside the house of the respectable citizens who had followed Eeyore and who must not be harmed, and said, in a voice that might have been despair or a whoop of joy, "Eeyore, so you finally did it!" Looking down at me, Eeyore's face was swollen to twice its size. Eyes like the eyeballs of a cow. The upward arc of his tongue extended to its full length between his thinly opened lips. And, above all, the abnormal massiveness of his shoulders and upper arms, and, covering the skin all over them, the scales.

Eeyore's expression and body in this dream, unquestionably him while not resembling him in the slightest, also had their origins in a painting by William Blake. The Blake series known as Visionary Heads includes a famous work titled *The Ghost of a Flea*. During a certain period in his later years, at the urging of the watercolorist John Varley, who was also an astrologer, Blake sketched portraits of mythological and historical characters who had appeared to him in visions. He always asserted that his art was based on apparitions and even that he copied down his verse just as he had heard it spoken.

Late one night, alongside portraits of imaginary and historical characters from David and Solomon to Edward the First who had appeared as visitations in Blake's studio, Varley discovered the painting *The Ghost of a Flea*. According to Varley's account to his friends, which was recorded, the story of the painting's creation was as follows. The previous night, when he had visited Blake as was his custom, he had found him even more agitated than usual. This was because Blake had just beheld something wonderful, the "ghost of a flea." Blake was however not able to capture it in a painting. As Varley pressed his friend to paint what he had seen, Blake, who had begun to stare into a corner of the room, declared, "It's here—*reach me my things*—I must keep an eye on it!" Describing the monster's tongue dart, expressing its malevolent appetite, from between its lips, the bowl for catching blood in its hand, the green and gold scales which covered its body, Blake proceeded to paint a portrait exactly as he described it, according to Varley.

In the horrifying image of *The Ghost of a Flea,* my dream had revealed a different Eeyore to me. But the malevolence of that image, no less than my bizarre scream, had its origin in me and no one else. This had nothing to do with my son. On the contrary, I felt like turning to myself and saying, "I see! So these are the twisted thoughts that occur at the outer limits of your consciousness when you consider the issue of your son's sexuality now that he's nineteen!"

Eeyore didn't tell dirty jokes or clown around about sex; when folio-sized monthly magazines full of nude photographs arrived at the house, he would throw them in the trash unopened as he helped sort the mail, and even assuming that his prudishness was an expression of the dilemma posed by sex at his age, I don't believe the incident in my dream could have occurred in reality. Finally, the images in my dream must have had to do with sexual issues of my own.

Nevertheless, I found myself unable to look my son in the eye the following morning and, for the same reason, I began avoiding *The Ghost of a Flea* in art books. But my son's reaction to M's severed head, which I described at the beginning of the chapter, led to an opportunity to refashion my relationship to Blake's painting. It came in the form of a letter from Martha Crowley in which she directed my attention to an essay on *The Ghost of a Flea* in a recent edition of *Blake Studies.* Her letter was as follows: "Thank you so much, Professor, for the wonderful time at your house. The food was delicious. I am ashamed of the position I took about Eeyore. I felt as if he were touching the head of M's phantom with his hand, and I was terrified. When I got home, I talked about you with my mother, whose field is European art history. We discussed Eeyore, and Blake. Mother pulled off the bookshelf a copy of *Blake Studies* that Geoffrey Keynes himself had sent her when she was young. Needless to say, she wanted me to see Blake's Visionary Heads and 'The Ghost of a Flea.' I'm sure you must have read this. Don't you think that Eeyore probably had his 'tongue in his cheek' when he pretended to be seeing a vision of M, just as Lord Keynes said Blake had? Wasn't he enjoying this huge joke on us? If that was the case, it was wrong of me to criticize you as if it were a serious problem. I'm sure you must have it already, but I'm sending the second edition of *Blake Studies* under separate cover."

In this way I came to read immediately the one essay I had skipped in the book by Lord Keynes, editor of the standard edition of Blake's verse, and was impressed by the elegance of his argument and by the manner in which Martha had applied it to Eeyore's case. No less than its prose style, the wonderful illustrations in this large, unhurried book reveal a man of culture and broad learning and reinforce its thesis, which is developed in the informal style of a journal. As Keynes's iconographic analysis is unique, I would like to summarize it here, avoiding repetition of the episode I have already described.

Keynes introduces the account by Varley, and includes as illustrations all the pictures related to *The Ghost of a Flea*. The tempera painting is overwhelmed by the virulent presence of the Ghost striding past stars and a comet, which are visible through a dark window. There are also two sketches; one is used as an illustration in what might be called Varley's "Zodiac Guide to the Stars." His description of how the flea painting illustrates the connection between human personality and the planets is also introduced. It appears that Blake's painting supports this astrologer's theories. The other sketch, in tempera, is an exercise focused on the upper body, and includes a detail of the area around the lips. These sketches convey a certain jocundity very different from the macabre mood of the tempera painting. Yet another of Blake's many sides as a painter.

After detailing the history of these paintings in a meticu-lous, unhurried narrative from the moment of their creation to their current whereabouts, Keynes develops the position, sup-ported step-by-step with references to the two sketches in par-ticular, that the painting supposed to be a sketch of *The Ghost of a Flea* as it had appeared in a vision was in fact based on the miniature of a flea in a book of "Micrographia" that had been published in the mid-seventeenth century, a copy of which Blake was bound to have seen. Apparently, Keynes had been a surgeon for many years: his approach was definitely that of a scientist. He suggests that Varley was motivated to accept Blake's expla-nation so eagerly because, if it were true, the painting would serve as an invaluable substantiation of his own astrological thinking. But there was evidence to suggest, Keynes continued, that Blake had been speaking *with his own tongue in his cheek* when he declared that the "ghost of a flea" had appeared before him as he moved his painter's brush.

Keynes's analysis showed me a new face of William Blake and gave me another way to think about Eeyore behaving as though he were face-to-face with M's phantom. Just as Martha had suggested. The liberating effect of this allowed me to look at *The Ghost of a Flea* without a tightening in my chest. Not that I was any better able to dispel my anxiety about a moment in the future when I might reveal the "ghost of a flea" inside my-self—it was I, after all, who had dreamed that grotesque dream.

That autumn, my wife and I made plans to take the children to our cabin in the mountains of Izu. Ten years ago we had seen a photograph—flocks of starlings exploding into the sunset sky from the zelkova trees on a tiny cape jutting into the sea—and had begun visiting the spot to enjoy that stirring sight with our own eyes. The land I eventually bought there was on a small hill back from a cliff covered in laurel and beyond a woods where the thin layer of earth covering the rocks was crisscrossed by the roots of old trees. There was a single bayberry tree on the hill; basically, I bought a small square of the slope that surrounded it.

The purchase of this land was in itself, considering the state of our finances, a reckless act, but I was drawn to it, above all, by the bayberry tree and also by the variety of the other trees and especially the giant zelkovas in the surrounding woods. Yet if that had been all, I should have been content to own a single bayberry, to approach it from time to time to examine the trunk and admire the foliage, to gaze up at the branches near the top and to survey the thick stands of trees in the near vicinity. Instead, I built a cabin on the property, adding to our financial burden, a step I took because of a premonition that some day before long my son and I would end up living together in Izu. I can recall a number of moments that led me to this feeling.

The year Eeyore entered his second year of special classes in middle school, as an experiment designed to cure his bed wetting, I began waking him up once in the middle of the night and taking him to the bathroom. In those days I was up until dawn anyway, working or reading, so this was easy enough for me to do; besides, the chance to see Eeyore again after he had gone to sleep felt rather like an added bonus for the day. Except for the following point of difficulty. As Eeyore lay in bed still half asleep, I would remove his diaper—if it was dry it was a simple thing to fasten the diaper again—exposing his lower belly. At that moment, reminding me of the animated film I had seen as a child in which the eight-headed serpent Yamata no Orochi bares its fangs to strike, Eeyore's penis sprang upward from its confinement. Every night, this terrible sight struck a blow at my heart. As it happened, Eeyore was at just that age when his penis seemed to be enlarging right before my eyes.

I witnessed another moment when I went to pick up Eeyore at middle school (as he was already beyond needing to be accompanied to and from school, it must have been an excursion day when he was coming home later than usual). In the evening shadows of the school yard, still excited from their outing and by the lateness of the hour, the children were taking reluctant leave of one another. Eeyore was bent over a girl perhaps two thirds as tall as he and less than half his weight who was crippled from polio, peering into her face as he repeated a leisurely farewell, *"Good-bye, good-bye, we leave you now, with a smile until tomorrow."* Although the lower half of the girl's face was an acute triangle that seemed twisted, it was easy to read in her broad forehead and large eyes her regret about the intelligence that had been broken by the demon of disease. Eeyore was treating her as carefully as if she were a fragile doll, and I could see, though she said nothing, that she was also pleased by his attention. Suddenly, as I stood there observing them, a voice exploded convulsively in my ear: "Enough! This is sick, this is creepy!"

Next to me, surrounded by several mothers who also had come for their children, a young woman teacher was voicing her disgust at Eeyore's parting words, grinding her teeth. "I'd say he's overdoing it a bit, wouldn't you! Don't you feel like saying 'That'll do nicely thank you very much!' This just makes me sick!"

I felt resigned; it was no surprise that this inexperienced young woman's feelings should by roiled by Eeyore's attitude, it was understandable. And so I stepped forward, spinelessly enough, to put an end to Eeyore's farewells, and saw the mothers lower their shoulders and hang their heads, as if the teacher's angry words themselves had slapped them in the face. I felt outrage seize me; the teacher, twisting atop her broad, firm hips a slender, comely back, glanced around at me defiantly, her face flushing darkly.

It seemed certain that this unmarried teacher had sensed the presence of a sexual motive in my son's behavior as he said his effusive good-byes. But I wondered if she wasn't simply frightened by the power of the sexual male who was growing up inside Eeyore's large body and would some day soon appear. As in my dream, this was a response rooted in the sexual darkness inside herself.

In addition to moments such as these, there was also the memory of an incident that had disturbed me deeply in my youth—as it happened, a mentally impaired person had been involved—but what made the incident important to me now was rather its bearing on my feelings about "place" and my sense that I would have to secure a "place" that could serve as a final abode for myself and Eeyore. It was the spring when I left the valley in the forest—I recall my feeling that this was a temporary move and that the time would certainly come when I returned to the village in the valley—and was boarding with a family in a provincial city. It was the final year of the Allied occupation of Japan, and there was a connection, at least in my imagination, between the incident and the presence of American soldiers.

The man of the house where I was staying, a career soldier who had lost his job when Japan was defeated, showed me a report of the incident in the local newspaper. On a small island in the Inland Sea, a youth with brain damage had murdered a little girl. With a long bamboo spear he had pierced her from her genitals to the back of her throat. When he was taken prisoner at the scene immediately after the crime, the perpetrator, who was my age, was wearing an imitation American GI cap made out of newspaper. A cap fashioned in this way had been in vogue for a time, and I also knew how to fold one. . . .

I remember the former colonel saying he hoped the incident wouldn't be putting ideas in our heads, but it wasn't the sexual details of the horror that upset me (to be sure, I was impressed, as by a new discovery, that the human genitals could be said to be connected, via the body's lumina, all the way to the back of the throat). It was the photograph of the crime scene appended to the article that rocked me on my heels—an island mountainside, a bamboo grove and tangled shrubbery, narrow fields that appeared uncultivated and, overall, part of the same hollow land that would be cold and damp the year round. It occurs to me now that my valley in the forest and this small island were topographically similar (even though the valley in its own sea of forest was to the island as hollow to rise); at the time, I had recognized that places like this were also to be found in the valley and had pictured them specifically. In this kind of "place," people committed cruel and degraded acts like this one. Or, perhaps, the place itself made people commit them. The article described the youth as an idiot; perhaps his idiocy was in his failure to resist the magnetic power of this "place." In my valley, the children avoided going to this kind of place, and the grown-ups who were obliged to labor there took themselves to work reluctantly with scowling faces. (Those whose livelihoods required them to cultivate the fields in those places seemed under a cloud, even to the children's eyes, and no one thought it strange when they died at an early age.)

My next thought filled me with terror: I had left the valley to live in a stranger's "place" where there was no forest and no landmarks, only a river that was huge out of all proportion and unfamiliar trees. I had no means of distinguishing an ominous place anywhere in this provincial city. Which meant that I might wander into one at any time and wouldn't know it. Perhaps I was there even now.

Then I recalled a minor incident that had occurred two or three weeks earlier. The landlord and his wife had left on an excursion and I had spent the night alone in the house with their daughter, a year or two older than I. In the middle of the night, when I came downstairs to use the bathroom, the girl was slowly combing her hair in the sloping handmade bed in her room, naked to the waist, with the door open. I urinated and went back upstairs without giving it a second thought. When her parents returned the following morning, the girl carried on about having been afraid during the night. I considered only then, with contempt, that she had been trying to attract me: if this boardinghouse had been built in one of those "places," I might have skewered her with a bamboo spear from her genitals to the back of her throat. I was aware of fear that made my head ring and of a twisted desire for dark passions. How I longed to return to the valley in the forest! To a world where every imaginable place was familiar to my body and spirit!

Years had gone by, and I had discovered for myself and Eeyore a place that was, in a sense, another valley in a forest, with topography that I could clearly read. That at least was what I had intended when I secured my own mountain bayberry on the slope of a hill bordered by virgin forest on the Izu peninsula, and built a house nearby. I sketched my image of a cabin and sent it to an architect I had known since my childhood. It wasn't until the actual cabin was finished that I realized with surprise that my image of a final abode had been unrealistic in the extreme. I had drawn a house beneath the luxuriant green of a large bayberry tree, but the lot was almost entirely on a slope, and the tree in question, together with a cypress at its side that had grown straight up through and above its leafy branches, were both located toward the bottom; the finished house looked down on the bayberry and the cypress from the living room on the second floor. This discrepancy served to teach me once again the sort of "place" I longed for.

We had planned to be at Izu on the Sunday that was the anniversary of the private middle school attended by Eeyore's younger sister and brother. But a large typhoon was approaching, and a weather report predicted the storm would move overland at precisely the Izu peninsula on the morning we would have been at the cabin. My wife and I abandoned the idea of the excursion and told the children. Eeyore was listening and did not react, so I assumed that a trip to the cabin was of no particular importance to him.

However, that Saturday, at just the time when we would have been leaving the house, Eeyore stood at the front door in the stiff, heavy leather shoes he normally refused to wear, a large pack on his back and a mountain-climbing cap on his head, and announced, as though he were trying to convince himself, "*Shall we get started? I'm on my way to the Izu house!*" In fact, by the time my wife came to me at my writing desk and said, after a silence when she seemed to be regaining her composure, "He seems to have reverted to—the way he was when you were away in Europe," she and Eeyore had already been engaged in dialogue for close to an hour at the front entrance to the house, in voices hushed so as not to be audible to me in my room upstairs. My wife had pleaded and cajoled. In response, she reported, Eeyore would say only, "*No, I'm on my way to Izu!*" Finally, my wife had threatened him with a scolding from me if I heard him sounding so unreasonable while I was at work in my study, but far from panicking he had looked away from his mother and from his distressed brother and sister and, in a curious display of obstinacy, had gazed at nothing at all with empty eyes. Then he had said the following, with a forcefulness that had recreated instantly for my wife the despair she had felt during my absence last spring: "*No, Papa is dead! He died, you know. I'm on my way to Izu by myself. Because Papa is dead. Good-bye, every-one. Farewell!"*

He had not unfurled this brand of ultimatum right away. He had merely positioned himself at the front door as if the family had not agreed to cancel the trip to the Izu peninsula. Then he had delivered himself of his first announcement in a loud voice and, when the rest of us failed to appear with our luggage, had continued waiting as though suspiciously. At that point, using their normal, everyday strategies, my wife and his sister and brother had attempted to convince him that the trip to the mountains had been canceled. My daughter used his interest in the weather map on television, reminding him of how he took notice every day of weather and average temperature in major cities all over the country: "Eeyore, a typhoon's coming! I wonder what the low will be—pretty cold I bet!" and so on. His brother shared knowledge, which he had probably acquired from a magazine, about the Izu peninsula having floated on the Pacific until it collided with its current location and became attached. "If that's the case, the peninsula might float back out into the Pacific someday. And we might never get back!" My son's response to this persuasion was simple and apposite and for that reason formidable: *"I have a winter sweater. I think we should get there before the Izu peninsula floats away. They say a typhoon is coming!"*

Eeyore was already aware from watching television that a typhoon was approaching the Izu peninsula. As he intended to make the trip in spite of the storm, dissuading him with talk of a typhoon was out of the question. What was needed was some other terrifying monster to replace the image of a typhoon in his consciousness. But what a futile, not to mention disagreeable, effort!

My wife droned on, and her vitality appeared to ebb away. When she reached the point where Eeyore had begun to insist that his father was dead, she turned half away from me and spoke quietly to the bookshelves against the wall.

I looked out the window. Among the few trees in our garden, the dogwood, the birch, and the young stewartia were swaying in the wind. Only the camellia with its thick trunk and stiff foliage was still; yet if you looked closely even the camellia was moving, but at a different frequency. The wind whistled through the trees and above them, wheeling slowly through the sky and moaning. Since morning it had been a little windy, and raining in fits and starts; it was as if fat dewdrops were hanging heavily in the air. Through the window glass that was streaking with rain and then clearing I observed the world outside. In the distance, the sky was pitch-black and ominous; inside banks of dark clouds darker clouds boiled and billowed. Even so, the wind wasn't so strong you couldn't walk against it—that's what Eeyore would say—and it wasn't raining hard enough to require an umbrella. In fact, he had already walked to the bus stop that morning and made the trip to and from his special school.

I had been working on an essay for a series I was editing with some friends and I put it aside and stood up. I sensed my wife flinch as though startled—she was still turned away from me in silence—but I was not at that moment angry at Eeyore. I was merely perplexed. I was experiencing the same feelings as my wife, at least I should have been. Nevertheless, I headed for the stairs. I believe I was assuming it wouldn't be hard to bring Eeyore around so that we could remain in Tokyo while the typhoon passed. But when I looked down at his large head, and at the bulky knapsack on his back that was as broad now as any adult's, and saw the ancient doll strapped to his right shoulder and side as he stood planted fiercely in front of the door, I felt myself letting go of common sense with a shudder of abandon and I began steeling myself for a departure with Eeyore for the wind-whipped storm that awaited us in Izu.

The large doll he had lashed to his body, close to three feet tall with abundant black hair, ogling eyes, and an overbite, was Tiny Chiyo, a filthy, damaged doll that had been lying abandoned in the shed for four or five years: Eeyore looked like a warrior on his way to a final, desperate battle with his child at his side.

"When I told him none of us were going to Izu, he dragged out Tiny Chiyo"—my daughter had sounded embarrassed as she reported the old doll's involvement to her mother. Her younger brother also appeared to twist away from the doll's shuttered-open eyes.

"I'm going with him. I'll unpack everyone else's stuff."

As I was repacking my suitcase in the living room, Eeyore's younger brother approached in silence and reached tentatively for his own things. Apparently he was prompted by feelings that accurately reflected my wife's own anxiety, which she now expressed: "That's a good idea; better that the three of you should go instead of just Papa and Eeyore!"

"No—Eeyore and I will go alone!" I said, aware that my loud voice seemed to be a hurtful blow to Eeyore's brother. I was asserting myself violently: the rest of the family, those who wish to continue existing in this world, are excused; Eeyore and I are free to behave as crazily as we want!

Eeyore's younger brother and sister, as if they were ashamed of themselves, though they had no reason to feel that way, retreated to their rooms. Without another word to my wife, in the grips of a "leap," I set out from the house with Eeyore and his doll as though we were knights departing for the Crusades.

We took the Odakyu line from Seijo Gakuen to the Odawara station and rode standing, jammed in among the commuters who filled the train. With all eyes staring at him, Eeyore declined to remove Tiny Chiyo or even his knapsack; he looked obstinately at the floor, his head down, behaving as if he had left on a trip by himself, and I couldn't even bring myself to hoist his pack into the luggage net above our heads. We stood back to back as if we were strangers, but Eeyore's body odor was curiously strong and I could tell even turned away from him that he had not alighted at a station along the way and was still standing at my side.

At Odawara, we transferred to the National Railroad, and, as far as Atami, the train seemed normally crowded for the hour; when we changed to the Ito line after buying box lunches for supper, there were very few passengers. The sea was already dark, and the mountainside was also in heavy shadow, but there were instants when light glinted faintly off the trees as they bent to the wind. As we crossed an iron bridge I glimpsed a swollen river; the wind-whipped trees and the tumbling water took me back to stormy nights in the valley in the forest. Eeyore was in the next seat with his back to me and had placed his troublesome pack in the aisle seat; I sat as though alone at the window curtained by the rain and the darkness of the night and recalled the wind and rain in the forest. On stormy nights I had felt anxious and somehow horrified, but the people in the village in the valley had seemed united. In a novel I had read as soon as I could read French there was a scene the day the Great War began when people experienced *"une grande communité,"* and I was certain I had understood that moment perfectly. Thoughts about the future course of the life I was to lead were included in the exaltation and uneasiness of those stormy nights in the valley, but it had never occurred to me that a life as unseemly as mine was waiting. Ashamed of my sentimentality, I took from my suitcase *The Life of William Blake* by Mona Wilson, a name I had been hearing for some time.

When we reached Ito, we learned that the track ahead was impassable. Eeyore was continuing to behave as though he were traveling by himself, but as this included listening carefully to the announcements inside the station there was no need to explain to him. When we came out of the station, Eeyore following two or three steps behind me, I made a deal with one of the taxis waiting for passengers in what was now a downpour to take us to our mountain cabin in Izu Heights.

"Checking up on your place? Shall I stop for batteries for my flashlight?" the driver asked, trying hard not to stare at Eeyore. "If it gets really bad I'm turning around, I can't be letting you off and not getting back myself! They say the typhoon'll hit Izu right between the eyes! You leave your place open?"

The storm became violent as we drove, but the driver managed to deliver us to our cabin. He even lit the way for us with his headlights from behind as we walked the thirty or so feet to our front door and got soaking wet. The path beneath us remained in darkness; what the headlights lit so brilliantly it hurt the eyes was the deep ocean of leaf on the frenzied branches of the bayberry, which seemed about to go up in flames as the wind whipped it against the trunk of the cypress tree. Opening the wooden door at the front entrance, I managed to get Eeyore inside before the wind blew the door shut, then went around to the rear of the house for an armful of dead branches to use as firewood. On the way back, the wood I was carrying caught on the branch of a tree, which snapped back and struck me a blow across the face, knocking off my glasses and bloodying my nose. What unexpected force this storm had, to stop me in my tracks to wipe my lips and search for my glasses!

But once I had closed the door behind me, I experienced a certain peacefulness very different from my painful thoughts until then. For one thing, Eeyore had grown alert as soon as he got inside and, with the electricity off, seemed to be using the flashlight to move around upstairs from the dining room to the living room. I got towels from the bathroom and brought them upstairs along with a mattress from my bedroom, which was plenty large enough for both of us if we lay down side by side. I had Eeyore get undressed and dry himself while I went back downstairs for bedding and blankets; guessing my intention to build a fire and sleep in front of the fireplace, he positioned and straightened the mattress, propping Tiny Chiyo on the floor alongside it.

I placed a bundle of the wet branches in the fireplace and lit some torn magazine pages on top of the wood. As I hadn't opened the valve in the propane gas shed at the edge of the property, we couldn't boil water. I gave Eeyore the box lunch from the train station and a cup of water, poured the sake remaining in a two-liter bottle in the kitchen into my own cup, and began drinking as I tended the fire. Eeyore, his large body hunched over in the darkness, squinted into the lunch box to inspect the contents as he ate them. He ate in silence, taking a long time to finish, then lay down in the very center of the quilt on top of the mattress, placing Tiny Chiyo at his side, and fell asleep, snoring loudly, as he did immediately after a seizure. I was left alone in front of the struggling fire.

The wind and solid sheets of rain rattled the wooden shutters. A large wind dragon whirled through the leaves of the shrubbery surrounding the house. High in the sky and in the space that rose steeply from the road along the kitchen side of the house—beyond, on the land across the road, the space was wide enough to accommodate a pine tree in which large crows were always perched—I could hear the screeching of the unimpeded wind as it chafed against itself, layer upon layer. At some point I also heard a cracking as though a large tree had been sheared off at the trunk (the following morning, because pines were scarce in this area, the only damaged tree, except for saplings, was the giant pine in front of the kitchen, yet the smell of resin was so strong it would give me a headache).

Eeyore's snores had changed as he slept to a sound like moaning. Lying flat on his back on the quilt atop the mattress on the floor where I was sitting, his legs straight out, he was like a mummy in its tomb. Next to him, his spring-loaded eyes also closed, Tiny Chiyo was a smaller mummy who had been interred with his master.

I banked the fire a little, so the wood would last, and read Mona Wilson by the light of the fire without the help of glasses, tilting the book toward the fireplace. I had reached the chapter where she interprets *The Four Zoas,* and I recalled my first encounter with this epic poem in my youth as I felt myself drawn into it again. Blake's pantheon of demigods explain that the world we know has fallen from primal bliss, and the two women among them, Ahania and Enion—they can be considered emanations of the principal demigods or brides to them, and also symbolize the various essences of this world—join each other in lament. They relate what happens in the "cosmic caverns of the grave." They speak of *Man, the eternal Man* who must remain asleep so long as we mortals dwell in confusion.

The time comes when *Man* surveys, as though in a dream, the tree, the herb, the fish, the bird, and the beast. Collecting the scattered parts of his immortal body, he thinks to restore the *elemental form* from which all things grow. This *eternal Man,* with a capital *M,* as in *That Man should Labour & sorrow & learn & forget, & return / To the dark valley whence he came to begin his labours anew,* was of course Albion, the ultimate human existence; there was a period in my youth when I saw my destiny in his, and in his grief my own. In the following passage, Albion laments the fate that requires him to suffer anew in this real world in order to redeem humankind through Christ, "the lamb of God":

In pain he sighs in pain he labours in his universe / Screaming in birds over the deep & howling in the wolf / Over the slain and moaning in the cattle & in the winds / And weeping over Orc and Urizen in clouds and flaming fires / And in the cries of birth & in

the groan of death his voice / Is heard throughout the Universe wher-
ever a grass grows / or a leaf buds The Eternal Man is seen is heard
is felt / And all his Sorrows till he reassumes his ancient bliss.

Taking a lesson from Blake, I could hear The Eternal
Man's existence and sadness in the sound of wind and rain en-
veloping the house. Though I knew the living room would fill
with smoke, I had left the damper in the fireplace closed to prevent rain from blowing down the chimney, but the moaning on
the other side of the damper was like a howl of pain from the
giant throat of Man.

As I went over the passage quoted by Mona Wilson, I became aware of a fact that seemed so unmistakable I was surprised I had missed it until now. In my novella *The Day He
Deigns to Wipe My Tears Away,* I had represented the "father"
as **ano hito** (that man). The significance I intended the Gothic
boldface to convey, if it were expressed in English, would be *Man*
with a capital *M*. I assume I had been influenced by my reading of Blake's language. On one level, the **ano hito** in my story
was "father" and on another he was a symbol, as in Blake, of
Everyman.

In my long novel *The Contemporary Game,* I named the
patriarch who comes back to life time after time *"Man who
deconstructs."* In this fallen, contemporary world which corresponds to Blake's real world, the body of *Man who deconstructs*
has been separated into small pieces and is buried in the forest;
in a passionate and painful dream, a young boy gathers up the
pieces one by one and attempts to bring them back to life and to
restore the Age to life as well but is finally unable to accomplish
his task and grieves. Martha Crowley had asked about the connection between this episode and the myth of Osiris and other
sources. But wasn't I simply mirroring the circumstances of
Blake's *Man* before he was reborn? Later I was able to confirm
this when I read Kathleen Raine's analysis of Blake as mystic.

Perhaps, in short, I had been writing novels for close to twenty-five years by simply restating in my own words the lines of Blake that I had glimpsed in the university library as I was entering my young manhood. Nor was it only a process of unconscious influence; I had been aware of using Blake's poetry as the source of my fiction any number of times.

Sitting between the fireplace and the mattress where Eeyore lay sleeping, I grew drowsy. The sum total of my work as an author felt shallow and simplistic, not equal to a single page of Blake; moreover, it seemed to me that I had failed to accomplish a single thing I should have been doing and now time was running out. I had declared my intention to define everything in and of this world for my son's sake, but I hadn't. The definitions were for me as well, yet I was neglecting them. Wasn't I using Eeyore's brain damage as an excuse not to be in earnest? If there was indeed something childish about me though I was nearly fifty years old—it was likely to be my childishness above all that my wife and Eeyore's sister and brother were resenting about our journey to the cabin—wasn't that due to my dependence on Eeyore's disability and my desire to remain with him forever in the domain of childhood?

Yet what if he were a college sophomore today, his brain undamaged, and came to me with the following question: "Father, give me your thoughts on death when you're being as honest as you can be. I've read every definition you've written until now and I am not persuaded. I'm not asking simply to pressure you. I am troubled! Please help me; show me the definition of death you've managed to derive from all your years of life." If a son of mine with a sound mind put such a question to me, could I sit there lost in thought while he peered into my face?

If I were to attempt a definition of death to an Eeyore whose intelligence had been restored, there is a verse in, once again, *The Four Zoas,* toward the beginning, that would provide a hint. As suggested by the title, taken from the "four living creatures" in the Greek version of Revelations, there are four fundamental principles of the universe, one of which is symbolized by the god Tharmas, who represents the material substance of this world, and whose wife, Enion, whom I have mentioned, is a symbol of material freedom. At the beginning of this epic poem, as a manifestation of the confusion of the world, Tharmas and Enion must separate, and their song of grief at the moment of separation haunts me. I feel a special poignancy in Tharmas's lines as he sits weeping in his clouds, trembling and pale: *& I am like an atom / A Nothing left in darkness yet I am an identity / I wish & feel & weep & groan. Ah, terrible! terrible!*

What if I were diagnosed with cancer at the annual physical at my health club—I say this because of an uneasy feeling that somewhere inside me there is malignancy—and had to prepare to die within two to three years no matter how desperately I fought? How could I possibly transcend in that time the current state of my soul! And how, accordingly, could I avoid saying to my son (I was now in the grips of the premise that my son, a college student in his second year who has asked me a question, was a healthy young man): "Eeyore! At the moment of death perhaps we can only repeat the lament of Tharmas! Pale and trembling, the high hospital bed feeling like our clouds. . . . *& I am like an atom / A Nothing left in darkness yet I am an identity / I wish & feel & weep & groan.*" Ah, terrible! terrible!

But how could the Eeyore whose intelligence was intact (in truth, my brain-damaged son had his own fears about unfathomable death and his own approach to transcending them) take heart from an answer such as that—"Ah, terrible! terrible!"—from the father he was counting on? The thought led me to picture myself adding the following explanation on my own behalf: "What I've been reading in Blake's biography makes me think he died a splendid death. He completed one of his unique illuminations, he painted his wife's portrait and spoke gentle words to her, his companion of many years, a woman he had raised from such ignorance that she was unable to sign the certificate when they were married, and his helper in the studio, and then, after singing a song in praise of God, he died. This is the man who long ago, as a young man, when his beloved younger brother died, saw his soul clapping its hands in joy as it departed from the body. *The Oak is cut down by the Ax, the Lamb falls by the Knife / But their Forms Eternal Exist. For-ever. Amen Hallelujah.* I wonder if living isn't just a process of preparation for this delightful half day before death? And what if that delight is merely illusion, since what follows is nothingness; why should we trouble ourselves with that! The problem is, in my case, I haven't managed to prepare for my half day of delight. Even though I'm approaching the age when my father, that would be your grandfather, died."

I seem to have spoken these words aloud (to be sure, I was surrounded by the roar of the storm, which showed no sign of abating), which must have meant that I was drunk. I think I was also half asleep. Presently, I felt the touch of a calm and gentle hand that was scarcely a touch at all on my shoulder and my arm and around my chest, waking me, and I heard a voice: *"It's all right! It's a dream, you're just dreaming! There's nothing at all to be afraid of, it's just a dream!"* And even so it seemed that I continued where I had left off, lifting my voice against the noise of the wind, speaking to the half-phantom that was my son. When I opened my eyes, Eeyore was kneeling at my side, quieting my body with both arms outstretched, holding me in the gaze of his ink-colored eyes beneath eyebrows that were thick and dark in the light of the fire. As I sat up, Eeyore moved backward with the nimbleness he sometimes displayed and, putting Tiny Chiyo to the side, made a place for me to sleep. Then he lay down again on his back like a mummy, his arms folded across his chest, and I lay down beside him and pulled the quilt over both of us.

With the momentum of the sake I fell asleep at once, before I could reflect on the curiousness of Eeyore's words to me. For an instant, I did seem to be aware of something quietly receding through the dining area that adjoined the living room and through the door, which had been left open into the darkness of the stairs beyond. . . .

When I woke up, Eeyore's body was not beside me, and the window farthest away from the fireplace where I was lying had been opened and light was coming in. Piercing the smell of smoke that filled the room, the acrid scent of pine was so raw it made my head pound. I twisted my body toward the light and discovered a darkly silhouetted figure slumped forward in one of the chairs in the dining area between me and the whitened window. It was my wife, and she appeared to be dejected. Through the frame of the sunlit window behind her I noticed there was something out of the ordinary about the view outside, something deficient. Moreover, something black and flat appeared and disappeared in that sparkling space, as though it were being thrown upward and thrown again. Groping out of long habit in the area around my head, I found the eyeglasses (which should not have been there) and recognized the blackness as a crow, I should say a great, fat crow, an old bird I knew well. It would perch in our giant pine and take flight at times as if to get some exercise, and glide out of sight, and then return and rest its wings. Now the exposed knot on a branch near the top of the tree where it was easy to perch was gone, and gone with it was the entire pine.

"Eeyore found your glasses and wouldn't let anyone else bring them to you. Everyone's outside cleaning up. They want to store the broken branches to use for firewood." My wife seemed to have sensed all along that I was awake.

"The big pine must be down! An ancient tree like that survives everything until now and then one night it suddenly snaps—it's strange. The crow is frantic."

"It fell right across the road and brought down the phone lines—it's as if they built a bridge to our property. Did you hear the noise?"

"I did—didn't you?"

"We just got here this morning."

"Really! I thought I saw you standing at the head of the stairs late last night."

For an instant, the silhouetted body seemed to tighten; then, in a voice that struggled to contain strong feelings, my wife said, "There's no way I could have been standing there watching you. The three of us stayed in a business hotel in Ito."

After Eeyore and I had left, my wife and the two younger children, in accordance with a proposal made by Eeyore's younger brother, had set out for Izu themselves via the bullet train from Tokyo Station. But even the bullet train was slowed down on its way to Atami as a result of the typhoon, and by the time they reached Ito and learned that the tracks ahead were closed, it was nearly ten o'clock. The taxi they found in front of the station happened to be the same one that had brought me and Eeyore to our cabin. The driver was not unwilling to bring them as well if they were determined to go, even though the wind-driven rain was worse at that time than it had been two hours before, but he insisted on stopping at the police station along the way to register us as a potential family suicide. He then took my traumatized wife and children to a business hotel teeming with commuters from Izu who were avoiding the storm, and helped them to check in.

"Family suicide, what a cheerful fellow!" I tried to cover with a laugh, but my wife's shadowed profile remained taut.

Early this morning, under a sky that was clear and bright, they had driven here in a cab through the raw damage left by the storm, but just inside the entrance to the resort-home area a fallen tree had required them to abandon the cab. As they made their way to the house on foot around and over fallen trees and boulders overturned in the road, my wife had stumbled and skinned both her knees. Just now, aligning two chairs, she had finished swabbing them. As my eyes adjusted to the glare and shadow, I noticed her two unexpectedly plump legs propped up in front of her.

I lay back again; the unfinished wooden beams crisscrossing at the ceiling glowed palely in the shadows. When we were building our first house I had joked that I would prefer to have no exposed beams since without them I couldn't hang myself. My wife had communicated this, literally, to the architect, and when we asked the same man to design our mountain house five years later, in what may have been a form of psychological compensation, she had requested exposed beams throughout the living and dining areas.

"I was thinking about what the driver said about family suicide," I began. "Don't you think it was more the fact that we were going to the mountains in the middle of a typhoon than anything he saw in me and Eeyore or in you that made him say that? There may have been incidents like that in the past . . ."

My wife declined my invitation to generalize and spoke instead the words she must have been considering deep inside herself until now: "You said you saw me standing here last night. I should be thankful it was me and not the 'ghost of a flea.' In her letter to me, Martha wrote that what frightened her wasn't just that Eeyore saw the ghost of M's severed head but that the professor also seemed to be seeing it with him. Yesterday, Saku said Eeyore would probably calm down when he got to the house, but there was no way of knowing what Papa might start thinking when he got to Izu. So we'd better go after them, he said, because of Papa!"

I could hear what was now a dry and even wind and the children's voices, particularly Eeyore's self-important instructions to his younger brother and sister to gather smaller pieces of wood while he took charge of the heavier. I lay there, puzzling over how I was going to approach my wife and explain why half my face was swollen. Given my behavior the day before, I would have to get right to work repairing the psychological damage between me and my wife and Eeyore's sister and brother. I sat up into the light and said the following, as if to encourage myself and the others, aware of my wife flinching once again as she noticed the swelling in my face: "Maybe Eeyore doesn't dream, but he does know that people have dreams! As he grows older, if the day finally comes when he dreams, I think he'll be able to tell it was a dream. Learning that made last night worth it."

I feared that Eeyore's first dream would be a painful one, and that I might no longer be alive and would therefore be unable to stand by his side. But I knew that Eeyore would be able to say, turning to himself as dreamer, *"It's all right. It's all right, it's just a dream."* Why should I torment myself? Eeyore would be able to turn to himself and continue, *"You're just dreaming! There's nothing at all to be afraid of. It's just a dream!"*

5: The Soul Descends as a Falling Star, to the Bone at My Heel

I t is extraordinary how the grotesquely odd and the familiar can reside together in Blake's invention. I have sensed this often, and have moreover come upon any number of passages that somehow accord with the details of my life with my son. The beginning of the epic poem *Milton,* for example, when the poet descends to this fallen world after having risen to heaven and attempts to bring about the salvation of his wife and daughters and, indeed, of all mankind. I have in mind the passage which relates Milton's descent to earth, and begins:

As when a man dreams, he reflects not that his body sleeps,
Else he would wake; so seem'd he entering his shadow.

Milton's soul enters the body of Blake, who resides in this real world, and they embark, in one body, on a journey through hardship and pain, but before they set out Blake writes that Milton's spirit arrives like a flame. When I began reading Blake again in Frankfurt I realized gradually that the illustration on the cover of my paperback volume of complete poems, a man who seemed about to fall with a shooting star at his feet, was one of the thirty plates that accompanied *Milton*.

Then first I saw him in the Zenith as a falling star,
Descending perpendicular, swift as the swallow or swift;
And on my left foot falling on the tarsus, enterd there;
But from my right foot a black cloud redounding spread over
*   Europe.*

I cannot resist comparing the notion that Milton's spirit entered Blake's body at the bone in his heel or instep with my son's unreasoning love for, or at least extraordinary interest in, his father's feet. Whenever he senses that our relationship is not going well, Eeyore attempts to restore communication between us through the agency of my feet. Milton's spirit descends like a star and arrives at Blake's core by entering through the tarsus. In the same way, Eeyore relies on the mediation of my feet in seeking to reopen the passage to my core. This practice had its origin in the days when I was suffering my first attack of gout and the power relationship with my young son seemed to reverse itself. At least that is what I have always assumed: that my definition of feet to Eeyore was based on coming down with gout.

But have I taken Eeyore's feelings fully into account? Was my definition valid from Eeyore's point of view? A wall rises between myself and Eeyore. He is terrified of looking into my face, of looking directly into my eyes in particular. If possible, he would prefer to move past the crisis with faces averted, as if we were unaware of the location of each other's face. A head-on charge directed at his father's "center"—a father who appears to Eeyore to be angry at him—would require more courage than he possesses, nor would the thought occur to him. Instead, he seeks a handhold at the "margins" of his father's body. The feet as the periphery of the human body. The feet which appear to protrude, as a man sprawls back with his legs thrust out in front of him, past the border of their owner's body. The head, face, chest, and other parts which constitute the body's center appear to be connected directly to the individual's, in this case to my own, consciousness, but the feet are at a distance, beyond the reach of consciousness. For this reason, they have the feel and tangibility of quintessential objects; even in their shape they are worthy of loving care as independent objects. It is as objects, therefore, that Eeyore clings to my feet. In this case, however, the feet in question are indeed connected to his father's center and thus by rubbing them he is able to discover a channel between himself and their proprietor.

The cultural anthropologist Y, whose theoretical work on the "center" and the "periphery" has earned him an international reputation, is a friend of mine and someone who cares a lot about Eeyore. My son was quick to sense this right away. It was therefore gratifying to discover that Y's theory could be applied, as above, to my relationship with Eeyore. With Y as my starting point, I thought to expand on the significance of Eeyore's use of my feet as "periphery" in establishing a channel to me as an approach to defining the function of my son's consciousness overall. My thoughts on the subject led me straight to the question of imagination. Here again, clearly, Blake seemed relevant. For that reason, while I have a theme to develop here, I want to begin by reviewing my personal history of writing fiction about my son and reading Blake.

I have described my chance encounter as a young man with a few lines from *The Four Zoas* that unsettled me deeply. Thereafter, as a student and after graduation, before I had ascertained that the verse was Blake's, there was a period in my life when I found his shorter poems highly evocative and wrote some fiction that was centered around them. This amounted to selecting a poem, or a few lines from a poem that I might not have read from beginning to end, and working them into my fiction in a manner that might be called arbitrary, or even willful. Looking back now, I find examples where I would have to say I had misunderstood the lines I used (even now, entering the forest of dense and twisted symbolism in Blake's long Prophecies with only my amateur, self-taught understanding as a guide, I am undoubtedly guilty of new errors). Nonetheless, when I notice as I make my way through Blake again a mistaken reading that was once powerfully evocative for me, it should lead me to a new discovery about myself at the time. Today, I know that Blake is a poet I shall continue reading until I die; this amounts to a feeling that Blake may enable me to construct a model for living my own life as I move toward death. As I confirm misinterpretations in my own fiction and am moved by them once again, I recall comprehensively the working of my imagination when I was young; in effect, my use of Blake provides the opportunity to take my measure today against myself in the past.

The first time I quoted Blake was in a novel I wrote just after Eeyore was born with a handicap and which I based on my actual experience at the time, *A Personal Matter.* From the so-called Proverbs of Hell in *The Marriage of Heaven and Hell,* I took the line, "Sooner murder an infant in its cradle than nurse unacted desires. . . ." The fact that I replaced the period that belongs at the end with an ellipsis, as if I were abbreviating a passage that followed, suggests to me that I had not actually read *The Marriage of Heaven and Hell.* Moreover, in translating the line, shifting responsibility to the young woman in the novel by having the translation come from her, I rendered it appropriate to my story. "Better to kill the infant in its cradle! Rather than ending up nursing unacted desires. . . ."

Looking back from my more comprehensive vantage of Blake's work today, I understand that *unrealized desires* represented a mode of living that Blake condemned violently, and that his emphasis was accordingly on the second half of the line. Clearly I should have rendered it as an impassioned appeal: "Compared to nurturing unrealized desires, even murdering an infant in its cradle is the lesser evil." There is no question that my translation is incorrect; what is unclear to me all these years later is whether I twisted Blake to meet the requirements of a scene in my novel, giving the line to the young woman in the story, or whether the experience of the birth of a son with brain damage was controlling my reading of the line.

The young woman in my story volunteers magnanimous encouragement including sex to the youthful protagonist, who is in regression from the trauma of having had an abnormal child. I portrayed her as a liberated young woman, quite the opposite of the "virgin" Blake rails against in the final chorus of "A Song of Liberty": *Nor pale religious lechery call that virginity / that wishes but acts not.* Even so, inasmuch as I failed to realize the connection between the "desire" I quoted and these lines, and must therefore have been unaware of Blake's idiosyncratic view of "desire," it seems likely that I had read—more properly, misread—that Proverb of Hell just as I translated it in *A Personal Matter.* Yet it was this mistaken reading that provided me one of my motifs in that early novel. I recognize the possibility, strange as it seems, that I have constructed an author out of myself from precisely this variety of mistaken certainty.

When my son was five or six years old and able to sit in a carrier attached to the front of my bicycle, during a period when

I was taking him every day to a Chinese noodle shop, I wrote a novella with a Blake poem as its "core," which I called *Father, O Father, Where Are You Going?* It was in the following kind of dialogue that I began using Eeyore as one of my son's names in fiction about him: "And as he rode home on his bike with his face flushed from the steaming noodles and burning in the wind, he would ask repeatedly, 'Eeyore, the pork noodles and Pepsi-Cola were good?' and when his son answered, 'Eeyore, the pork noodles and Pepsi-Cola were good!' he considered that complete communication between father and son had been achieved and was content."

The "I" in this story, who is in part superimposed on myself when I was young, is a writer attempting to write a biography of his father. "I" works on his draft as though he were dictating it into a tape recorder. In that section, I quote from Blake: "Father! father! where are you going? / O do not walk so fast. / Speak, father, speak to your little boy / Or else I shall be lost." The poem is from the widely known *Songs of Innocence*. To this I added the last stanza of "The Land of Dreams" from the *Pickering Manuscript*: "Father, O father! what do we here? / In this land of unbelief & fear? / The Land of Dreams is better far, / Above the light of the Morning Star." (*Father, o father, what are we doing here? In this land of unbelief and fear? And the land of dreams so very far as it is, beyond the light of the morning star!*) After mistranslating Blake in this way, in the same style, as if the poem were continuing, "I" speaks into the tape recorder about himself: "Father, Oh father! What are we doing here? What were you doing here? And what do I think I'm doing in the middle of the night, in this land of unbelief and fear, seated earnestly at a tape recorder as if it were a device to send signals to you, eating pigs' feet with mustard miso Korean-style and drinking whisky, what kind of an appeal am I supposed to be making all the way to the land of dreams so very far as it is, above the light of the morning star!"

Reading this novella that I wrote in my early thirties, I discover today that the protagonist "I" is identified with the child represented in Blake's poem. "I" is of course Eeyore's father, but more than that he is a lone child and, together with Eeyore, two baby birds screeching in the same nest, is calling out for his lost father.

I have relied on Blake's thought not only in my fiction but also in my literary criticism, in which I have quoted passages from Blake. Perhaps this was the painful groping of someone who had become an author with no experience of life. From early on in my career, I have thought about imagination. I have proposed that imagination is at the core of the function of language in fiction and is critical to observing the circumstances of our contemporary world. This has required me to study the theories of imagination of my predecessors. Beginning with Jean-Paul Sartre, I arrived, after a number of detours, at the work of Gaston Bachelard; when I wrote "A Methodology of Fiction," I quoted the following passage from Eiji Usami's translation of Bachelard's *Air and Dreams:*

> Even today, Imagination is considered to be the ability to form images. But it is rather the ability to deform images presented by perception, the ability to liberate us from basic images, the ability in particular to change images. If there is no changing of images, no unexpected merging of images, there is no imagination and the act of imagining does not occur. . . . If a present image does not recall an absent one, change images, liberating us from, in particular, basic images. As Blake proclaims, "The Imagination is not a State: it is the Human Existence itself."

In my early readings of this passage I paid scant attention to the Blake line. I was ignorant of the importance of the word "imagination" in Blake's mythological world, and I also felt in my arrogance that since my own thoughts about imagination seemed to connect to Bachelard directly I had no need of Blake's mediation. However, since the spring, when I began reading my way through Blake's complete oeuvre, I have reconfigured my own construction of the word "imagination."

The line quoted by Bachelard appears in *Milton,* which I mentioned at the beginning of the chapter. The capitalized words in this passage, Imagination, State, are in each case used by Blake idiosyncratically to connote meanings unique to himself, which, once understood, sweep away from the text the impression of mysticality or ambiguousness. What remains, and can be read, is a tangible, lucid presentation of Blake's basic thought:

> *Judge then of thy Own Self: thy eternal Lineaments explore*
> *What is Eternal & what Changeable & what Annihilable?*
> *The Imagination is not a State: it is the Human Existence itself.*
> *Affection or Love becomes a State, when divided from Imagination*
> *The Memory is a State always, & the Reason is a State*
> *Created to be Annihilated and a new Ratio Created*
> *Whatever can be Created can be Annihilated Forms cannot*
> *The Oak is cut down by the Ax, the Lamb falls by the Knife*
> *But their Forms Eternal Exist, For-ever. Amen Hallelujah.*

Locating the word "imagination" in Blake's texts is easily accomplished: "The Eternal Body of Man is the imagination, that is God himself; the Divine Body is Jesus, we are his Members." "Man is All Imagination God is Man & Exists in Us and We in Him." "For All Things Exist in the Human Imagination." For Blake, the substance of God is founded on the Imagination. The same is true of the ultimate Man. Man reaches God through the agency of Imagination. Man will be redeemed from this fallen world of illusion when all Mankind becomes the single body of God, and it is Imagination which is the means of achieving this State: when all Men at last conjoin with the Eternal Body, that is, with God, that moment in and of itself will be the fulfillment of Imagination.

It is from these thoughts on imagination that the earlier quote proceeds: "The Imagination is not a State: it is the Human Existence itself." Once the ultimate man is envisioned as conjoining with God, a conjoining enabled by the imagination, it should be possible to accept straightaway the view of "Imagination" as substantial, human existence itself. Where Blake becomes difficult to understand is in his singular use of terms like "State" and "Forms," the "State of Man" in this fallen world, or the "Forms" that express the essence of what will become the ultimate Man.

Now then, if imagination is human existence itself—I find myself compelled to use Blake's definition as the basis of my own thinking—in what form does imagination live in Eeyore? The following question looms to the surface as a major issue (in truth, I have taken this detour in order to arrive at it): "Eeyore—do you have an imagination? Assuming you do, how does it work?" Again and again I have experienced the pain of posing this urgent question. Until it has seemed to me that discovering an answer was life's most difficult challenge, not only to Eeyore himself but also to me!

In *Jerusalem,* his last "prophecy," Blake wrote: . . . *as in your own Bosom you bear your Heaven / and Earth, & all you behold, tho it appears Without it is Within / In your Imagination of which this world of Mortality is but a Shadow.* Reading these beautiful words, was I able to acknowledge with a calm heart and mind that the fundamental source of existence in this world was lacking in my son?

Since about ten years ago, during the period correspond-
ing to Eeyore's puberty, what we have been able to see of his
interior life has been revealed chiefly through music. That said,
I must add that I personally have been unable to connect these
stirrings in Eeyore's soul in response to music with either the
exercise or the development of imagination.

As a child, Eeyore was an expert at identifying bird calls. In
my novel *The Flood Has Risen Unto My Soul,* in which I call the
character modeled on my son "Jin," I described this as follows:

"Whenever he was awake, Jin's life consisted of listening
to bird calls his father had transferred to tape from stacks of
records. And it was the bird calls that drew 'words' from the
toddler for the first time. From the tape recorder next to his
pillow on the cot where he sits or sprawls, a bird call issues at a
volume just perceptible. Through scarcely parted lips, his voice
even lower, Jin sighs, 'Thrush—it's dusky thrush,' or 'Titlark,
it's titlark, it's flycatcher, nightingale, it's nightingale . . .' In this
way the child with dimmed intelligence learned to distinguish
no fewer than fifty bird calls and discovered in listening to them
the same pleasure he took in eating."

When I became aware of Eeyore's budding interest I poured
effort, perhaps wasted, into nurturing his inner affinity for the
sounds of birds. When he entered a special class at elementary
school and began to make friends, his passion shifted to the
music of Bach and Mozart. But it lived in him throughout the
preschool years of his childhood. Hearing the strong, high-
pitched "peep" that dipped gradually lower in the scale, for example, he would say, "*Kingfisher—it's ruddy kingfisher.*" Since I
was operating the tape recorder and Eeyore was receiving my
signal and responding with words, I took this to mean that communication had occurred. Perhaps, but did that mean that my
son's imagination had been engaged? There was no possibility
that Eeyore was picturing the shape of the bird from the sound

of its voice on the tape. His vision was impaired in a way that could be corrected only by a complex configuration of prism and lens. In those days before he was wearing glasses, he couldn't possibly have resolved the shape or figure of a bird; even so, I went to the trouble of pointing to photographs of birds on record-album jackets and repeating for him, "This is a magpie; this is a starling." But it seemed never to occur to him to look at the photographs on his own as he listened to the tape.

In short, the bird as object did not exist; the signal of the bird call was merely invoking the name of a bird. Nor did providing Eeyore with the signal of a name elicit a bird call from him. In other words, the excitement of conjuring the concrete existence of the bird in question in the space between the bird call on the tape and the name spoken in a whisper by my son was being experienced in the father's imagination only.

As Eeyore encountered other children with handicaps similar to his own, his interest shifted from bird calls to music created by people, and although this transition unmistakably occurred and was an important event in our family's life, I don't believe I could explain its significance satisfactorily to an outsider. I have the same feeling about the special procedures for communication that have developed between Eeyore and me over time: I am certain they will also appear strange to an outsider, and I feel that I am losing my nerve even as I prepare to describe them. To my wife and to Eeyore's younger brother and sister, our procedures, which were spoken aloud, were familiar sounds. We had two, and both began as games. Once evolved into a kind of joyful acknowledgment; the other concealed a threat of punishment that makes me reluctant to describe it.

It is now seven or eight years since a young Korean woman paid me a visit to deliver a request from a writer in Seoul on her way to New York. Her errand required only a brief conversation, and when it was time for her to leave, the person she was to see next who had arranged to pick her up at my house failed to appear. He was a Korean resident in Japan, and I knew his name, but he was not the sort of person whose address was available so there was no way I could take her to him. The hour was already late, and as the young woman began to show signs of real distress, Eeyore came up with a game to keep her entertained. She spoke no Japanese, but when she sang stanzas from Korean songs, Eeyore would play them on the piano and add chords to the melodies. During and after our conversation the young woman had seemed guarded, an almost stern expression on her face, but gradually she became caught up in the game, adjusting the pitch on Eeyore's bongo drums, his favorite instrument when he was young, and thumping out Korean rhythms along with his piano.

The young woman went on her way to America, and a number of Korean folk songs and melodies that were based on them remained in Eeyore's repertoire. Presently, I added lyrics to one of the melodies he liked to play. As the result was a simple ditty, I'd like to print it with the musical symbol at the beginning of each line that we used to see in popular magazines just after the war when they published a hit tune.

> ♪*Don't fret. Nothing to fear*
> *Not when my dear boy Eeyore is here*—♪

Originally I had written lines leading up to these, but somewhere along the way Eeyore had forgotten the words and I had forgotten the melody and we ended up singing only the refrain. Over time, the song came to serve as a signal of acknowledgment between Eeyore and me. "Do-oo-n't fret," I would begin singing, drawing out the first words, and from whatever corner in the house he may have wandered into Eeyore would appear, timing himself to arrive at my side as I finished, "Ee-ee-yore's here," and say, extending an arm to touch me as though we were a tag team in a wrestling match, "*Thank you very much!*"

The origin of our game was spontaneous, it was not something I had contrived with a purpose in mind. I would sing the lines offhandedly, as if to myself—"Don't fret, nothing to fear, not when my dear boy Eeyore is here"—and Eeyore, hearing me, would return to my side and respond with "*Thank you very much!*" and an exaggerated gesture to go with it, and that was all. I do recall that just about this time, whereas until then he was rarely out of my sight, burrowing under my desk while I was working or waiting at the front door for the sound of my returning footsteps when I went out, Eeyore had begun discovering things to do all by himself in out-of-the-way corners of the house. Before long, I had begun using our song, not always but often, as a means of summoning him to my side when he failed to appear when he was called.

Next door to my study in his bedroom, having laid out a change of diapers, my wife is waiting for Eeyore. But he dawdles downstairs, listening to music on an FM station or thumbing through a sumo magazine in the family room. I leave my desk, walk to the head of the stairs, and sing: "Do-oo-n't fret, nothing to fear, not when my dear boy Ee-ee-yore's here." Instantly, Eeyore sheds his lethargy and comes bounding up the stairs to slap my open palm exuberantly. "*Thank you very much!*" And the changing of the diapers is accomplished without incident.

This procedure of ours was invariably so effective that when I left the family in Japan and was staying in Mexico City I began humming "Do-oo-n't fret" and stopped myself short. If I sang the refrain, I feared that Eeyore might find a way to travel a quarter of the way around the world without a thought for the distance separating us and arrive at my side in a sad state of exhaustion after his monthlong ordeal to slap my hand as I stood there dumbly and shout *"Thank you very much!"*

Our other procedure was unmistakably intended as a form of chastisement. Unless he was responding to an invitation to do something that suited him, such as listening to music, my son moved only in slow motion. When told to do something or to stop doing something he complied sluggishly (to be sure, it took time for him to comprehend what it was he was being ordered to do and to take action, but that wasn't the whole story). And so, when his mother had asked him to wash his face and put on his shirt and pants and he showed no signs of moving, an almost daily occurrence, I turned to him and began to count: one, two, three, four . . . Most of the time, Eeyore was on his feet by the time I got to "six."

I counted playfully. But if I seemed too amused and the count advanced to the point where it began to appear that Eeyore's lethargic progress toward action was slowly driving him into a corner, the specter of "punishment" turned the situation grotesque. There were times when I got as far as "twelve, thirteen, fourteen, fifteen," and still Eeyore had failed to do as he had been told. Obviously, I would never strike him, but the natural and unavoidable development was that my aggravation became audible in my voice as I counted and threatened him.

When Eeyore has failed to get enough sleep he is likely to have a seizure that may or may not be a symptom of epilepsy (my wife and I disagree about this), especially during the morning, when he loses his sight for a minute or sometimes two. It is important that we get him to bed by eight-thirty. The problem is NHK's *Classical Favorites,* which begins at eight-fifty. If we can get Eeyore into diapers before eight-thirty, he resigns himself to going to bed, but when his mother becomes involved in something else, such as talking on the phone to other mothers at his special school, and fails to summon him to the bedroom by eight-thirty, he will do what he can to stall for another fifteen or twenty minutes. He may try moving in slow motion to and from the kitchen with the glass of water he needs to take his antiepileptic pill before bed, or he'll pretend to have misbuttoned his pajamas and painstakingly button them again. Meanwhile, his mother's voice summons him repeatedly from upstairs, and when at last he does start up the stairs he may turn around halfway for one more trip to the bathroom and then arrange to pass in front of the TV on his way back. If *Classical Favorites* should happen to come on at that moment, he will become an immovable boulder in front of the screen, and so there is no choice but to begin counting before that occurs, in a manner that is clearly a warning from the outset, "one, two, three, four . . ."

One Sunday, a few of Eeyore's younger brother's friends were playing at the house. They were aware that something about their friend's big brother was at variance with their own normality, but with the politeness that was part of their middle-class upbringing they refrained from active investigation; in what appeared to be a natural way, they avoided looking at Eeyore. For his part, though he was irritated at their amusement about things that were a mystery to him, Eeyore contented himself with peering at sumo magazines and a Bach discography in the corner of the room where he always sprawled and did not attempt to join in their games. Presently, I went upstairs to my study to work, and when I came back down, although my wife and daughter were not aware of it because they were preparing to change Eeyore's diapers, a bizarre situation had developed.

Eeyore's brother and his friends had assembled a set of Merculin electric train tracks in a circle that occupied half the family room. The tracks were old and bent (and some of the joints were broken) and fitting them together must have been a difficult task. Nonetheless, the locomotive was chugging around the round of tracks pulling a freight car behind it, but the children appeared distressed. The problem was Eeyore: inside the circle, his large rear plunked down between his legs in his customary manner of sitting down, his head thrust forward as if he were preparing to snatch a playing card from a deck, he was glaring at the transformer with one hand poised menacingly in the air in front of him. His brother's friends were pretending to be engrossed in watching the train circle the track; his younger brother sat facing him across the transformer, his own body thrust forward somehow defiantly though it was only a third the size of Eeyore's hulk, and he seemed to be taking the brunt of Eeyore's hostility. It appeared that he hoped to alter the course of the situation by maintaining resistance if possible.

I understood at once the source of the tension that had led to this curious stalemate. Moving the lever on the transformer in the + direction caused the train to accelerate. Naturally enough, moving it the other way decreased the voltage and caused the train to slow down and finally to stop. When the lever was depressed further, past zero to S, the current reversed and the train began to move backward. But for just an instant, when the lever reached the S mark, the transformer buzzed. Eeyore was hypersensitive to certain sounds, and this buzzing was apparently one he found difficult to endure. In fact, we had packed up the Merculin train set and stored it away in the shed for just this reason. The boys must have found it there that afternoon and Eeyore's brother, in his eagerness to accommodate his friends, had apparently assembled the tracks and begun playing with the train without stopping to recall the effect of the transformer noise on Eeyore. The boys had sent the locomotive chugging around the tracks exuberantly—until a few moments ago I had heard their excited shouts and laughter in my study upstairs—and when they reversed the lever to move the train backward and the transformer had buzzed, at that instant

Eeyore must have intervened with a nimbleness he rarely displayed. Positioning himself in the center of the tracks, he was now standing guard lest anyone try to so much as touch the transformer again.

"Want to listen to the new Glenn Gould in the other room?" I suggested. "If we take the amp from here, our other speakers will really sing!"

Eeyore looked up at me for just an instant and returned to guarding the transformer with immovable finality. Recently, we had observed this variety of intractability beginning to reveal itself as one of his standard attitudes: "There's nothing I can do to prevent myself from behaving this way so kindly refrain from trying to coax me out of it, you're wasting your time." That sort of attitude. Sitting around the circle of the tracks, the boys faced the immovable mountain that was Eeyore, their eyes downcast, and I stood there watching them and trying to think of something more to say. It was then that Eeyore's brother spoke as he faced Eeyore defiantly across the transformer: "Papa, how about trying one-two-three-four?"

Before I could respond, his face flushing with his shame at having recommended that the threat of punishment be deployed against his brother, my younger son glanced around at his friends as though apologetically, already punishing himself, stood up abruptly, and went into his own room. Like athletes with no intention of reproaching a teammate even though his error had cost them the game, his friends rose and followed him without a backward glance at the tracks they had labored to assemble.

Eeyore continued to guard the transformer with one hand poised in the air as though in readiness for a rat that might leap out at him at any moment. Alone with him, I watched the train maintain a constant speed around the track. One-two-three-four: the procedure I had intended as a game was now perceived by the entire family, including Eeyore and his younger brother, as a technique for issuing orders that conveyed the threat of punishment. I felt like a tyrant who had resorted to disguised punishment to control my feebleminded son's disobedience out of a concern for what others might be thinking. A cruel tyrant!

If I were able to detect Eeyore's imagination at work in his spontaneous modes of expression I would be able to encourage him to develop it. I have had this thought since the days when he was listening to recorded bird calls, and I cherish it still. Currently, Eeyore finds pleasure in expressing himself through puns and composing music. He indulges in two varieties of word play, both related to television: puns on TV commercials and take-offs on specific individuals who appear as the stars of TV variety shows. When I was applying a plaster bandage to a boil that had developed on his side, he said, partially to thank me, "*o-deki kangeki!*" (boil, grateful!). This was a reference to the shout of joy in an instant-curry commercial that is delivered by a famous singer whose name is Hideki. On another occasion, when the American student I have written about was having dinner at our house, and my wife had been supplying her with the English names of the vegetables she was deep-frying and was at a loss to translate navy beans (*ingen-mame*), Eeyore volunteered a word in a manner that was plausibly English and might be transcribed as "*Ingen shim border!*" The earnest young woman confessed her ignorance of the word, but hastened to add that many plant names came from American Indian languages. I understood Eeyore's outrageous pun; it was a takeoff on a line delivered in a TV commercial by a sumo wrestler he liked: *Ningen shimboda* (Life is persevering!).

When he went to work on a musical composition, Eeyore began by writing "Composed by Hidan Toru" above the first staff on the score paper. He created his pen name by combining the first name of the composer who had always loved him as though he were his own son, "Toru," and the epileptic-seizure suppressant he had to take every day, "Hidantol."

On one of Eeyore's favorite programs, traditional storytellers responded with quips and puns to questions posed by the comedian who was the master of ceremonies. Replies that were judged superior were rewarded with a *zabuton* cushion. At the beginning of every program, the emcee lampooned the unshaven giant with a red face who was the bearer of the prize cushions, describing him with a series of comic metaphors full of grotesque leaps. Eeyore relished this performance, and eventually applied the technique to creating a name for an NHK sportscaster with a baby face and wide-open eyes and a shiny bald head: "The Kewpie doll who knows his sports." Another example that will make sense only to sumo fans who follow the matches closely on television, and which may also require a note focusing attention on the connection between the color and feel of a poached egg and the shape of a tea cup, is Eeyore's choice of name for the sumo wrestler Hakuryu, "Poached tea cup."

Eeyore's puns were not complex intellectual manipulations. The teachers' notes from his special class at middle school included complaints about his frequent punning and requests that he be cured of the habit. Nonetheless, Eeyore had discovered a means of evoking laughter by separating words into their sounds and meanings and creating a distortion. And who was to say this was not an example, however trivial, of his imagination at work? When he encountered an image of a newscaster or a sumo wrestler on the television screen, he created metaphors in his own words to recapture those images. I prefer to think of this activity as the work of a bright and cheerful imagination. So what if his puns and comic metaphors were barren efforts, good for one-time laughter only, and would not add up to anything real in his daily life!

Shortly after Eeyore entered third grade, I learned that the wife of an editor I had known for many years was a piano teacher, and asked if she would give him lessons. Writers had been acknowledging their gratitude to this editor in new books and paperback editions that had been important to me since my high school days, and when he was finally assigned to me I was overjoyed. During the war years when he was growing up, he had suffered as a consequence of coming from a Christian family (with no affiliation to a particular church), and as an adult he lived a strictly principled life; his wife, Mrs. T, had her own singular views on teaching music that seemed to resonate with her husband's values. Though Eeyore's fingers were long and well shaped, he moved them clumsily, yet she did not focus on developing his technique. Her lessons were about creating a route to communication with Eeyore through music that sometimes seemed superior to my own relationship with my son.

The time came, under Mrs. T's guidance, when Eeyore began to compose. Shortly after he had entered middle school, Mrs. T played one of their exercises in a key different from the one in which it had been written and Eeyore, listening, said with conviction, "*This is better!*" Thereafter, when he encountered a melody that pleased him, he asked for it to be played in various keys. Mrs. T incorporated this in her lessons, devising exercises in "shifting keys" and "melody building blocks." If the former was about tonality, the latter amounted to practice in composing: Mrs. T would begin the fragment of a melody, and when Eeyore picked it up she would take it back. Eventually, this led Eeyore to create entire melodies on his own. Mrs. T went on to teach him how to render a melody he had created in four-part harmony, and before long he was changing the melody in the process. Soon they were playing together, Mrs. T taking the right hand and Eeyore the left, and Eeyore's fingers were bringing beautiful melodies to life.

His specialty was memory. Blake held that memory was a negative function and placed it in opposition to imagination: Blake would have said that a defect called memory bound Eeyore and constrained him from giving flight to his imagination. In any case, once a melody and harmony had roused in him, he did not forget it. After a lesson, sprawled on his belly on the floor of the living room, he filled the staves of a manuscript page with elongated notes like bean sprouts. Nothing distracted him, not even his younger sister and brother watching TV at his side.

On his eighteenth birthday, I had Eeyore's longest composition to date made into a book and printed twenty copies for his friends. I photocopied and bound the pages of his handwritten score and carved the name of the piece and an illustration into a rubber eraser that I used to stamp the cover: The Hikari [Eeyore's real name] Partita in D Major, opus 2. The piece began with a prelude and six variations: an allemande, a courante, two sarabandes, a siciliana, and a gigue. Not surprisingly, the structure of the piece followed closely the Bach that Eeyore listened to repeatedly, but his melodies and harmony seemed to me to reveal a degree of originality. In Eeyore's daily progress with the writing, Mrs. T perceived growth that went beyond the development of his piano technique. In fact, the demands of a piece Eeyore referred to as a partita, while he had strictly observed the rules of piano fingering in writing it, exceeded his own technical capacity to perform it.

In mid-autumn we received a request for a collaboration between Eeyore as a composer and myself as a writer. Across a stream full of trout from the mountain cabin in Gumma prefecture where we spent our summers, there was a facility where physically and mentally handicapped children grew their own vegetables and practiced communal living. My wife and I had taken Eeyore there for a tour ten years earlier. Though he had never been cowed by anything before, on that day Eeyore had clung to my wrist and refused to let go. At the time he was only as tall as my waist. Presently my wife and I had realized that he was afraid of being abandoned there.

Now the facility was planning a festival to celebrate its fifteenth anniversary this coming Christmas and had asked us to consider creating a musical play for the handicapped children to perform. As time was growing short, they would leave the format to us. They asked only that we avoid music too complex and drama too full of action to be performed, and that we take as our theme the role played by the weak in helping to avoid the horrors of war. I accepted their proposal right away and was excited about writing a libretto.

The theme we had been assigned prompted me to reconsider a question having to do with the handicapped that had been posed to me as a kind of homework assignment the year before. Eeyore had just been promoted to the high school division of his special school, and the national meeting of the PTAs from special facilities all over Japan had convened in Tokyo. As the father of a handicapped child, I addressed the meeting. On my way to the train station afterward, a pair of female teachers with their vigorous legs stuffed into rugged jeans overtook me to ask for my help in solving a problem. The year before, the senior students at their special facility had traveled to Hiroshima on their annual excursion. The exhibits at the Peace Museum replicating the horror at the time of the explosion had jolted the children. And it seemed to their teachers that all the children had somehow changed. This year they wanted to return to Hiroshima, but some parents were opposed; what advice could I give them on how to change their minds?

The young women were convinced that I would be in favor of a school trip to Hiroshima for their handicapped children, but when I pictured Eeyore and his classmates filing through the dimness of the Peace Museum I felt uncomfortable. I told the young teachers that I couldn't be certain that either position was correct. Assuming that a large number of parents were on the opposing side, it would be hard to say that calling off the trip was wrong. If it were true that the shock of visiting Hiroshima had produced healthy changes in the handicapped children, then last year's journey to Hiroshima was undoubtedly an excellent learning experience. But how had the horror of nuclear weapons been explained to the children, particularly those who were gravely afflicted, and what evidence had they seen of healthy changes resulting?

Handicapped children were not among the ranks of those who created nuclear weapons and deployed them. Clearly, their hands were not stained. Moreover, in the event of a nuclear attack on the cities where they lived, they were certainly the most vulnerable to harm. Handicapped children were entitled to oppose nuclear weapons. I had seen people in wheelchairs participating in antinuclear demonstrations in Hiroshima and had been deeply moved by them and by the student volunteers helping them.

Apart from all that, there was the question of Eeyore the individual. With his sensitivity to death he might comprehend the tragedy of an atom bomb incinerating an entire city, of hundreds of thousands of people dying in that instant and for months afterward and many more than that wounded. Undoubtedly, he would be shocked by the photographs of the dead and the wounded. Given the fear of death already inside him, he might even find himself being driven into the darkness of an enormous shadow of death. And certainly he would change. But this particular change might amount to receiving a wound even his father could never heal for him, to experiencing the destruction and death of a part of his own physical body. "*Uh-oh! One hundred and forty thousand people died from just one bomb! And more died after. There were people who evaporated, the flash of light burned people's shapes into stone steps! Oh, it's really frightening. All those people died!*"

What if Eeyore began expressing thoughts like these habitually? Would it be possible to turn him away from his interior gloom into the light? Even when his own father felt devastated whenever he surveyed the state of nuclear weapons in the world? These were the thoughts that occurred to me and that I expressed. I tried persuading the female instructors that if they were going to expose handicapped children to cruel and terrible realities, they must first consider carefully a mechanism for converting the shock the children were certain to receive into something akin to hope. Children with normal minds might be considered capable of discovering such a mechanism on their own—though surely there were those among them who could not, not only children but also adults—but to expect seriously handicapped children to perform an operation of that kind would be to saddle them with a heavier burden than they could bear.

The disappointed teachers eventually fell silent and moved away; but the problem they had presented me with remained alive. Hadn't I myself failed to create a mechanism that would allow the consciousness of the tragedy of war including nuclear weapons to open on the prospect of hope? Hadn't I failed, in other words, to provide Eeyore with a definition that would permit him to convert the shock he would receive into something positive? I could feel these concerns pushing me toward a musical about powerless people and their role in avoiding the horrors of war.

That week I wrote a script I called "Gulliver's Foot and the Country of the Little People." A stage was to be created in the gymnasium at the facility, and a curtain would be lowered halfway. Installed in the center of the space that remained visible below would be a single, giant, papier-mâché foot that was cut off by the curtain just above the ankle. The chorus of handicapped children, including those sitting in wheelchairs, would be grouped around the foot. Gulliver's voice was to echo down from speakers high above his giant foot and behind the curtain.

   I. On the beach, brandishing hoes and sticks, the little people stand at the base of Gulliver's giant foot and raise a cry of lament. There is news of an approaching warship from the neighboring country. From above the clouds Gulliver's voice booms down: Has such a crisis occurred in the past and, if so, what was done about it? The people reply: Defending themselves with these weapons they retreated into the mountains and waited for the invaders to go away. Even so, each little skirmish inevitably produced its own dead and wounded on both sides. To be sure, there has been peace in the land for some time now. People seem to have realized there was no profit to be gained from occupying a country as poor as this. But why had their neighbor chosen this moment to attack again? A war would bring suffering to them as well.

  II. The king and his ministers arrive from the city. The king calls for a ladder to be leaned against Gulliver's foot and disappears behind the curtain. The ministers explain to the people. The king has come to ask Gulliver to annihilate the enemy ships in the offing by throwing boulders at them. Or to encircle them with rope and capture the entire fleet.

 III. Gulliver's voice attempts to persuade the king to reconsider his battle strategy. A victory in this war would only deepen the people's hatred in the neighboring country.

And even Gulliver could not massacre all the little people in the neighboring country. War would break out again and by that time Gulliver might be long gone. Better to adopt the old policy of fleeing into the mountains. If they needed help transporting things he would gladly be of service.

IV. The angry king climbs down the ladder and delivers a speech to the people: Gulliver is ungrateful. His gluttony has made the country poor yet in a time of crisis he does nothing. Those of you who are close to him must entreat him to go into battle! So saying, the king withdraws with his ministers.

V. With no other recourse, the little people call out to Gulliver to fight for them. Gulliver's silence conveys his perplexity.

VI. A representative of the people of the neighboring country arrives. He explains that his king is calling on his subjects to attack because he fears that otherwise Gulliver will join forces with the king of this country to attack him.

VII. Gulliver declares that he will not participate in war. The king and his ministers return to arrest the representative of the neighboring country as a spy, but the little people unite to drive them away.

VIII. The representative promises that his country will disarm. The little people and Gulliver watch him sail off across the sea.

When it was time to entrust the script to Eeyore, I drew a diagram of the stage as I explained the action. Eeyore knew about plays: his special class at middle school had staged *The Giant Turnip,* and I tried using examples from that experience to talk about the large papier-mâché foot, but I couldn't be sure from what he said, and this troubled me, whether he had understood the story: "*Oh boy: That's a big foot! That's a good one. Is it Papa's foot? I can't write music for a story so long. It's a major work, wouldn't you say? It's difficult, wouldn't you say? I can't do this one. I always forget everything!*"

Mrs. T and Eeyore's younger sister encouraged him to begin work. His sister broke down the script into short scenes and drew a storyboard. Eeyore had chosen to see Gulliver's foot as identical to his father's, but his sister drew Gulliver's face to look exactly like Eeyore's own and this seemed to awaken his interest. Mrs. T selected from among Eeyore's compositions the strongest melodies and organized them in a kind of inventory catalogue. At each piano lesson, she helped Eeyore choose melodies that seemed to fit verses in my script and pieced them together to build the score. When they had sounded out a melody and the harmony to accompany it side by side at the piano, Eeyore's job was to transcribe it on five-stave paper in time for the next lesson.

I made only one request regarding the music. I had written the lines of the king's speech to fit a song Eeyore had already composed for another occasion, the first track-and-field-day ceremony of his own school, Bluebird Special Facility. "The Bluebird March," as it was called, began slowly and then at the refrain became an allegro using triplets in a way that conveyed tension. I asked that the march be transposed to a minor key and made to fit my lyrics. As I had expected, the music conveyed perfectly the blend of panache and whininess that was the king's special flavor. Once Eeyore began working on the tune I often heard my wife singing the king's speech in the kitchen:

> *Gulliver's gluttony has made us poor*
> *Yet he does nothing to help . . .*

The whole family participated in completing the musical. Eeyore's younger brother pronounced my script too long and wanted it pared down until only a logical framework remained. He also discovered on my library shelves a book on stage design and devoted ten days to building a model of the set. In this way, with everyone pitching in, "Gulliver's Foot and the Country of the Little People" was completed. But shortly after we had sent it off to the facility we received a request to simplify it further in consideration of the children's ability and performance time. Once again we went back to Mrs. T, and with her help we created a final version. I succeeded in convincing Eeyore of the need to revise the script, but when it came to actually redoing the arrangements he couldn't be bothered. Apparently, it was in the essential act of creating the composition that he found his pleasure and his ability to concentrate.

Two days before Christmas Eve, when our musical was to be performed, Eeyore and my wife went to our cabin in the mountains. At the house for his final piano lesson of the year, Mrs. T had taken the time to remind Eeyore, who was restless with excitement about leaving, that the children performing Gulliver were not only amateur musicians but also handicapped, and that he must not be angry even if the beat were uneven and the singing off-key. On another occasion, conducting his own composition for chorus at his special class in middle school, Eeyore, who enjoyed watching not only concerts but orchestra rehearsals on television, had provoked complaints from school mothers by whipping the stand with his baton and shouting orders to repeat. Informed by Mrs. T that he would attend rehearsal as the composer but would not be conducting this time, Eeyore had indicated his agreement by removing the baton he had packed in his backpack. His compliance was almost certainly due to his high spirits at the thought of having his mother all to himself for the two days of their journey together.

Alone in the Tokyo house with Eeyore's younger brother and sister, I realized how long it had been since Eeyore and his mother had spent the night away. After an early dinner, my daughter remained at the dining table to do her homework and my son disappeared into his room and gave himself away with the stealthy beeping of a computer game. The house felt calm and orderly. Eeyore's sprawling absence here and there kept entering consciousness as an empty, chilly feeling that required us to acknowledge the degree to which his large body with arms and legs spasmodically akimbo like a baby's overshadowed our daily lives.

That evening, putting aside a letter "from a reader" that had continued to trouble me, I was making my way through Erdman's principally social and political critique of Blake. Somehow, a cloud of gloom seemed to be hanging over those of us in the family who had stayed at home. Recently, I had received a number of anonymous letters of the sort that people addressed to particular individuals because the media ignored their own assertions about this and that. While the letters were informed by feelings of victimization, they were also forceful and assertive in their way; today's, postmarked from Mikawa in the Yamaguchi prefecture, had been provoked by a collection of my speeches at student antinuclear protest meetings and handicapped children's parent associations. Those who were responsible for the nation and for society, the letter began, whether in America or Europe or Japan, must survive nuclear war by hiding in giant shelters so they would be able to rebuild the world after the Soviets had been destroyed. In normal times, entertainment may be important, but in times of crisis authors are useless parasites of society, and handicapped children the more so. In honesty, could an author and a handicapped child rebuild the world after a nuclear war? Wasn't it more likely that they couldn't build even a single house? Those who feel powerless tend to fall into defeatism. "And where do folks like that get off criticizing the leaders in the freedom camp who dedicate themselves each day to the inevitable nuclear confrontation with Soviet totalitarian fascism! I'm not suggesting that you and your retarded son commit suicide, but have you ever considered keeping your mouth shut instead of spewing your poison into our world?"

It wasn't as if I felt unable to refute the author. It was rather that his logic quickly detached from my consciousness, leaving behind only an image, assuming we had survived the nuclear war together, of building a hut for myself and Eeyore in which to escape the onslaught of the black rain. That night, we three house-sitters went off to our rooms to bed without so much as a decent good-night to one another. The following day, Saturday, happened to be the last day of school, and although we had not planned to attend the performance I arranged to meet the children at the station after their closing-day ceremony and we decided on the spot to join Eeyore and my wife.

Our cabin in Gumma looked naked and exposed; the silver birch had dropped their leaves, and the first typhoon of the summer had swept down from the plateau and uprooted the pines that grew in the shallow soil that covered the lava rock. We arrived at sunset and set out down the path toward the facility on the opposite slope, the leaves covering the ground beneath our feet glowing redly in the failing light. The view from the path that wound up through the mist from the last rays of light pooled at the stream in the bottom of the valley was so unnaturally clear that we could make out the figures of my wife and Eeyore returning toward us side by side, their eyes on the ground in front of them, from five hundred meters away.

"Let's call out to them," Eeyore's sister suggested, but her brother stopped her: "He might think we're here because something bad has happened." A sense of danger of this kind lurked in the children's minds at all times. This was the variety of daily life the family was taxed with, I thought to myself; but the children had already shifted to an untroubled mood and ran down the hill together, Eeyore's sister moving as always with the ease and grace of a prancing colt. Reunited, the four of them began climbing back to where I waited, looking up in my direction as they came; and in my lingering melancholy I imagined them as they would be when I was dead, just as they were now, gathered around Eeyore though he was the largest, protecting him, managing. Up the hill they marched in high spirits, singing, and in a minute I could hear the words:

> *Gulliver's gluttony has made*
> *our country poor . . .*

When we had returned to the cabin, my wife told me about the dress rehearsal Eeyore had attended early that morning. In the very first scene, as he listened to the little people singing their chorus, his elbows had lifted and tightened against his sides and he had leaned forward from the waist with his head in his hands. *"Oh boy, this is surprising. This is a problem. What shall we do, Mama?"* This time, Eeyore wasn't venting his anger as a haughty composer; he was deeply perturbed. To an observer it might even have appeared that he was mortified about a mistake of his own. Nonetheless, the music teacher, a small man who seemed to have his wits about him, came down from the stage with the score in hand and explained to Eeyore that he had further simplified the arrangements during the rehearsals to match the children's ability to sing in chorus, and had even converted a number of solos into group recitations. My wife listened with growing apprehension, but Eeyore had surprised her by agreeing readily: *"I understand. There are times when the performer will leave out repeats, let's see, Glenn Gould is one; and in mono-aural Lupatti did the same thing!"*

The rehearsal had resumed, and this time Eeyore sang along as he watched—he had a beautiful singing voice, clear as a young boy's before it changed and without vibrato—but each time the action onstage was late or a new singer began off-pitch he shook his head discreetly. The music teacher also appeared to notice, and as the piano would have to be removed to the side of the stage on the day of the performance, the problems he and Eeyore had identified together seemed to concern him. At that point, at my wife's suggestion, Eeyore had accepted the job of prompter beginning at the rehearsal that afternoon, and had made a big difference. The place he had chosen to install himself was a surprise in store for us at tomorrow's performance. Eeyore's younger brother, whose model of the stage had been used in building the actual set, was certain he knew the answer to the secret.

Using wood from the pine trees that had been felled by the typhoon early that summer and was still green, I managed with difficulty to light a fire, and the family sat around it in a semi-circle and ate the vegetable rice and chicken in ceramic pots that we had bought at the Yokohama station. I felt content, but it was a different sort of contentment than when Eeyore and I had traveled to Izu in the typhoon. As we continued our conversation, Eeyore jumped up with the agility he possessed when engaging in an action that pleased him and opened wide the window on the valley side of the cabin. The deep, silent chill that precedes snow on the plateau flowed into the room. Shivering, I was about to instruct Eeyore to close the window when he silenced me by exclaiming, with a theatrical gesture, *"Shhh! Listen everyone!"*

> *Ships of war draw near to where we stand*
> *How can we know what terrible fate is at hand?*
> *What is to become of us?*
> *Gulliver, what are we to do, where to flee?*
> *Keep us free.*

From the facility on the slope across the valley, the sound of singing voices reached us faintly through the stillness of the resort community. It was the first chorus Eeyore had composed, to words I had written right after we had decided to collaborate on a musical play. I reproduce here the score in its original form:

Inasmuch as the music teacher is preparing to publish an account of the entire project that goes back to asking me and Eeyore to become involved, I shall be brief about the actual performance of "Gulliver's Foot and the Country of the Little People" that Christmas Eve. I shall limit myself to certain impressions of the individuals onstage that moved me, and to Eeyore's behavior that day.

Mr. M's mise-en-scène was based on his interpretation of the country of the little people as literally a gathering of handicapped children. Although they were costumed as peasants from medieval Europe, the children made no attempt to conceal their handicaps, appearing onstage in their wheelchairs, or on crutches, or not so much sitting as having slumped to the floor; and as their performances appeared to be merely an extension of their every-day behavior, it was rather like watching an ordinary holiday celebration at the facility. When handicapped children are over-coming their handicaps to behave normally, the more so if a group of them is involved, they infuse the space around them with a deep humanity and with a vitality that feels valiant. Here, too, the choruses had force and presence precisely because each of the singers was overcoming his own difficulty to achieve a natural performance as he moved about or sat motionless on the stage.

Our play was put to use to demonstrate how the children were dealing with their individual handicaps. One example was the casting of the king, performed by an infinitely lovable Down's syndrome child with a round, pudgy face. He was re-splendent in the reddish berries of the wild briar that was a fa-miliar sight in the thickets in this area, not only in his crown but garlanding his shoulders and his chest. For this child, ascend-ing a ladder appeared to be a major undertaking that only re-cently had become possible at all with great effort. In the scene where the king climbs the ladder leaning against Gulliver's foot, everyone onstage cheered him on, and when his round, cautious legs and feet finally disappeared behind the curtain, the play was interrupted by applause. It therefore seemed entirely natural in the finale that the king, who had been driven off by his little sub-jects, should appear among the crowd together with his minis-ters waving farewell to the envoy from the neighboring country.

When it was time for curtain calls, Mr. M rose from where he had been playing the piano to one side of the stage, beneath the large fir that had been cut nearby for a Christmas tree, and said, addressing Gulliver's papier-mâché foot, "I'd like to intro-duce the composer—would you please join us."

The audience filling the chairs that had been set up in the front half of the gymnasium seemed to go silent with expectation:

handicapped children from the lower grades, parents who had come to pick them up for the New Year's holiday, and adults and children from the settler families clearing land for farming nearby. They were waiting for Eeyore to appear from inside the paper foot where he had successfully accomplished his task as prompter. Sitting next to me in a row, my wife and Eeyore's younger brother and sister were also waiting with a bright and eager excitement in their faces that I had not observed for a long time. As the back of the foot was open, Eeyore might easily circle around to the front of the stage whenever he chose. Mr. M called out a second time: "Please hurry out now—we're all waiting." But from inside the foot Eeyore's loud voice replied with conviction: *"I think I'll stay in here, thank you very much!"*

The laughter that erupted was good-natured: the rest of the family and I laughed along. Shaking his head as though nonplussed despite his own laughter, Eeyore nonetheless waited for Mr. M to return to the piano and for the laughter to subside before speaking out in a booming voice one final time. He began by addressing the handicapped children onstage who were kindred to him, then spoke to the entire room, lifting his voice another level: *"For a curtain call let's sing the sad chorus at the beginning. Then we'll sing the last chorus in our biggest voices. After that we hope the audience will join us in 'Silent Night.'"*

The chorus rang out, and at just the moment when the key changed, the spotlight on Gulliver's foot was turned off and handheld lights illuminated waveringly the giant foot of paper stretched over a wooden structure and bamboo ribs. Inside, his hulking body seeming to occupy the entire space, Eeyore like the other performers was waving his right arm slowly back and forth above his head as he sang along. As the shadow puppet that was Eeyore appeared, the applause swelled, filling the space in front of the stage that was meant to be the sea the envoy sailed across on his journey home.

Until now, it had been my goal to provide definitions of things and people for Eeyore's sake; but at this moment it was Eeyore, presenting me with a stanza from Blake's *Milton* as a lucid vision, who was creating a definition for his father:

> *Then first I saw him in the Zenith as a falling star,*
> *Descending perpendicular, swift as the swallow or swift;*
> *And on my left foot falling on the tarsus, enter'd there.*

This vision went on, however, to unfurl an urgent, baleful image of a black cloud redounding from my right foot to cover Europe, my contemporary world. And as if in hopes of finding courage to confront that ominous image, I lifted my own voice and truly began to sing.

6: Let the Inchained Soul Rise and Look Out

We signed Eeyore up for occupational therapy at the Setagaya Welfare Center for the Disabled. For two weeks, on leave from his school for handicapped children, he would be commuting to an actual job. The homework he was assigned to help him prepare was inserting wooden chopsticks—the kind you pulled apart— into their paper sleeves. When he returned from school and removed from his satchel a large number of white wooden sticks and a sheaf of paper sleeves, it was as if the world of the diviner—purity or defilement was unclear—had been brought into our daily lives. At an appropriate distance from two audio speakers, Eeyore hunkered down like a reclining walrus, his legs drawn up alongside his large rear. Then he spread the wooden chopsticks on a patterned mat and proceeded slowly and painstakingly to sheathe them in their paper wrappers. But not before examining them closely. When he discovered one that was broken or split he would exclaim regretfully, *"Too bad! This chopstick's missing a piece!"* and carry it to the kitchen where he would respectfully bury it in the garbage.

When he finished one hundred pairs and had counted them again, my wife would line them up so that the printed surface of the sleeves was visible from any angle and then apply a label and package them in plastic wrap. This final step was difficult, but apparently it was a technique readily mastered by an adult. When we went to the supermarket as a family, my wife would halt in front of shelves we normally would have ignored, appraising similar packages of one hundred wooden chopsticks with an artisan's critical eye before pushing our basket slowly down the aisle.

It came time for my son to go to the job training center, the first time in his life that he would be participating, however quirkishly, in society. I had some thoughts about this, and apparently my wife was thinking along similar lines. Late one night, when she had finished preparations for the opening ceremony, she said to me as I sat reading at her side, "I think I'll put Mr. F's pamphlet on the constitution in Eeyore's smock pocket—that's sort of what he asked us to do."

I went upstairs to my study and brought back from a cabinet where I kept mementos of friends and associates I admired who had passed away a booklet that had been published by the Okinawan Teachers Union twenty years ago, when Okinawa was still under U.S. military jurisdiction. The man who had presented the pamphlet to me, someone who definitely belonged in the category of colleagues whom I loved and admired, an Okinawan named F, had been dead for some time: early this year an important Okinawan folk ritual commemorating the thirteenth anniversary of the man's death had been celebrated on his home island of Iejima. F was an activist in the movement to repatriate Okinawa to Japan, and he had died in a fire at a hotel where he had been staying after a demonstration. A heavy drinker, he had been in an alcohol coma when the fire broke out. I had never seen him under the influence when we were working together and was surprised to hear after his death that he loved to drink and that he was sometimes abusive when drunk. I remember only one encounter with him that made me think he might have been drinking, a scene in which Eeyore had also played a role.

There was a period when Eeyore was a child when he and I were devoted to eating pigs' feet. I can still hear him ordering in his lucid bell of a voice: *"Pigs' feet with spicy miso."* I enjoyed taking him to Korean restaurants here and there and feeding him pigs' feet that were the specialty of the house in each place with slight differences in the preparation of the miso and how the meat was steamed. When he was served a single pig's foot split down the middle on a plate, Eeyore would eat the thick skin first, then the meat, then the gelatinous tendon underneath, and at each joint in the foot he would remove the small knuckle and line it up on the table with the others. One day I noticed him staring at a knuckle with a quizzical expression, apparently at a loss for where to place it in line; when I picked it up and examined it, I saw that one of his baby teeth had fallen out. Young as he was, Eeyore's approach to pigs' feet was governed by principle: he was not finished until he had aligned the knuckle bones in their proper order.

One winter evening—I recall having had to travel some distance from home to find a Korean restaurant that served cold noodles out of summer season—we were walking down a street of bars and restaurants in the district called Sangen-jaya on our way home when a small man with a hulking head and barrel chest and strikingly short legs emerged from an eatery that served the biting liquor the Okinawans call *awamori* and turned in our direction the face of a tired child. Bundled as we were in our winter clothes over the corpulence we had in common, Eeyore and I must have looked a strange pair, but there is no question the man saw and recognized us. He stopped dead in his tracks as though glued to the street, and as I hailed him—"Mr. F!"—he appeared to sob, and pushed through the awning at the entrance back into the eatery from which he had just emerged.

The late Mr. F and his comrades in the movement against U.S. control of Okinawa had carried in their breast pockets a pamphlet about the constitution. To my wife, who was not given to theatrical behavior, slipping that same pamphlet into Eeyore's smock as he was taking his first step into the outside world may have been a tribute to the life of a man so tenderhearted that he was wounded by the mere sight of an acquaintance walking down the street with a handicapped child.

My wife went upstairs to the bedroom she shared with our daughter; I placed the pamphlet with its brown paper wrapper on the dining table and reflected, as I drank my whisky nightcap, on my plan to create a collection of definitions for handicapped children relating to our world, society, and mankind, a project that was to include a retelling of the constitution in my own words for Eeyore's sake. I had not achieved my goal, but not because it was too difficult. It wasn't even that it lacked interest as a challenge to a writer. Nevertheless, while I talked about it often enough, I had left it untouched. Even now, I was writing a series of short stories and attempting to transform them into a collection of definitions, but as I had released myself from the condition that the language must be comprehensible to handicapped children, this was not the project I had originally planned.

There was a concrete reason for my thinking to have developed in this direction: David V. Erdman, the definitive editor and commentator on Blake since Keynes and one of the compilers of the *Blake Concordance* I relied on. Recently, I had been reading Erdman's book *Prophet Against Empire*. Based on exhaustive research of newspapers and pamphlets written in Blake's day, the book interprets the poet's language in the long poems he called Prophecies in the context of social issues of the time and against the background of the Napoleonic Wars. I found the book to be filled with new hints and provocations, but I was particularly interested in Erdman's analysis of Blake's poetic expression of the philosophy of the Declaration of Independence in his long poem *America, A Prophecy*. According to Erdman's reading, in the lines following the sixth of eighteen illuminations in the folio edition, Blake reconfigures in poetry the assertions in the Declaration of Independence. He begins with "Life":

> *The morning comes, the night decays, the watchmen leave*
> *   their stations;*
> *The grave is burst, the spices shed, the linen wrapped up;*
> *The bones of death, the cov'ring clay, the sinews shrunk*
> *   & dry'd;*
> *Reviving shake, inspiring move, breathing! awakening!*
> *Spring like redeemed captives when their bonds and bars are*
> *   burst.*

Then "Liberty":

> *Let the slave grinding at the mill, run out into the field:*
> *Let him look up into the heavens & laugh in the bright air;*
> *Let the inchained soul shut up in darkness and in sighing,*
> *Whose face has never seen a smile in thirty weary years;*
> *Rise and look out—.*

The "pursuit of happiness" follows:

> —*his chains are loose, his dungeon doors are open.*
> *And let his wife and children return from the oppressor's*
>   *scourge;*
> *They look behind at every step & believe it is a dream.*
> *Singing. The sun has left his blackness, & has found a fresher*
>   *morning.*

The conclusion proclaims that overturning oppression is a right and a duty:

> *And the fair Moon rejoices in the clear & cloudless night;*
> *For Empire is no more, and now the Lion & Wolf shall*
>   *cease.*

Readers are likely to divide into those who find these lines exalting and others who hold that Blake has merely refigured the *ideology* of the Declaration in overwrought verse. Perhaps the latter response is the more natural: for the mood of Blake's age has nothing in common with that of our own, nor do we relate to mythological metaphor from the Bible. Nevertheless, I am among those who are deeply moved by these verses. And my feelings about them echo the shivers of emotion I experienced as a youth at the radical changes that came just after the war—perhaps I should say during and after the war—and most particularly at the promulgation of the new Japanese constitution that was the climax of that upheaval. I have described my experience at the time in commentary and essays that have been the target of criticism by those who dispute the importance of the five years of real democracy that followed the Surrender. How, they argue, can someone who was eleven or twelve years old when the constitution was promulgated have been so moved by its abstract language!

A desire to respond to this variety of criticism and ridicule must have figured in my determination to use the constitution as a point of departure for a collection of definitions for Eeyore. And I must admit that my difficulty in getting started has been due at least partly to the fear that I would not be able to convey adequately my excitement at the time. This is not an impossible task, nor did it lack interest as a literary undertaking: what had prevented me to this day from sitting down to work in high spirits was the presentiment of unavoidable and specific difficulty.

Such were my thoughts late that night as I gazed at the pamphlet on the table in front of me and consumed a quantity of whisky that far exceeded the dosage I normally required to fall asleep. Presently, I recalled in vivid detail a scene that had slipped from memory and that now, reviving, revealed to me the source of my wife's remark about the pamphlet that had seemed abrupt and unaccountable. Several months after our bizarre encounter with Mr. F, he had visited us in Tokyo to ask for my support in the first Okinawan election to be held under U.S. occupation jurisdiction. As he made no reference to the incident at Sangen-jaya, I began to wonder if I had been mistaken about the man who had emerged from the restaurant. On the other hand, he was clearly nervous around Eeyore, looking up as though startled every time Eeyore wandered through the living room where we were talking.

We served Mr. F a simple meal that night; I recall that he drank only some beer, emphatically declining my offer of whisky. As my wife was serving us, he said to her abruptly, speaking as a former teacher, "Your boy's handicap doesn't seem that serious; if this were Okinawa, you could put him in a regular class!"

My wife was feeling low at the time and replied that she and the other parents of handicapped children had only one thing in mind wherever they happened to be—at home, at PTA meetings, wherever—and that was living even one day longer than their children so they would always be there to care for them. Hearing this, Mr. F thrust forward his wasted baby face with the dark, soft look of an old man's penis and declared: "Mrs.! You mustn't think that way! That's defeatism! In the society we must create, your boy would carry this pamphlet in his shirt pocket, and whenever he had a problem he'd hold it up and say 'Look here!' and the problem would go away! Anything less than that goal is defeatism!"

Mr. F had died in a fire at the hotel run by the Japan Youth Center before the reversion of Okinawa had been accomplished. And my wife had slipped the pamphlet he had left for us that night into Eeyore's pocket on the day he set out to be trained to participate in society for the first time. Needless to say, she was painfully aware, though ten years had passed since our friend's death, that we had not succeeded in creating a world in which a handicapped child in a moment of distress had only to produce a pamphlet on the postwar constitution. More likely, she was simply saluting her memory of the little man who had lurched along with the gait of a corpulent dwarf but who had opposed defeatism with giant finality.

In the verses I quoted above, Blake weaves political principles into Christian symbolism; and this direct expression of his political position differentiates *America* from his later prophecies. Sparks from the American Revolution ignited France, and eventually the fire spread even to England. Blake prophesied: *And the fair Moon rejoices in the clear & cloudless night / For Empire is no more, and now the Lion & Wolf shall cease*; but reaction set in before this vision could become real, Blake's gloom deepened, and he stopped writing about politics explicitly.

In the real world, Blake's political arch-antagonist was King George III. But could the same age that produced despondency in Blake have gradually restored the king's bright spirits? Recalling the British history I had read in preparation for my college entrance examinations—Pitt the Elder and the Younger; Admiral Nelson's glory and his undoing—I spend time trying to position Blake among his contemporaries. I realize this is not the place for a review of English history; with Blake as my guide, I must return at once to my son. But I want to set down just one episode from history. It was commonly held that the shock of losing the American colonies had driven King George insane; in his intriguingly entitled book *America's Last King,* Erdman introduces a scene that foreshadowed a second bout of madness. On February 13, 1801, while at prayer, the king abruptly rose from his knees and startled the church full of people by shouting the 95th Psalm at the top of his lungs, words that seemed well suited to his frenzied mind: "For forty years I loathed that generation and said 'They are a people who err in heart, and they do not respond to my ways.'" As it happened, 1801 was indeed the fortieth year of George's reign. It is worth noting, Erdman writes, that George was identifying with Jehovah. Kneeling again, the king went back to prayer and prayed for a long time despite the cold stone floor and the icy winter air that set his bones to shaking.

Rumors of this incident reached Blake, and are reflected in additions he made at the time to *The Four Zoas,* which he revised frequently. King Urizen, who attempts to control all things with reason, is a representative figure in Blake's mythological world; and a hint of the mad King George shadows Blake's portrayal of Urizen:

> *Outstretched upon the stones of ice the ruins of his throne*
> *Urizen shuddering heard the trembling limbs that shook the*
> *strong caves.*

What attracts me to Blake so powerfully is that he not only formulates his own unique mythological world based on a tradition that extends from Christianity to esoteric mysticism, he also empowers his mythology to develop on its own by infusing it with energy from his life and times. And the motion he achieves in this way allows him to drive his mythological world through and beyond his motifs of contemporary politics and international relations to a place beyond time. For me, these two facets of the same achievement account for Blake's magnetic power.

When I began reading the vast and richly articulated mythological world of Blake's Prophecies, I couldn't help wondering what force in particular could have driven him to produce this voluminous quantity of verse day after day. The booksellers had published *The French Revolution* only, and at that, only one of the seven volumes Blake had originally planned. The fact remains, Blake composed these massive poems in isolation, revision after revision, without orders from the bookshops or response from readers. And, with the censors in mind, he concealed his true meaning beneath complex layers of mythological invention. This was in consideration of George III's oppressive monarchy; at the same time, Blake's disapproval of the king drove him each day to hone and polish his verse to its utmost brilliance. Erdman draws on his reading of contemporary sources to re-create this process persuasively.

Erdman's disclosures leave me wondering whether Blake and his faithful, lifelong companion, Catherine, might not have engaged in biting criticism of the king's reign in their private moments together at home. That prospect leads me in turn to what feels like the discovery of a new truth about a famous episode that ended with Blake being brought to trial.

In 1800 Blake left London and spent time in a house by the ocean that he later characterized as "three years of sleep at the Atlantic seaside." During that time, supported by the dilettante poet William Hayley, Blake painted miniature portraits and printed illuminations that were unrelated to his mythological world. Gradually his discontent grew, and toward the end of his stay at Felpham, Sussex, he was charged with a crime. Had the ensuing trial taken a wrong turn, he might well have been sentenced to death for treason. Based on the sworn deposition quoted in Erdman, the incident may be summarized as follows: One day, Blake discovered a soldier unknown to him wandering in his garden. The garden was a sacred place to Blake, for he had beheld wood sprites attending a funeral in the shadow of fallen leaves. The soldier symbolized to him the crudeness and cruel bestiality of this fallen world. Blake pushes the soldier out of his garden; the soldier seeks revenge by claiming that Blake cursed the king and his subjects in a loud voice and accuses him of plotting to overthrow the monarchy. Britain's highest court eventually finds Blake innocent. Even so, portions of the deposition struck me as likely to have occurred. As Blake and the soldier are shoving each other around, Catherine appears and eggs her husband on. She declares moreover her intention to join battle herself so long as a single drop of blood remains in her body. "My dear," Blake exclaims, "surely you don't intend to fight against France?" "Of course not! I shall do whatever is in my power for Bonaparte's sake!"

Judging from Blake's sketches, Catherine was a large, buxom woman with plain features. Uneducated, she had signed their marriage certificate with an X; but in later years she acquired the skills she needed to assist Blake in inking and printing his engraving plates. It seems unlikely that Blake or Catherine used the crude language that appears in the soldier's testimony. On the other hand, the content of the language ascribed to them corresponds, to a curious degree, to the thinking they shared. Blake was terrified when he was shown the deposition, Erdman supposes, and likely felt obliged to bemuse the spies who seemed to be watching him by obscuring his criticism of King George with enigmatic metaphors. Erdman places the incident at the beginning of the transition to the long silence that Blake maintained until his later years.

What I imagine is that Blake and his wife did have the conversation the soldier remembered, but not in the coarse and vulgar language that he claims he heard. Napoleon was not yet emperor at the time, and Blake still viewed him as a liberator carrying the firebrand of the French Revolution. In his version of the future, the essence of his longing, the power of the revolution would extend to England and enable liberation there (not that it took Blake long to become disillusioned with Napoleon and account him a hateful oppressor).

Inasmuch as the High Court pronounced Blake innocent, there is no basis for believing the soldier's story; nevertheless, when I picture Blake reduced to creating work that was antithetical to his beliefs while relying for support on a gentleman poet of mediocre talent even as he critiqued the times in long Prophecies understood by fewer people than understood his paintings—Hayley ridiculed them as works of madness—and when I imagine that he might have possessed, even in his midforties, the physical strength to repel a soldier, and that, as the soldier insisted, his wife Catherine might have had recourse to violent language in expressing a radical purpose of mind, I feel deeply moved. In fact, it seems likely that Blake and Catherine were both silent as Blake struggled with the intruder; and that the language reported by the soldier had passed wordlessly between their souls—somehow, the vanquished soldier had managed to hear the voice of silence.

As I allowed my thoughts to circle this episode of violence, a scene from my childhood surfaced in my memory. I was taken there by the power of certain words Blake used repeatedly. The scene involved my father, who died during the war. I have written about my father's death numberless times, not explicitly perhaps but alluding unmistakably to him. Now for the first time, a scene I had forgotten came back to me, and in its vivid light I seemed to discover something new about my life: that my chagrin as a child at wartime authority, and my father's death, and my response to Japan's defeat at the end of the war were of a piece, a single context. My experience of things through Blake's mediation continues to feel mysterious.

Before and during the war years, my family was in the bark business. We bought up Mitsumata bark from neighboring farms and paid the farmers to soak it in water until it softened and then to peel away the rough outer layer and the pulpy yellow layer underneath with scrapers we supplied. When the underbark had been bleached white in the sun, we picked it up in small bundles, which we compressed into flattened oblong bales and delivered to the national mint, where the bark was used in making paper currency.

As a child, it appeared to me that my father revealed different aspects of himself as he worked at the various facets of his business with scarcely a word spoken. In negotiation with the farmers, partly as a function of my naive assumptions about him, he seemed to have the air of a patriarch. Sitting with his legs folded beneath him on the wooden floor as he bundled the strips of bark, peeling the remaining pulp away with his darkly gleaming knife, he appeared to be an artisan, the image that feels closest to me and my daily work with pen and paper. In the final stage of the process, as he operated the bark press in a dark corner of the warehouse alongside the prefectural highway, he struck me as a factory worker. Watching him contain and direct the violent force that issued from inside him, I had my most vivid sense of my father's physical body as an adult.

The bark press was an oak plank that was bevel-geared at both ends to vertical iron bars ten centimeters around. The handles that operated the gears were also iron bars that extended from both sides of the contraption. As the handles were pushed forward by two men standing on either side of the machine, the warehouse echoed with the crunching of the bark bales beneath the plank; when the brake was released and the handles were pulled back in the opposite direction, the gears that moved the plank clanked back to the top of the iron bars and the process began again: *crunch, crunch, crunch, clank, clank, clank.* When the bales of bark had been compressed to one fifth of their original bulk they were bound in tough bark cord and thudded heavily to the wooden flooring that was laid beneath the press only.

The press was installed at the rear of the warehouse in shadows as dark as the corner where my dog had whelped her pups. When I see words like "grinding mill" or "wheel" or "wine press" that have a negative connotation in Blake, I recall the crunching and clanking noises it made. Blake used "wheel" and "mill" to evoke the taxonomy of reason, with Urizen at its apex, that was responsible for mankind's delusions; "wine press" and "grinding mill," as in the verses from *America* I quoted above, are symbols of labor that is not appropriate for mankind just expelled from Eden. Seeing the words on the page, I recalled an incident involving the bark press that occurred the year before my father died, and thought I could also see that it was somehow linked to the episode of violence in Blake's garden.

For the first time ever, the governor of the prefecture visited our village in the valley on an inspection tour. The gesture was probably intended as an encouragement to local cottage industry, part of the government's wartime campaign to increase production "on the home front." My father must have received advance notice from the village office: jacketed in a brand-new smock of thick cotton stiff as a board and looking like a different person—now that I think of it, he was my current age—he sat waiting in a wooden chair with his back to the press in the darkness, a bale of processed bark glowing softly at his side, his head lowered pensively. Peering in at him in the pale light from where I stood outside at the edge of the road, I was already feeling uneasy.

Having stopped along the way at the lumberyard and the soy-sauce brewery downriver, the governor and his entourage came up the high road with our village headman and the police chief from the neighboring town leading the way. Just inside the warehouse everyone stopped to listen to our village headman describe for the governor's benefit the history of bark processing in our village. My mother was peering into the darkness from just under the eaves at the entrance, and even from where I stood at the rear of the group of adults I could see the reason for the worry I could read in her face and the tension in her body. The plan was undoubtedly to follow the headman's explanation with a demonstration: small bundles of Mitsumata were already loaded into the press. But the machine required two operators, one on each handle, and my father's partner had gone off to war ten days ago. A replacement had not been summoned. The governor's party waited, heads thrown back as they peered imperiously down their noses into the semidarkness where my father sat alone, his chin buried inside the stiff cotton collar of his smock, his eyes on the ground in front of him.

"You there!" a voice snapped at my father. It was the police chief, in an officious tone of voice he never used with anyone, certainly not with my father, not even with the livestock—it felt like a tone of voice that had never been heard in our valley in the forest. I shivered, and I felt my mother shivering at my side. But my father remained seated, and as he lowered his head again the police chief stepped toward him and delivered a reprimand: "You there! What are you waiting for?"

Slowly my father rose, threw his weight against the iron handle, tightened down on the crunching bark, and then cranked the oak plank clankingly back to the top of the press. He repeated the process, moving back and forth with the handle, staring into the space ahead of him as if he were not being observed. Forcing the horizontal axis down on one end only seemed to be bending the machine; if the iron bars came loose from the oak base in which they were seated, the crank handle would spin backward out of control and knock my father off his feet. I shuddered. Just then, my father released the handle and moved to the front of the machine on his way to the other side, approaching the governor and the others quietly. Standing at my side, my mother, who was ten years younger than my wife is today, made a mournful sound as though she were swallowing a scream in her throat. At the hip of the cotton jacket that gave my father the look of a foreign soldier in uniform, he wore a hatchet he used to trim the stiff cords that bound the bark; as he moved toward us quietly the hatchet handle was gripped in his hand, his elbow jutting from his body. But he walked past the adults as though lost in thought, seized hold of the other handle, and continued his work, with difficulty at first and then with powerful motions that became more fluid, flattening the crunching bark and reversing the handle with a clanking of gears. Presently the governor and his party filed off toward the chestnut collection station upriver, but my father continued to work, moving back and forth to operate the cranks on both sides of the machine until he had completed the baling.

My memory resumes a year later, early in the spring before the end of the war, on the day that began with my mother coming downstairs early in the morning to announce that my father had let out a scream of rage in the middle of the night and died. I have no memory of the intervening year: as I recall what happened, the day of my father's humiliation in front of the governor's party is followed directly by the night of his angry scream and death. I have only a faint memory of what followed. I do recall my mother's reply to the head of the neighborhood association when he paid a visit to discuss arrangements for the cremation and observed as he expressed his regrets that my father's last year had been "a haze of drink." My mother had been responding in a feeble, teary voice; now she pulled herself up to her full height and said in a curious basso, "My husband drank his fill at night; but early every morning before any of you was awake he read his books, and heaven knows he worked the long day—is that what you'd call 'a haze of drink'?"

My other memory of that long day is that my head was filled with terrifying thoughts. Reviewing them now, in the light reflected by the episode in Blake's garden, I can organize them as follows. The police chief had ordered my father to the press as though he were scolding a dog, and my father had labored there. The machine had seemed about to come apart under the lopsided force he had applied to it, but it was actually the violence inside my father that was on the verge of exploding. To relieve the pressure, the violence had to be channeled outside his body. I wondered whether my mother might not have read in my father's movements and expressions that day an intention to stand up to his abusers no matter who they were, the police chief, our village headman, the governor, even His Imperial Majesty—I'll get to my basis for that notion in a minute—a determination to match their abuse with abuse of his own even if it meant wielding his hatchet. And whether that might explain how frightened she had seemed to be when he had moved toward us from the machine with his hatchet at his waist.

But my father had submitted to the police chief's scolding and had grappled with the bark press single-handedly. The machine had survived, but one year later the violence inside my father that had lost its outlet had broken the mechanism of his body and he had died with a bellow of anger. But what if he had raised his hatchet, I asked myself that day, and shouted back at the police chief? To the child that was me at the time, it seemed clear that he must have been killed on the spot by the police chief or tortured to death in jail. Because once he had begun to behave menacingly, opponents would have stepped between him and the adults, one after the other, in ascending order that reached all the way up to His Majesty the Emperor! My logic didn't present itself to me clearly in words, but when I assembled the thoughts that rose in me like bubbles that day, this is where they pointed.

The evening of the surrender, when my mother learned of the emperor's radio broadcast long after it was over—since my father's death, insisting there was no such thing as good news, she had stopped reading the newspaper or listening to the radio—she approached me with her cheeks flushed from agitation and whispered hotly in my ear, "It's just like your father said: The top are on the bottom now, and the bottom are on the top. It's just that way!"

A few days later, I had secluded myself in the river in the early afternoon; not only was I alone in the water, there wasn't a child in sight on the riverbank or on the bridge in the distance (the peculiarity of the circumstances suggests this may be the memory of a dream). And I was struck by a bizarre thought. The day the governor toured among his constituents and the police chief had lashed my father with his tongue and driven him to make a spectacle of his labor, what if, in that instant, the emperor's proclamation of the war's end had blared from a radio across the entire valley? Then my intrepid father in his cotton smock would have raised his hatchet high in his right hand and ordered the police chief and the governor to take their places at the crank handles and to begin the crunching and clanking. And three or so places back in the line, His Majesty the Emperor would have been removing his white gloves as he waited his turn to go to work.

About ten days later, when my mother permitted me to carry the radio into the big room on the occasion of a broadcast for "junior citizens," I realized that the social order with the emperor at its apex had not turned upside down entirely, at least not to the extent that His Majesty could now be forced to labor at a bark press. My contemporary, the scholar K, must have been listening to the same broadcast because he later included it in his history of postwar education. I have copied out the portion that gave me the impression I have just described:

> The important thing is to realize His Majesty's value to us and to follow his bidding. The way we surrendered could not have happened in any other country: His Majesty had only to speak once, bidding us lay down our arms, and even though we had battled the enemy with all our hearts and souls until the day before, we ceased fighting without complaint—what makes our country so very special is that we Japanese obey our emperor's bidding with all our hearts! Hereafter, no matter what difficulties we may encounter, our country will prosper so long as we continue to heed Our Majesty in this way. Moreover, as a land blessed with such a magnificent Imperial Majesty, it is our duty when dealing with foreign nations to avoid causing strife and battle, and instead to labor to ensure that all countries join hands in strength and exist happily together.

These experiences carved into my life a fundamental definition of violence that reading Blake has made me acutely aware of. There is something inside the body that resembles a condenser. When the electrical charge exceeds its capacity, the mechanism begins to warp and, as the strain increases, breaks apart from the inside out. The only way to control the distortion is to find some means of discharging the violence to the outside from time to time. I wondered whether the behavior I still referred to as "leap," using my name for it as a child, wasn't a sort of drill or exercise that anticipated the future while my own charge was still relatively low? So far, I had done nothing even close to removing the hatchet at my hip and shouting back at the governor and his party as my father might have done that day. Did that mean that I was heading for the moment when I, too, would relinquish my body's mechanism to destruction from the inside following a scream of indignation? I was, after all, only one year older than my father's age when he died. Not long ago, as Eeyore lay on the couch recovering from a seizure, his face darkened with exhaustion and fever, I discovered something in his face that reminded me of my father. I was drawn to examine my own face in the mirror; I had always felt that I alone among my brothers didn't look like my father, but with my image of Eeyore's face as a guide I was able to see a resemblance to a photograph taken shortly after the governor's tour, the last photo of my father's life.

But that summer when the war ended, alone and away from the eyes of the other children, in the river in what may have been a dream, I had resolved in my imagination an approach to dealing with violence that was neither being destroyed by it internally nor releasing it savagely to the outside world. If I had to express in words the passions that live in my memory of that moment, I could hardly do better than the Blake verse I have already quoted:

> *Let the slave grinding at the mill run out into the field:*
> *Let him look up into the heavens & laugh in the bright air;*
> *Let the inchained soul shut up in darkness and in sighing,*
> *Whose face has never seen a smile in thirty weary years;*
> *Rise and look out—.*

And then:

> —*his chains are loose his dungeon doors are open.*
> *And let his wife and children return from the oppressor's scourge*
> *They look behind at every step & believe it is a dream.*
> *Singing. The sun has left his blackness, & has found a fresher*
> *morning.*

Eeyore continued to commute between home and the occupational therapy center and presently he was put to work assembling the paper boxes used by the Nakamura-ya restaurant in Shinjuku for take-out picnic lunches. When spoken to by one of the teachers or a handicapped adult he replied politely, forming his words with deliberate care. At recess, he listened carefully and applauded when one of the little girls played the piano or sang a song in the rumpus room. Sometimes he even corrected her fingering or showed her a chord to play with the melody until before long she and the others were relying on him. Observing this side of Eeyore's behavior, the teacher in charge summoned my wife for a conference. Eeyore was considerate of his comrades and worked hard at his job, but at the end of the day, when it was time to clean up, he would seize a broom or a mop as if he were eager to get started and then stand there doing nothing. Was he lazy, or was this kind of work simply too much for him?

Shocked, my wife immediately began training Eeyore to clean at home. My son was by this time a large man, tall and hulkingly built, yet I observed him puzzling over fallen leaves on the stepping stones in the garden, or scattering leaves he had swept carefully into a corner. Now that it had been noticed by someone on the outside, it was impossible not to see that something was lacking in the competency training we had given Eeyore at home.

One day when my wife was groaning with a cold and a toothache, I went in her place to wait for Eeyore at the bus stop in front of the therapy center. I got there early, and began walking up and down the street to keep warm in the chill wind that was blowing as the sun went down. There was another reason I preferred not to linger at the sign in front of the bus stop. A woman fifteen or so years younger than I was already standing there; her corpulent body was wrapped in a bulky overcoat buttoned up to her chin, her face was sallow, and she gave off an air of enclosed, unapproachable melancholy that told me right away she must be a mother with a child at the facility.

Recently, there had been two deaths at Eeyore's special school. One of the children had gone with his father to watch the parade of portable shrines at a neighborhood festival, eaten some grilled beef, and gone to sleep with his father lying at his side. The next morning he had appeared to sleep late, and when his father had gone in to wake him just before it was time to leave for school, he was already cold. Reading the principal's announcement, I was moved by the quiet time the boy had spent with his father on his last evening, and by what felt to me like the merest whisper that was his death, like a faint light going out at a great distance. The other child, who wore his hair in a Mohawk that looked as though he had been his own barber, I remember with a smile; having reached a point where he was able to bathe himself, he had suffered an epileptic seizure when he was alone in the tub and had drowned.

When news of one or the other of these deaths reached the school my wife happened to be there, getting ready for the annual bazaar. The discussion turned to organizing a consolation visit to the family and a young mother had said, "Let's make that on a volunteer basis—what happened was a blessing!"

When my wife reported the young mother's words to me she communicated not so much disapproval as a feeling of misery she shared with the younger woman. I suggested to her, as she appeared to be turning the words over in her mind, that the young mother had spoken in that instant out of the despair that repeatedly renews itself and is always unexpected; if she hadn't cared about the community of handicapped children why would she have volunteered to work at the bazaar? What she had said was better forgotten if possible—no doubt the speaker would remember the line longer than anyone who had heard it.

For no good reason, I had the feeling that the woman leaning despondently against the bus stop sign in her bulky overcoat was that same young mother. As I walked past the entrance to the center for the second or third time, I ran into three even younger women peering in at the main building through the gate. They appeared to be a team and were dressed alike, in suede coats and reddish-brown boots, a fashion choice designed to accent the reddish tint they all wore in their hair—stylish, vivacious girls. As I passed them they were commenting emphatically, as though speaking among themselves but clearly with the intent of influencing passersby, "Do you believe how fancy it is!" "Like a palace or something!"

As I returned along the same course, past the center to the crosswalk at the intersection and across the street, I thought idly about the curious remarks I had just heard. Then I realized there was nothing curious about them, or the least bit unclear. The young women's observations about the building being too fancy had seemed strange to me because I had assumed they were here as parents intending to enroll their own handicapped children. On the contrary, they were almost certainly critical of municipal policy on welfare facilities and were reconnoitering the center before organizing a protest. If that were the case, the remarks they were grandstanding to anyone within earshot made perfect sense: my wife in particular had been thrilled the first time she had seen the welfare center; it was a beautiful building.

At just this moment, Eeyore happened to appear at the front gate and, as I watched from across the street, was surrounded by the three young women and began responding to them with what appeared from his gestures to be his customary politeness. I continued on my circle past the school to the corner, across the street and back again without even quickening my step, observing the scene from a distance. Eeyore was talking, shaking his head slowly as he spoke, and then he stopped: hunching his shoulders and thrusting out his chest he appeared to stiffen into something as implacable as a wall and went silent, his head hanging. As if they hadn't noticed, the three women went on talking at him, preventing him from moving away. By now, other children had emerged from the center, but the women continued to direct their inquiry at Eeyore alone.

I quickened my step, but before I could reach Eeyore the doleful mother who had been waiting at the bus stop had rushed up the street to where he stood with the other women. During the short argument that ensued, the mother in the bulky overcoat had her arm around Eeyore's shoulder like a giant bird and appeared to be pulling at him as if to deliver him from the women. At that point I arrived and the young women hurried away at the sight of me. With one arm around Eeyore and the other around a girl who had also emerged from the center, her face darkly blotched in agitation, the mother glared at me and said, "You just stood there and watched! You should be ashamed of yourself!"

Eeyore returned my gaze with a look of prim superiority that made it appear he agreed with his friend's mother wholeheartedly. I bowed and expressed my thanks and felt as if my son were being entrusted to me reluctantly.

On the bus I tried to learn what Eeyore had been asked by the women but he remained grimly silent. The mother who had hurried to his aid had taken the same bus and, in a tone of voice that had every passenger listening, offered me an explanation: "Those women are fighting to stop a welfare center from being built next to the town houses where they live. They were here today to reconnoiter. They interfere with construction, they write letters to the paper about depriving their children of space to play, a while ago they offered to donate seventy-five thousand dollars and to volunteer their own time to care for the handicapped. They promise to do all that and more in return for not having a welfare center in their neighborhood! They treat our children as if they were unclean!"

My wife joined me in questioning Eeyore at home but he declined to say a word about what he had been asked. It wasn't even clear that the women were part of the movement to stop a welfare center. Four or five days later we saw the construction site in question on the evening news. As work resumed, a bell was rung to alert the protesters in the neighboring apartment building, and housewives hurried down the fire escapes. As they shouted protests at the city workers on the other side of a chain-link fence with their children joining in beside them, their standard of living was plain to see in their expressions, their gestures, their grooming—clearly, the three young women in suede coats and leather boots had not "dressed up" when they had come to see the center. Listening to the commentary, Eeyore had exclaimed, *"Gosh! Are they against building a new center? That's terrible!"* I took the opportunity to ask him yet again what the three women in front of the center had asked him or said to him that had made him hang his head in anger or maybe embarrassment. *"That's enough! Let's stop!"* he said emphatically, and looked away. My wife had been watching, and when she spoke she also seemed to be subtly avoiding my eye: "The parent who helped Eeyore said they saw our children as unclean, but I think they feel they're being attacked by something frightening. I think they feel their lives are being invaded by something that terrifies them. And I think their feelings will infect their children. From what we just saw it looks as though it's already happened. What if it gets to the point where terrified children start throwing stones. I'm worried about the plastic plate in Eeyore's head. He may have to start going to the center in a helmet the way he did ten years ago. When he graduates this time, he'll be going to that building they're trying to stop. . . ."

In my novel *The Pinch Runner Memorandum,* an accident in the special education class at elementary school launches the protagonist on a campaign to train his and others' disabled children to defend themselves. The hyperbole of the speech he delivers is in keeping with the "grotesque realism" that underlies the novel's comic tone:

> The only real help a teacher can give to children venturing out into the world is to hold society up for them to see and to show them, "Here it is, kiddies, and here are the places to watch out for!" Is that possible? And will *our teachers* deign to do that for *our children?* Because all they're being taught here now is how to keep their arms and legs out of harm's way—they're being prepared to survive in some corner of future society as imbeciles that require only minimal looking after! And who knows, maybe the society of the future will adapt our approach to suit its own priorities and teach them how to take care of their whole bodies instead of just their arms and legs, to keep them out of the way, you get my drift, by killing themselves, yes! Yes! Yes! Wouldn't that be something! So if we're truly concerned about *our children,* we must teach them how to arm themselves against the force in future society that will seek to relegate them to that outlying corner. And this will become ever more critical because the number of children like ours is bound to increase in quantum leaps so long as this planet

continues to be contaminated, and when children like *our children* multiply throughout the population until they are everywhere you look, they will be seen as symbols of everything negative about the future and become the focus of mass hatred! The hatred of the enfeebled and the discriminated against who have had to survive the threat represented by *our children*! And some of that weakened and excluded race will eventually rise up—what are we doing about showing *our children* how to defend themselves when that happens!

In the opening of the novel, which is similarly overwritten, a handicapped child gets lost in Tokyo Station; in describing the father's franticness as he tries to find his son I quoted lines from Blake. As he searches for his lost child in the throng of people at the station the father feels that he is the one who has been abandoned:

"Father! Where in the world did you go when you abandoned me?" I whispered the words to myself, and the next thing I knew I was speaking as though in a prayer for that occasion only, as if I were an atheist seeking help from someone whose identity was unknown to me (from my Father, perhaps?—just joking!): Father! Father! Where are you going? O do not walk so fast / Speak, father, speak to your little boy. / Or else I shall be lost. I walked all over that station in circles, faster and faster until I was out of breath and almost running, chasing the person who was trying to abandon me, in pursuit of my father maybe?— just joking!

At the time I was writing this book, two or three years before it was actually published, in the winter of Eeyore's tenth year, something similar to the incident I have just described actually happened to us. Except that Eeyore didn't simply wander off: a certain party took him from us and then left him stranded. I chose not to use the incident in the novel in just the way it had happened because I was afraid, paranoid perhaps, that it might inspire some reader to try the same thing. Wishing to avoid coverage in the press for the same reason, I did not go to the police. To be sure, my wife would have reported the incident if we hadn't located Eeyore by the end of the first day. And I wouldn't have tried to stop her.

At the time, my wife lived in fear that my paranoia might drive me to defend myself with a degree of violence that would have to be considered unjustified even though the other party was the aggressor. I'm not trying to shift responsibility for my paranoia at the time toward someone else. What I will say in fairness is that it was triggered by a tenacious campaign against me in the form of letters and telephone calls that had been going on for four or five years already and was a long way from being over. In the beginning, I had assumed that the letter writer, whose name and address I knew, and the telephone caller at the other end of the silent line when I answered his calls five or six times a day, were different people. As I also assumed the phone calls were the work of more than one person, I even felt that they were an expression of hostility directed at me by society in general. Later, I learned that the silent phone calls, not all of them perhaps but most, were from the letter writer.

I prefer not to go into details of what was already a nightmare of long duration. I will say that the person behind the letters and calls was a student in the commerce department at a well-known university who wrote to me requesting that I facilitate his debut as a professional critic, and suggested I might begin by helping him free his pen from the writer's block that kept him at his desk from morning to night without producing a single line. The arrogance of his letters, which never faltered from beginning to end, was possibly their only merit. Before long, he was addressing them not only to me but also to my wife and fulminating against us for attending to the needs of a handicapped child while dismissing the request of a healthy person. Our thoughts were frequently occupied by the letters and phone calls for days at a time, yet the student demanded to know as he maintained his attack on the family why he should be the only one to suffer. When he began hinting at suicide, I wrote him a letter suggesting that whether he planned to continue his studies or find a job, his first priority must be to regain his mental health, and urged him to see a psychiatrist. This resulted in a new pattern of phone calls that made it clear to me that the caller and the letter writer were one and the same person: the phone would ring from morning to early evening—while the student's parents were out of the house, I assumed—and when I answered, a voice would whisper, before the line went dead, "Take your own sick ass to a mental hospital!" When my wife answered and reported that I was not at home, the voice would ask her questions, for example, had she read in the papers about the man whose head was bashed in with a blunt weapon by a stranger sitting next to him on the train? It got to the point where my wife and I would steel ourselves every time the phone rang; the situation reminded me of another telephone attack more than ten years earlier, and reviving memories of that politically motivated assault drove me even deeper into paranoia.

About this time, an incident occurred. It was past the middle of the night and I was writing at my desk in my windbreaker with the hood over my head (because I had turned off the heater when the family went to bed) when I heard an insistent voice outside. At first I thought it was a conversation between two people but, no, the voice seemed to be calling my name. When I looked outside from the front entrance to the house, I saw the figure of a large man speaking into the broken intercom at the side of our gate. "Is anything wrong?" I called out. "As if you didn't know!" replied a voice that sounded drunk and spoiled, as though it issued from a peevish child. I asked the figure to return in the morning unless it was urgent, and closed the front door. But the young man continued speaking into the intercom. Unable to work, I began the bodybuilding routine that had been my nightly treatment for insomnia for several years. On top of the weight I still carried from the last years of my youth, the regular thirty-minute workout had given me a robust look. When I had finished the routine and the young man was still in the middle of what sounded like an argument with the intercom, I felt anger rising in me uncontrollably. I resolved to seize the youth by his shirtfront and walk him forcibly toward the station (naturally I knew better than to take along a barbell that could serve as a weapon). I suspect the incident in Blake's garden at Felpham may have been influencing my behavior at the time. As I emerged from the house and stepped into the circle of light from the lamp at the gate, my head hooded in the jacket, two voices screamed, one behind, the other in front of me. My wife had screamed at the sight of my hooded figure as she looked toward the gate from her bedroom. The source of the other scream had raced away down the street like mist before a wind. My wife's reaction was evidence of her fear that paranoia might impel me to do someone harm in a spasm of what I took to be self-defense.

Not that my life in my mid-thirties was entirely closed to interaction with outsiders. Consider, for example, a meeting at my house with two students and the fact that it resulted in the most terrifying day of my life with Eeyore and did very nearly drive me beyond the realm of acceptable behavior. My gloomy entries in my diary at the time allow me to reconstruct the day of their visit in some detail—the student, Unami, who said he came from the Kyoto-Osaka area, and his guide to my house, Inada, his high school classmate, now at college in Tokyo, who hardly spoke at all.

When I awoke late that morning and went downstairs from the study where I also slept, Eeyore appeared to be playing the Mozart game with some visitors in the family room. The object was for Eeyore to identify the composition and the key when someone read a K-number from a Mozart discography; as it happened, I had just published a short essay about the game. My wife was busily preparing lunch in the kitchen, bowls of rice with chicken and eggs on top in sufficient quantity to feed the family and the visitors. As she worked, she informed me that the students had been introduced by Professor W. The garrulous one reminded her of a municipal assemblyman from the Soka-Gakkai Party; the other was taciturn and shadowed. But together they seemed to be doing an excellent job of amusing Eeyore, whom she had kept home from school because he had awakened feeling out of sorts. Apparently, one of the students had interned in a special class for handicapped children.

I helped my wife carry the food into the family room and talked with the students over lunch. Eeyore seemed reluctant to interrupt his game with Unami, and remained in the room with his mother. His mood was cheerful, a rare occurrence at the stage he was in: in the brief time since he had arrived, Unami, whose hair was unfashionably short for those days, cropped so closely you could see his shiny skull, and who fit my wife's description so perfectly that I couldn't help smiling, had managed to charm both Eeyore and his mother with his ebullient chatter. The saturnine Inada, a type that was familiar from the days of the student riots, observed his friend's performance with what appeared to be a certain bewilderment.

The conversation that day, and specifically what Unami had to say, developed in three distinctly different stages, like a well-directed performance. After lunch, while my wife and Eeyore were still in the room with us, he reported recent news about a number of eminent scholars in a familiar manner that conveyed their regard for him. I had started this by asking what Unami had told Professor W about wanting to meet me. I inquired because I knew that the professor was no longer entirely trustful of student activists as a result of a series of incidents in the course of the past several years when students had carried books out of his offices at the besieged university and sold them to secondhand bookstores.

Unami reported that he had found the professor outside in the pale winter sunshine, painting floor slats alongside a tiny pond in back of his house, and that it had been his impression that he lived more modestly than the French literature scholar in Kyoto who had his own Noh stage at home. By way of letting me know that he had read Lévi-Strauss's *Pensées Sauvages,* as yet untranslated into Japanese, he added how charmed he had been to see that Professor W had time for "bricolage."

Getting down to business, Unami told me that his introduction to Professor W had been provided by the French literature scholar in Kyoto he had mentioned; the purpose of his visit had been to request a copy of the précis in French of my graduation thesis, and to ask for an introduction to the political scientist Masao Maruyama (the original connection between the two professors was their mutual friend Herbert Norman, the Canadian diplomat and Japanese history scholar who had committed suicide in Cairo toward the end of the McCarthy era). Professor W had told Unami that Professor Maruyama's poor health prevented him from receiving students; regarding my thesis, he had suggested that Unami approach the author directly.

As I listened carefully to what Unami was saying, I realized it was not precisely the case that he had come to me with an introduction. In any event, in the few days since his arrival in Tokyo from Kyoto, this student had met with a number of the scholars, writers, and critics who had championed postwar democracy in the academy and in journalism (I belonged to the generation who had grown up under their influence). "We've been meeting with people who are being held responsible by fighters on the front line for reducing democracy to a slogan," he began. "What they've actually done is declare bankruptcy, surrendered in the middle of the battle. And to be honest, one of our standard tactics when we criticize their ideology is to hold up your essays as an example of what the Americans call a *laughing matter*. But as we see it, this battle is going to produce a backlash. And if it does, we may have to do some making up with the people on the other side of the fence who see us as having terminated relations with them. When we showed some professors we still know in Kyoto a rough plan for how to proceed, they were impressed with our ability to look forward to the darkness that lies ahead—we got all the introductions we wanted!"

In my diary entry that day I identified three distinct shifts in Unami's attitude as reflected in his language and delivery, I, II, and III, and the above appears at the beginning of II, shortly after my wife had coaxed Eeyore out of the room. Until then, Unami had spoken politely about his professors and had avoided mention of his fellow students' evaluation of me.

"It's a fact that we consider your essays *laughing matters,* but since you don't touch political theory and you're not an activist, I personally think we're mistaken to make someone like you the object of doctrinaire criticism. But you do make us crazy! Because no matter how cold we are to you or how we mock you, you don't budge from your position, you just keep on writing the same stuff that was in your essays when we began reading you in high school. Nothing we say or do seems to smoke you out of your hole and move you any closer to the realists; but you don't step away from the phantom of postwar democracy and join us in battle either—who cares if people would call it an old man's folly! And ten years from now will your thinking have changed one bit? That's what's so irritating about you—you're like molasses! And what grounds do you have for thinking you're fine just the way you are and will never have to change? We tried thinking about that from your point of view, and we concluded that your grounds are your handicapped child. There's a movement we support, to put handicapped children in regular classes. I'm sure you know all about it, but you don't join, your child is enrolled in a special class that separates handicapped children from the others. And when we attack you for promoting discrimination, we get molasses again! There are different approaches to raising handicapped children; some should be enrolled in regular classes but special classes are better suited to your child's needs, isn't that how it goes? Your whole life revolves around your child, you've designed it that way, and your judgment is based on your experience, so outsiders can criticize you until they're blue in the face. Can you deny that? You've taken an oath to yourself that you're prepared to look after your handicapped child on your own steam no matter what happens to society, isn't that right? Anyone who reads *The Flood Has Risen* knows that. So as far as you're concerned, there's no reason to join the movement. That's what you do, you hunker down into a position like a hulk and you don't budge, that's what we mean by molasses!"

When Unami broke off, as if to observe my reaction, I asked the silent Inada whether he included himself in Unami's "we" and he spoke what may have been his only words that day: "I agree with everything he said, it's what we think."

What could I say? And Unami's analysis of my state of mind at the time, that portion of it that I classified under II when I wrote it down, would feel like elaborately devised flattery in light of what was to come: before long, his tone shifted abruptly away from I and II to provocation as plain as raw meat. "We know you donated royalties from your books about the atom bomb to 'Second-generation Survivors.' The organization told reporters the money was being used to buy a vehicle for campaigning around the country. The truth is, they bought a jalopy with a fifth of the money. And when it broke down the day before they were supposed to leave, they came crying to you again for money to repair it. But what had happened to the money that was left over, did it occur to you it might have ended up in some pockets at the top of the organization? A while ago, they sent some students to Tokyo to demonstrate, and when it looked as though they might get themselves arrested, they asked you and the acting chancellor of Hitotsubashi University for plane fare so they could get back to Hiroshima. And you ended up paying for the whole thing, isn't that so? They were afraid the opposition party might get violent on them so they went crying home to Daddy and you paid for it! It seems there's no limit to the money you're willing to waste, but what about the other side? And speaking of money for buying cars, which you seem to have for them, how about donating a car to us? We're planning to install a short-wave transmitter in a minivan and broadcast live as we drive around. The crooks in the government and high finance get dragged into the Diet to testify but they hardly ever tell the truth. We plan to build a little torture chamber in our van and to broadcast our interrogation live. We're going to drive all over Tokyo grabbing politicians and industrialists and bureaucrats along the way and torturing them and broadcasting their testimony live while we're on the move. Our van is going to cost a lot more than the pocket change you gave the second-generation survivors, perhaps you'd consider coming up with some seed money?"

When I saw, without having to ask him again, that Inada concurred with everything Unami was saying, I lost the desire to continue the conversation. Unami was eerily well informed: he not only referred to things that were known only to those who had been in communication with me, but certain developments made sense to me for the first time in the light of his interpretation. Yet he was also perfectly aware, no matter how grounded in fact his argument was, that I was not about to take his proposal seriously. From the way he spoke it was clear that his intention was merely to provoke me, and he was succeeding at that. As I sat there wondering sullenly what I could do to get the students to leave, my wife, concerned that the lengthy visit might be leading me toward the excessive self-defense she worried about in those days, came back into the room. And the minute she appeared with tea on a tray and Eeyore in tow, Unami abruptly transformed back into a charmer. "Eeyore, while I was talking with your dad here I thought of another one for you. Ready? What's Mozart's smelliest key? It's simple: B-flatulence. Get it?" A minute later the students excused themselves and left.

In those days, my wife accompanied Eeyore to school in the morning and I went to meet him on my bicycle at the end of the day. Having started in elementary school when he was eight, he was now in a special class for third-graders. In response to his teachers' concern that he might never develop the ability to go to school by himself if we continued accompanying him from door to door, we had been having him walk the last part by himself, gradually extending the distance along a route followed by other students on their way to the same school so there was no possibility that he might take a wrong turn. Down the hill from Seijo Gakuen where we lived there was an area of heavy traffic surrounding the empty lots that were a part of the Toho film studios, and the students had to take a pedestrian overpass across a main thoroughfare to reach the school just on the other side, but their route had been carefully considered. As I waited with my bicycle in front of the telegraph office at the top of the hill, Eeyore, looking smaller than he did at home, would climb slowly up the street in my direction with that unmistakable gait of his that appeared to be both casual and intent. Every day, joy rang out in me at the sight of him. Standing at the curb—he walked along the side of the road against traffic as he had been taught—I waited. Because the lenses in his glasses were still being adjusted, he didn't notice me until he was just ten feet away. His expression as he stopped in front of me was invariably flat, unmoved, but tension left his body like steam disappearing into the air and he turned back into a creature so soft that exposing him to the outdoors seemed unthinkable. Installing him in the metal seat attached to my handle bars, I would peddle home with his back against my chest.

That day, I waited at the telegraph office but Eeyore did not appear at the bottom of the hill. Gradually, the stream of children from the lower grades moving past me thinned out. Two girls who were older than Eeyore but in the same special class came up the hill holding hands and I asked if they had seen Eeyore, careful not to startle them, but they stiffened like boards and passed me in silence. I jumped on my bike and rode down the street past other children climbing the hill. Leaving my bike at the overpass, I ran through the tunnel to the school entrance, up the steps, and across the school yard to the special classes building. A young teacher was still there, working at her desk, and she told me that Eeyore had left thirty minutes ago. I ran all the way back to my bike and pedaled home along the route we always took, searching for a sign of Eeyore. When I reached the house, I learned from my wife that he had not returned.

My wife went into action immediately. She phoned the teacher in charge and reported that Eeyore was missing, and she contacted the network of mothers whose job it was to organize search parties of two and three parents when someone's child failed to appear. Until she set out to join the search, which was beginning in the immediate vicinity of the school, there was little I could do to help; as I knew that she and the network of mothers would operate more efficiently without me, I remained at home to look after Eeyore's younger brother and sister and to wait for calls from the teachers and parents.

Minutes after my wife had left, the phone rang once only. I remember glancing up at the clock as I started out of my chair and feeling inexpressible misery and rage at the same time when I saw that it was precisely three o'clock. Could it be starting again now, I remember thinking, at a time like this, could this be the literary hopeful with his familiar telephone routine, call after call all day long and silence at the other end when I answered until finally he cursed me and hung up? The student's fixated, tenacious personality was evident in the minute handwriting in hard pencil that made his letters impossible to read without holding them up to a light. He would begin calling at two or three in the afternoon and call every thirty minutes. Before long, he had conditioned me to the point where I was aware of the sound the telephone made in the instant before it rang, like a sudden intake of breath. With his sustained telephone attack, the student had instilled in me a fixation similar to his own.

That afternoon, when the phone rang a second time and then went silent I was seized by regret that made my head pound. What if the caller had Eeyore? This was the person, after all, who had written letters accusing us of caring about our own handicapped child to the exclusion of everyone else and who had heaped abuse on us for what he called the privileged life that allowed us to ignore uncaringly our obligation to others. It was clear that he had been hanging around the house: a few weeks earlier he had placed in our mailbox notices of having failed the employment exam at a savings bank and elsewhere. If I had questioned the silent caller just now, I might have gotten him to tell me "Yes, I have your son, and here are my conditions for his release." What if this were his last phone call, his final appeal to me, and now he'd turned instead to acting on the horrific thinking in his letters?

If I wanted his address I had only to look at the letters I had stored in a manila envelope. But how would I convince the police of my suspicion? Standing at the phone, I counted out the thirty minutes. At four o'clock, the instant it rang, I seized the receiver and said my name. Silence at the other end. "Hello! Hello!" I said. A second later came a murmured "Yes——." I searched for something to say, but before I could speak the youth said to me in a voice dark with anger, "You go to a fucking mental hospital!" and hung up. So he was cooped up in his house and engaged in the same telephone harassment as before! This was the first time I felt liberated by a phone call from him, and it would be the last.

It was after six o'clock and already pitch-dark when, following a report from my wife that Eeyore was still missing, I received a call from the student Inada. Beginning with "I thought I should let you know," the student who had sat silently alongside the fluent Unami on the occasion of their visit delivered himself of the following account. His tone was somber but revealed no sense of guilt.

His friend Unami, acting entirely on his own and using information he had learned from my wife about our daily coming and going from school, had that afternoon taken charge of Eeyore. Unami was angry about my refusal to take political

action, and angrier still that I used my handicapped child to jus-
tify my position righteously. He had decided, therefore, that by
getting rid of the child he could force me into a place where I
could no longer defend my lack of action or, alternatively, that
he could extract from me a promise to take certain action as a
condition of releasing Eeyore unharmed. He planned to retain
my son while he opened negotiations to determine how far I
would be willing to go. However, according to a communication Inada had just received, after trying without success to speak
with me on the phone, Unami had given up in disgust and had
taken the bullet train back to Kyoto, leaving Eeyore on his own
in Tokyo Station. Although he had nothing to do with any of
this, Inada thought it would be better to let me know.

My wife had just returned; she and the other mothers had
taken a break from searching in the vicinity of the school, and
she had decided to come home for an hour to prepare dinner.
Probably she was worried about my ability to take proper care
of Eeyore's brother and sister, who were still infants. I was able
to control the anger that rose in me at the thought of Inada's
opening and closing remark—I thought it would be better to
let you know—but as I attempted to convey to my wife what I
had just heard as she stood there giving off a frozen, metallic
smell with snowflakes in her hair and on the shoulders of her
coat, I could feel the miasma of blackness bubbling inside my
chest spewing into the air together with my words. "The student who visited us, the one who talked a lot, kidnapped Eeyore.
He planned to force me into action by finishing Eeyore off—by
finishing Eeyore off!—or by releasing him under certain conditions. He kidnapped Eeyore to control me. But he gave up in
disgust. He—gave up in disgust and went home on the bullet
train."

I was on my way out the door to Tokyo Station but my wife
said she wanted to come with me and went next door to ask a

woman we didn't know particularly well to look after the children. It didn't occur to me at the time, but she was terrified that if Unami reappeared, while I might not have killed him I would certainly have hurt him badly. So together my wife and I walked all over Tokyo Station looking for Eeyore, for more than three hours, and I had precisely the internal experience I described in *The Pinch Runner Memorandum.*

It was after ten o'clock and the station was nearly empty when we found Eeyore on the platform for the bullet train. Sitting on the concrete platform with his back molded to an indentation in the wall of a newsstand, he was quietly watching the snow falling heavily on the tracks. His boots were filled with urine that had wet his pants and run down his legs. When I squatted at his side and peered into his face he looked back at me blankly as always, as though unmoved, but tension melted from his face and body and the soft creature that always appeared in this way rose to view with a radiance that was blinding. We went home in a taxi through the night snow, stopping to outfit Eeyore in new pants and boots. Later, I vomited into one of the boots that was still soaked in urine and let out a scream of rage. When I had finished and was sitting limply in my chair, my wife told me that she had been light-headed with fear as we searched for Eeyore that I would attack and injure Unami and might even be sent to jail.

On the first day after the New Year holiday this year, in the early hours of the morning, a cram-school teacher and a civil service employee in the municipal office who lived in a bedroom town on the outskirts of Kyoto were bludgeoned to death with a lead pipe. I happened to be on a trip to Hiroshima and read about it in the Kyoto edition of the newspaper. I said nothing to my wife, who seemed unaware of what had happened after reading the

Tokyo paper. According to the article, the victims, former members of a faction in the student movement, were Sankichi Unami and Akira Inada, both thirty years old. Three days later, just after six o'clock, when I was at my exercise club swimming, my wife received a long-distance phone call from Kyoto. "A friend and I paid you a visit about ten years ago," the voice said tactfully. "I'm the one who called himself Unami."

He explained that he was calling about the killings that seemed to be a carryover from the internal lynchings during the former days of the student movement. His purpose was to prevent a misunderstanding on our part. Reading in the paper that Unami and Inada had been murdered—as she related the phone conversation my wife told me for the first time that she had seen the article but had kept it to herself—we might be feeling the relief of knowing that poetic justice had befallen the men who had taken our child away and abandoned him. Or we might be sleeping uneasily because murder seemed excessive even for poetic justice. In any event, he wanted to correct a mistaken assumption. When he and his friend had visited our house, they had used the names of two activists in an opposing faction. The victims a few days ago were the real Unami and Inada. Perhaps they had been plugging away as political activists; more likely their past had caught up with them while they were in hibernation. The caller was still engaged in the movement. His current life had nothing to do with literature, but he gathered that my wife and I and our son were alive and well.

Having contained herself to this point, my wife now revealed her anger: the student had done a terrible thing to our son; what if he had fallen off the platform onto the tracks, or what if he had wandered onto a train leaving for some distant place and we had never been able to find him! But the man calling himself Unami who had opened a cruel wound in our memory shot back: "Mrs.! Frankly speaking, wouldn't it have been better that way! You'd have been spared ten years of bondage to your son and might have enjoyed your life! And think of your husband, he's still singing the same old tune we pointed out ten years ago, maybe he would have found a way to break out of his rut. Mrs., everybody knows that a child with a damaged brain can't ever be productive. You might say his social metabolism doesn't work quite right. But your husband uses the child as justification for not facing the tumult in society head-on. In ten years, he hasn't changed one bit! Isn't that what a critic wondered about him recently, whether he intended to go to his grave just as he is, without ever growing up philosophically? Your husband tells himself he's living life for two, himself and his child, but the truth is that in their codependence they manage to avoid putting in the effort and the suffering that even one life would normally require. For my part, I've transcended politics and social upheaval and reached the next stage. I head up the young men's association in a religious group, putting everything I have into figuring out how to save a human soul. When your husband was my age, he was writing really irritating things like *Come to think about it, there is such a thing as salvation. . . .* But your husband doesn't seek salvation with any urgency, he prefers to stand on this side in peace and quiet and feel uneasy. The political battle ten years ago was child's play compared to our struggle to find salvation for the soul. We're talking life and death, and without salvation we can't even die in peace. And I'm responsible for the young people who have suffered through that battle and come out the other side. But I need to say this to your husband directly—he'll be back by ten, won't he? I read in the evening paper, maybe it was last year, that he goes to his swimming club in the evening. I'll call again around ten."

I swim 1000 meters freestyle at my swimming club every evening and then come home and begin drinking the whisky I need to fall asleep. For close to seven years, this has been my daily routine. But if I had started drinking that night, I would have been drunk by ten o'clock. And although Eeyore's brother and sister would have gone to their rooms, it was likely they would still be awake and able to hear their drunken father's angry voice. I wanted to avoid this. I lay down on the sofa and glanced at pages in Erdman's book that I had already annotated, too distracted to read ahead. Eeyore, who had been in the family room with his brother and sister when my wife was recounting the phone call to me, went upstairs to his own room at nine. Lying there watching the clock and waiting for the phone to ring revived memories of the long telephone siege that had climaxed ten years earlier, and I felt once again the stirring of enlarged paranoid feelings and the latent aggressiveness that accompanied them.

While I rejected the fake Unami's appraisal of Eeyore, it was certainly true that we had been fettered by his presence for the past ten years, or for that matter for the past twenty years since the moment of his birth. *Let the slave grinding at the mill run out into the field: / Let him look up into the heavens & laugh in the bright air; / Let the inchained soul shut up in darkness and in sighing, / Whose face has never seen a smile in thirty weary years; / Rise and look out—*. Reading the Blake verse in the darkness I felt as though I were in chains. Eeyore would never be free of brain damage; for Eeyore and his mother, escaping the whip of that oppressor to return happily could never be. *They look behind at every step & believe it is a dream. / Singing. The sun has left his blackness, & has found a fresher morning.* But Blake had come to realize that his joyous certainty was only an illusion, freedom and emancipation would not appear in this world, and this awareness had led to his long silence as a poet.

My wife's frazzled nerves had sent her upstairs early to bed, but she came into the family room at two minutes before ten, or so I thought. When I looked up from my book, it was Eeyore in a nightshirt from throat to feet that made him look like a foot soldier in a medieval scroll. "Did you forget your medicine? Take it now and go back to bed."

Eeyore turned obediently toward the kitchen. But he was taking his time, and at the moment I read the intention in his hesitation the phone began to ring. By the time I was on my feet Eeyore had planted himself between me and the phone, and as I reached for the receiver he threw his weight against me with a grunt. It was after a long swim and I should have been quick on my feet, but the body blow threw me off my balance and I fell backward against the dining table. I noticed as I fell that my wife had hurried into the room from her bed and was observing the effect of Eeyore's violence with a frightened look in her eyes. *"Yes, yes, this is Eeyore."* Pushing into the wall with his head so as to avoid our eyes, the receiver tight against his ear, Eeyore was speaking into the phone. There was a pause. Then he spoke again, more forcefully than usual: *"You are a bad person! Why are you laughing? I can't talk anymore. Absolutely, I can't do anything!"*

Eeyore slammed down the receiver as if it were a blunt weapon. His head still leaning against the wall, he appeared to be waiting for something that had boiled up deep inside him to subside. I sat down in a chair at the overturned dining table and my wife stood at my side, shivering with cold in her pajamas, and tried to comfort Eeyore in a voice that sounded like a throttled scream. It was like the sound she had made when she saw me emerge from the house late that night, and it also put me in mind of the sound that had emerged from my mother in that instant when my father had approached the authorities with his hatchet. "If you get so angry you'll have a seizure! Eeyore, do you remember him? Are you that angry about something that happened ten years ago?"

"Are you able to grow so angry?" is what I heard. "Do you have the capacity to get angry about something you remember?"

My wife turned to me as if in an appeal, her fear deepening as she spoke: "I'm worried! He could have a seizure over this, or he might injure someone. Why is he so angry? If he does remember what happened at least he'll be careful not to go off with anyone again—he never mentioned what Unami did to him but he remembers, and he's furious about it—"

Eeyore stepped back as though he were peeling his head away from the wall and turned to face us. I realized that what had seemed strange about him when he had come downstairs in his nightshirt was his tension, but now the tension seemed to have melted away, and there was even an echo of confident consolation in the words he spoke to my wife: "*I always remembered! He was a bad person. But you don't have to worry, Mama. I won't be angry anymore. There's no bad person anymore. Absolutely!*"

Every man has the right to his own illusions even if they are nothing more than that, and the right to express them powerfully: *And the fair Moon rejoices in the clear & cloudless night; / For Empire is no more, and now the Lion & Wolf shall cease.*

7: Rouse Up O Young Men of the New Age!

I have braided my life with my handicapped son and my thoughts occasioned by reading William Blake into a series of short pieces. My purpose, on the occasion of my son's twentieth birthday this coming June, was to survey the entirety of our—mine and my wife's and his younger brother's and sister's—days together with him until now and into the future. I also wanted a book of definitions of the world, society, and mankind based on my own life. Attempting now to complete the series, I have been thinking about the rain tree, my subject in an earlier book of short stories. I have a feeling it has its own place in the circle connecting my son and Blake. I have been led to that discovery by a sort of poem, "Beyond the Rain Tree," that I wrote when I was in Java.

When I published my rain tree stories in a single volume a certain critic wrote that I had created a metaphor for universalism but had failed to carry it outward to a place where it would have relevance for anyone but myself. "You say you've seen the universe in the rain tree. I'll give you that, because you also wrote that your metaphor reached the composer, T, and came back as an abundant echo. The problem is, you remain unchanged even after the rain tree has been lost from this earth. In other words, the 'rain tree' in your vision neither evolves nor expands. What do you intend to do, hold onto your aging rain tree metaphor as if it were a talisman until the moment of your own death?"

I had finished serializing my rain tree stories and could only respond with silence. Presently, I sensed my thoughts turning to another rain tree about which I had not written. The actual rain tree. When, standing in a grove of tall trees, I had heard a guide say rain tree, as though by way of explanation, I had glanced quickly over my shoulder in the direction of the voice. In that instant my next action, directly connected to my son, was determined, and I conceived the sort of poem I have just mentioned.

The place where I gazed at the rain tree from a distance in this manner was the Bogor Botanical Gardens. If I ever revisit Indonesia with Eeyore along, I shall go straight to those gardens and almost certainly confirm that the tree in question was a samaan tree of the genus *Samanea*. This is the tree the Japanese refer to by a variety of names, including the American mimosa; in America, it is commonly known as the monkeypod or rain tree. It is possible that the tree I had in mind was the American mimosa after all, but I preferred to think of it as a samaan because what I had read of the American mimosa, that it folds its leaves before a rainfall, created a problem for me. I doubted that such a tree would be capable of storing raindrops as they fell, and, as is clear in the following lines from my novel, my image of the rain tree required that special quality: "It's called a rain tree because when it pours during the night the tree sheds raindrops from its foliage until past noon the following day, as if it were still raining. Other trees dry right away, but the rain tree's branches are covered in tiny leaves the size of the pad of a finger and each one can hold a few drops of water. It's a clever tree, wouldn't you say?"

I had spent three hours alone in the Bogor Botanical Gardens on my way home from a trip to Bali with friends. My encounter with the climate and topography and the mythological folk arts of that astonishing island, and being in the presence, even as a passerby, of natives who seemed descended from the universe itself, had triggered in me what I can only describe as a transcendental experience that involved both my spirit and my emotions. I was also aware of a connection being made deep down with Eeyore, from whom I had been separated for ten days for the first time in a long while. I felt the connection being made at the Buddhist excavation at Borobudur, on the way to Bali, and, after arriving at the island, at the "temple of death" in Pura Darem—moments that seemed to strike at my very soul. Later, when I had left my traveling companions and was visiting the Bogor Botanical Gardens on my own, the distillation of my accumulated experiences on the trip flared up to compel me toward a choice. In the instant I learned that the rain tree I had been longing to see was right next to me, I chose to walk in the opposite direction, toward the maze created by a variety of other trees growing in orderly rows.

With no map to guide me I had been wandering through the gardens, making my way down one path or another when my intuition told me it would lead to trees I wanted to see. I had come upon an area that seemed more like an English garden than a tropical island, bright and open rather than lushly overgrown, and was standing in front of a baobab tree. A group of refined-looking men and women who appeared to be Ameri-

can tourists, the men in linen suits, the women in white summer dresses, was halted down the path in front of me. Their
guide, speaking heavily accented English with a confidence that
suggested his pride in the job, said with emphasis, as though he
were interrupting himself to make an announcement, "This is
the famous rain tree." In the bright Java sunlight I shuddered.
For an instant, I squinted up into the sun at the airy canopy of
slender branches that had shed their leaves, then lowered my
head and moved away in the opposite direction. I had to see this
rain tree with Eeyore, I thought, I couldn't look at the tree alone
having abandoned him. Beneath the thought was another, that
eventually I would be leaving Eeyore behind and setting out
alone for a more peaceful world. I felt certain that looking closely
at the rain tree without Eeyore at my side to bear me up would
be more than I could endure; I felt wobbly on my feet.

I mentioned experiences that had planted this feeling in
me so it was there inchoately, waiting to be activated by the
words "rain tree." I want to describe those moments. The stone
Buddhas beyond counting that covered the mountain of stones
at Borobudur were in the process of being restored; the coexis-
tence on the mountain of a construction site and an archaeologi-
cal ruins side by side struck me as impossibly valiant. At the
bottom of a long flight of stone steps, in the very best location
for a vendor's stall, a little old man—or was he roughly my own
age, I wondered, withered in appearance, not only his skin but
even his posture, by the tropical sun and exposure to wind and
rain in his life out of doors?—was selling thick tea and purplish-
silver frogs made of paper and clay. The frogs were toys: the
head was hinged like a bellows, and when you tilted it up it
croaked like the Indonesian frogs I had heard frequently along
the way.

The man wore a faded batik shirt with long sleeves, and
on his left hand where it protruded from the sleeve I glimpsed

a baleful sixth finger like a spur. Doubtless, that finger had secured him the prime location for a stall at one of Java's top excavation sites. Accepting a paper-and-clay frog and my change
from his six-fingered hand, I stepped into the meager shade of
a tamarind tree and imagined that Eeyore had been born and
raised in Java; the object attached to his skull like a second head
would likely have earned him his own prime location for a
vendor's stall. I reflected wistfully on the communality of Indonesian society.

The philosopher N, the principal authority in our party,
has written about the universal significance in island folklore
of the "temple of death" in Pura Darem, the scene of my moment on Bali. If I can summarize the gist of his essay, it will help
me to convey my own sense of just where I was when I stood in
the courtyard that day. In every Bali village there are three
temples that together comprise a single institution. The seaside of the island has negative value and stands in opposition to
the mountains, which are positive. Pura Darem, at the sea, is a
temple for the souls of the dead before they have been purified,
that is, before their funeral. When they have been purified, the
souls of the dead are celebrated at a second temple. And there
is a third temple that directs the communal life of the village.
The patron spirit of Pura Darem, the witch Randa, invades a
variety of people and possesses them. She also uses her magic to
cure the sick. Following is a direct quote from N's essay that
reveals the creativity he applies to developing a thesis that is
grounded in Bali folklore: "The persona of the witch Randa
permits human weakness and evil to be rendered manifest and
even celebrated rather than suppressed or ignored, and this su-
perbly effective mechanism in Bali folklore protects the island-
ers from *pathos* even as it vitalizes their culture."

We entered the village of Pura Darem. It must have been
a festival day; girls with flowers in their hair moved across the

ground still wet from a cloudburst in their bare feet and entered
a high stone gate bearing offerings on banana leaves. In the
courtyard, little girls wearing sashes of red cloth watched from
a thatch-roofed building resembling a barn. As we walked around
inside the temple grounds, pausing here and there to observe the
function of holy space, the young women and the little girls
began to leave, perhaps because the sun was setting. Finally, only
one girl remained, with two children who seemed to be her siblings, and appeared to have no intention of leaving. It was as if
they intended to offer a special prayer in the interior of the temple,
and were waiting for everyone, including us, to leave first. We
became aware of this all at once, and in a subdued mood that was
clearly a response to the temple space, conversing in lowered
voices, we walked toward the entrance to the courtyard. But I
had left my notebook on the sturdy, raised floor of the thatch-
roofed building. When I went back alone to retrieve it, the girl
and her younger brother and sister had just descended to the
courtyard and were heading for the stone gate that rose in the
dusk like a pagoda. As the girl turned toward me I saw that one
half of her lovely, charming face was horribly disfigured by what
must have been a congenital deformity. Even so, she exuded a
calm and graceful naturalness that included her deformity and
was somehow reinforced by her bearing, which was elegant, and
by the obvious respect and intimate affection for the siblings accompanying her. As if I were again a child crossing the grounds
of a Shinto shrine by myself, I bowed respectfully to the space
of the enclosure where I was standing, and withdrew. Had
Eeyore been born on Bali, we would have made it our solemn
custom to present ourselves each evening to Pura Darem to offer
a prayer to the witch Randa. I felt certain of this deep inside me,
and my certainty encouraged and even inspired me.

Returning from Bogor to my hotel room in Jakarta, inside
a loneliness that was close to panic and not the variety that could

be left behind by an early round of predinner drinks, my first
and only such attack on the trip, I worked on my sort of poem
until it was time to join my friends for dinner downstairs, and
I called it "Beyond the Rain Tree":

> *Toward the rain tree*
> *And through it to the world beyond*
> *Our spirits merged, consubstantial,*
> *Yet selves as free as they can be*
> *We return. . . .*

Later, I realized that these lines had been influenced by my
longtime mentor and my friend, the composer T. Even the title,
"Beyond the Rain Tree," was based directly on a piece for violin and orchestra that T was composing at the time and had
spoken to me about, called "Beyond the Distant Call." Later,
when I was working on the rain tree stories that had their origin in my sort of poem, revising my manuscript, I would encourage myself by singing aloud, "*Somewhere over the rain tree way
up high / there's a land that I heard of once in a lullaby,*" or again,
"*Somewhere over the rain tree blue birds fly / birds fly over the rain
tree, why then, oh why can't I?*" and both the melody and the lyrics were from T's arrangement for guitar of "Over the Rain-
bow." T had not accompanied us to Bali, but he had visited the
island earlier, and it was his talk of the deep and lucid beauty of
gamelan music that had laid the ground for the trip. Accordingly, as I sat in the courtyard of that temple whose stone pillars
and even the trees pointed toward the sky as though by design,
raptly watching royal Balinese dancing to the accompaniment of
gamelan music with the stars high above me in the dark sky, I
could almost hear T's quiet voice as though he were squatting
beside me in the Bali night. In my rain tree series I related how
he had been inspired to compose his rain tree chamber music

by the metaphor I created in the passage I quoted above, and how in turn I had been inspired to create a series of stories when I took my wife to hear a performance of his composition.

As it turned out, I didn't include my sort of poem in the rain tree series: in the heat of writing one story after another, my "rain tree" caught fire and burned to the ground. I did make notes for a draft of a full-length novel that was intended to bring the rain tree back to life, but I decided to leave things as they stood at the end of the collection:

> I still commute to the pool every day and wonder as I swim freestyle laps without resting whether the day will ever come when I discover the lost rain tree once again, even as a metaphor? I have no idea, and also wonder, that being the case, what led me to believe that if I continued writing this draft I would eventually get to a concluding chapter in which the rain tree was reborn? What led me to cling to the pathetic hope that something fictional rather than actual could guarantee me the encouragement I need in real life? No doubt my momentum would carry me to a concluding chapter, but how could the rain tree that appeared there be anything but a fake? And how could a fake carry me outside my ailing self to a genuine experience no matter how hard I swam and continued to swim?

Today, at work on the concluding chapter of this chronicle of William Blake superimposed on my life with my son, which I intend to complete for his twentieth birthday, I sense that I am fully aware for the first time of the meaning lurking inside that sort of poem I wrote on the island of Java four years ago (I would almost rather say, imitating Blake, that I had merely copied down what was passed on to me by the spirits of the trees in the Bogor Botanical Gardens). Having completed my initiation into

Blake with a tour of his mythological world, I am also certain that I shall continue reading him for the rest of my life. I need hardly say that my own lines had become clear to me through reading Blake. I was already aware of the importance of his esoteric thought, which subsumes neo-Platonism, when the cultural anthropologist Y, who was on the trip to Bali and gave us a lecture on the mythological universalism in the island's folk arts, loaned me Kathleen Raine's book *Blake and Tradition*. The subject of this monumental work was precisely that aspect of Blake which I hoped to understand in more detail. It helped me bring into consciousness and reformulate the scene in the final chapter of my novel *The Contemporary Game,* which I recall having completed the day before I left for Bali, in which I described a landscape I had pictured to myself in the valley in the forest and then had actually discovered in a dream. Raine also delivered into my grasp the significance of my vision in "Beyond the Rain Tree." I went so far as to consider that Blake's esoteric thought had found a new expression in my rain tree metaphor.

Perhaps the chapter I am writing now about Blake and my son might also serve as the conclusion to my "rain tree" novel: "Toward the rain tree and through it to the world beyond"—when I wrote these words I was thinking of my own and Eeyore's deaths. "Our spirits merged, consubstantial, we return. . . ." Eeyore and I cross over into death's domain and remain there beyond time. As though illuminated by a reflection from that image itself, the significance of my life with Eeyore in the present seems to rise into the light.

The wooden gate opens with a clatter that no one else produces. Large shoes shuffle down the path to the house and the front door slams open. Gym shoes are shaken off, first one foot and then the other, and thud to the concrete floor just inside, and finally Eeyore appears in the doorway to the family room in his student uniform as though he were stepping onto a stage, filling the space, a beaming smile on his face and his briefcase in his hand. This was a moment late in the afternoon, almost a ritual, that I awaited eagerly every Monday through Saturday.

One day early this year, as I lay on the couch reading Raine's new essay collection, *Blake and the New Age,* a dictionary and pencils on top of a wooden box at my side—my son had spent a full year in his special class at middle school painting the box orange—Eeyore, who had appeared in the doorway as always, looked down at me with troubled and somehow mournful eyes and, with the merest nod at my words of welcome, hurried past me into the kitchen and reported the following to my wife:

"It's my turn to go to the dormitory! Are we ready? I'm moving in next Wednesday!" He paused, then continued: *"Will Daddy be all right while I'm away? Will he make it over this next hurdle?"*

At this my wife laughed aloud, but I was unexpectedly moved, and while I smiled involuntarily I believe I felt like sobbing.

"You sound like an announcer at a sumo match. But the pressure will be on you, not Daddy. You've been having seizures in the morning because you stay up so late—at the dormitory you'll have to take your medicine every morning as soon as you wake up!"

Each of the students at Eeyore's special school was required to spend one term in the dormitory on the campus. We had known for some time that Eeyore's turn was coming up, and he had been apprehensive about it. During the New Year's vacation, when we had assembled as a family for late breakfasts, his normal dispatch at table had gradually slowed until he was barely moving. He did manage to finish his meal, but the tension in his face as he lay on the couch after breakfast made him look like a different person—he appeared to have transformed all at once into a man past middle age with somehow ancient features. I found myself recalling the solemnity, I want to say the aboriginal solemnity, that appeared in Professor W's face when he was on his deathbed. Presently, a flush appeared in Eeyore's upper face, his eyes seemed to gleam with an amber light, and his expression revealed a suffering that he did not understand and thus could not complain about in words. When I placed my hand on his large, prominent forehead it felt hot with a leaden heat. He had forgotten to take his epilepsy medicine and was having a seizure. My wife had continued to insist that Eeyore was not epileptic, and although I knew that this kind of seizure was considered a form of epilepsy, I refrained from asserting what I had read.

The day he was to move in to the dormitory, as Eeyore studied the weekly FM program guide that was inserted in the newspaper, I tried to determine what was behind the words he had spoken to his mother. "Eeyore, you asked whether I would make it over this next hurdle. When was the last hurdle?"

I had half expected him to say "*I forget,*" his standard reply at times like this. But he lifted his face from the page and, narrowing his eyes in what appeared to be a glare as he rolled them upward at an angle, responded with a lucid answer: "*When Mr. H died of leukemia! Saku had cancer at the same time! It was a terrible thing. But you made it over—good work! It was a whole week around the twenty-fifth of January three years ago!*"

It turned out that Saku—Eeyore's younger brother—hadn't had cancer after all. He had urinated blood in sufficient quantity to notice it himself though he was only a child, and when tests at our local clinic came back positive for blood in the urine for several days in a row, we had begun commuting to Tokyo University Hospital. He was given a battery of tests which lasted for days but which failed somehow to prove conclusively that Saku was, in the words of the doctor in charge, "not guilty." Even when Eeyore's younger brother had to endure an agonizing bladder examination, he was unfazed. I did less well; gradually our visits to the hospital together had worn me down.

We rode the train to the Ochanomizu station and then waited at the bus stop on top of the bridge for the bus to the campus. Twenty years ago, I had waited countless times in the same spot for the same bus with my classmate H, who now lay dying of leukemia in the hospital directly across the canal from the bus stop. For a time he had shown signs of recovering, but at the end of last year he had suffered a brain hemorrhage and had been in a coma ever since. When Eeyore's younger brother had finished his tests for the day, I sometimes left him in the outpatient waiting room at this hospital and paid my friend "a visit," a conversation standing in the hall with his wife, wasted from the effort of nursing him and in a kind of frenzy, after which I returned gloomily to the waiting room downstairs.

H died, and I accepted the role of host at his funeral. At the wake, as I sat on the porch around the house greeting guests in a cold wind, I was troubled by thoughts of my son still undergoing tests, and further troubled by a remark an older writer who was one of the guests was said to have made: "It's a terrible shame; this time it's his younger boy that's sick and not the older brother." I must be honest, the remark seemed to have caught nimbly and skewered and pushed into my face a cruel thought that had glimmered for just an instant at the back of my consciousness: "Better Eeyore than his younger brother!"

At dinner that night, I asked Eeyore's brother a question. "When they tested your kidneys because they thought that might be where the trouble was, we discussed me or your mother or Eeyore giving you one of our kidneys if yours had to be removed. Which one of us would you have chosen?"

"Good question." Eeyore's younger brother always paused to consider before speaking and now he was being even more deliberate than usual. "Eeyore's taking Hidantol . . ."

I seethed. How could he say such a thing! How could he be so egotistical! Maybe it was hard not to think about how healthy the donor's kidneys were, but to make that the basis of a judgment against his own brother! Abstracting somehow the words that rose in my gorge, I asked the following question: "So you're assuming that Eeyore's kidneys are damaged?" Once again Eeyore's brother paused to deliberate, visibly flushing. He must have been ashamed of the image of himself reflected in his father's misunderstanding. "Eeyore's taking Hidantol," he repeated, wanting accuracy. "I assume that an epilepsy suppressant must be full of harmful ingredients. Wouldn't he need both his kidneys to process all that toxin?"

I apologized, and I acknowledged that his concern for his brother was appropriate. After dinner, Eeyore tried to respond to my suggestion that he choose the records he didn't have on tape so that he could record them and take them with him to the dormitory, where he would be allowed to use a tape recorder. But he seemed stymied by this task: sitting on the floor with his legs beneath him, he had been staring at the pile of records in front of him for more than an hour but hadn't selected a single album. "You can't dawdle this way when you're in the dorm or you'll be a nuisance to the others," my wife cautioned. Eventually, his younger sister said, "To Eeyore the whole thing is music; maybe he can't choose a part of the whole." "*That's right! Exactly! Thank you kindly!*" Eeyore said.

I told Eeyore's sister that I thought her observation was accurate. That night, before they went to sleep, the younger children were talking in the bedroom. Eeyore's sister seemed to be looking for confirmation from her brother that I had praised her. After his customary pause, I heard his response: "It felt good, didn't it! I was praised, too!"

Partly because of Eeyore's imminent move to the dormitory, my wife and I had been concentrating our attention on him. Apparently his younger brother and sister were feeling overlooked, by their father in particular. Downstairs, still seated in front of his records with his legs tucked beneath him, Eeyore was mumbling to himself as though he were speaking for me: "*This is a problem. This is truly a problem!*"

After H had been hospitalized with leukemia, during the period when he seemed to have survived the first crisis and had recovered however slightly, I visited him a number of times. The people around him, including his wife, had not informed him of his diagnosis, but I had the feeling he was signaling me obliquely that he knew. Shortly after he had gone into the hospital, he had shown me the bruises covering his still robust body. Sometime later, as a result of radiation therapy, his hair fell out and left his splendid skull exposed with just a few tough white hairs glistening on top of it. His eyes were frightfully clear, and they shifted restlessly as he spoke to me (in the brief interval when his wife had left the room): "We injure some people in the course of our lives, and we get injured by others. And we settle accounts along the way. We make it up to some and require others to compensate us. In that way we close the books— that's how the future appeared to me when I was a student. Now I realize it's not really about closing the books in the course of your life. In the end, all you can do is ask those you've injured to forgive you and of course forgive others in the same way. It seems to me there's no other choice. Take Jesus, he forgave the sins of mankind. They say that Christianity introduced that

notion into European thought for the first time since ancient
Greece. Have you ever thought about any of this?"

"I don't know a thing about Christianity," I had replied,
appalled at how spineless I sounded. "But Blake goes even further; in his view, sin is merely a reflection of presumptuous reason, an illusion mankind labors under, so that denouncing or
retaliating against sin is meaningless—the only thing of any
importance is Jesus Christ's forgiveness of sin."

"Christ's forgiveness? I suppose thinking that way would
make things easier. Our sins against others and the sins that
others commit against us are painful, and so is rancor that burns
and is never extinguished."

After his death, I heard that H had turned to his wife when
he had fallen ill and said to her: "I made your life a mess, didn't
I!" At the time, I recalled our conversation. When I heard a
rumor about a physical fight between H's widow and the pro-
prietress of his favorite bar—who held the opposing view that
H's life had been ruined by his wife and apparently had said so
to his widow when she showed up at the bar one night—I recalled our conversation again with a bitter taste in my mouth.

I remember another conversation that we had late in the
fall of the year when my friend got sick, when it seemed clear
that he was on his way to recovery and his hair had grown back.
Learning that I had finally managed to publish a novel I had
been working on forever, *The Contemporary Game,* he expressed
a desire to read it immediately. But he was under doctor's orders to moderate his reading, and as it seemed to me that reading this thick volume while lying in bed on his back would drain
his energy, I had promised to take a volume apart and bring it
to him in lighter sections without covers after the New Year.
But I went to visit him one day and discovered that he had sent
his wife out to buy the book and had already read it from cover

to cover. With a smile in his eyes that had stopped darting but remained so crystal clear they were bizarre, he praised the book generously. Later, he recounted a memory, which had meant nothing to me at the time, of something that had happened when we were students. "When we were on the bus on our way to support the Sunakawa strike, you said it wouldn't bother you even if you got smashed in the head with a billy club and died, and then you talked about practicing 'soul takeoffs' when you were a kid. You had the whole bus laughing, and I remember wondering if maybe you were just a clown. Why did you leave that episode out of the novel? When I think back about it now, it strikes me as a story with some urgency about it, not just funny but poignant, and I missed it in the novel."

It wasn't until several weeks later, when H was critically ill again with no prospect of recovery and I was paying him a visit in his cramped hospital room, having retraced my steps to the Ochanomizu station after taking Eeyore's younger brother to the university hospital and then dropping him at home, that I finally remembered clearly the story he had been referring to. Complaining of a violent headache, H had slipped into a coma several days earlier, and although his kidneys had now ceased to function— when I learned this my thoughts shifted to Eeyore's brother— he was still receiving Ringer's solution intravenously and his whole body was swollen with fluid. Later, the autopsy revealed that blood vessels had burst in both H's brain and his lungs and that blood with nowhere to go had pooled in heavy, sloshing balloons throughout his body. Even so, the heart that had been conditioned by playing rugby at Hibiya High School was still beating inside his chest, and the respirator that looked like the handiwork of an amateur with its hard rubber valves and soft accordion rubber tubes continued to hiss like a bellows.

As I gazed down at H in this condition, the meaning of his words to me two weeks earlier became clear. I had for a fact

told my friends on the bus on the way to Sunakawa about practicing "soul takeoffs" as a child. But that was a memory of a
dream in a sequence of dreams that had appeared to me when
I was young. Gathering here and there along the road where it
climbed the hill, the children from the valley in the forest were
practicing running down the road and soaring upward into the
sky as if they were on gliders. We were practicing "soul takeoffs" to ensure that our souls would be well prepared to escape
from our bodies when death arrived. When the soul broke away
from the body, it climbed into the sky above the valley and glided
through the air as it observed family and friends below disposing of the husk of the corpse that it had shed. Presently, it soared
higher in larger circles until it reached the very tops of the trees
in the forest that surrounded the valley. And there it resided
biding its time until the day when it glided down into the valley to enter a new body; it was to ensure that this process of death
and rebirth would proceed smoothly that we practiced "soul
takeoffs," extending our arms from our sides as we ran down
the road making a noise like a diving plane.

I must have omitted this dream from *The Contemporary
Game* because, working on the book, I hadn't been thinking
about death and rebirth as urgently as H as he lay in his sickbed
with leukemia. And that had been his point, his final observation about me.

I was frequently criticized for stuffing *The Contemporary Game*
with imagery and symbolism I had borrowed from mythology,
folklore, and cultural anthropology. In fact, according to Y, from
whose books I took most of what I learned, the imagery and
symbolism at the heart of the novel were original to me. And
certainly as I wrote I was aware of continually following hints
and leads from a storehouse of dark dreams from my childhood

days in the valley. As I put words to my dreams, I was thrilled to discover their connection beneath the surface to the mythologies of other places and other countries.

The imagery-symbolism at the core of the mythological world I depicted in *The Contemporary Game* appears as the reverie of a youth (who is myself) wandering in the night forest with a high fever and, at the same time, as a vision, which is actually observed. At the height of the war, the youth=myself explains the following notion to two astronomers who had evacuated to our village: "If it were possible to perceive all the galaxies in the universe at once in a single glance, perhaps we would discover an infinite number of worlds existing as units of space multiplied by time, and perhaps we would see inside the vastness of those units an infinite number of slight variations on our own world, though we believe it to be unique, whose histories were developing in parallel with our own. In other words, how do we know that what we consider history isn't simply a version of history selected at will by a godlike entity as if he were playing a game and revealed to us as if it were our own; how do we know that we ourselves aren't merely an element in the mechanism of that game?" Although I had spoken lightly of my notion as if it were a joke, it had obsessed me since I had become fascinated with astronomy as a child. The following passage, a scene which the youth=myself re-creates for his "sister" as though he has beheld it in a mind addled with fever, is in fact a summary of the dreams that had recurred to me over time as a child in the valley, with only slight variations:

And then, sister, during those six days I experienced in the forest, I saw with my own eyes as a reality the vision I buffooningly described to Apogee and Perigee [the nicknames we had given the astronomers]. As I walked around covering up the fragments into which the *Man who deconstructs* had broken apart, a space as clear as the glass balls in the model of a molecule revealed itself to me, and inside that lucid space surrounded by trees and shrubs and bushes I could see the Herdsman and the Weaving Girl. In this way, in the spaces as clear as glass balls that continued to appear before me, I saw every one of the characters that are passed down to us in our local folklore. And I saw them to be existing simultaneously in the same moment, even those who will figure in episodes in the future. As I walked through the forest day after day and watched the figures revealed to me, I realized there was no need to search outside the Milky Way, that, just as Apogee and Perigee had said, everything that was and is and will be could be found right here in the forest. I understood that what was here in front of me now was precisely that panorama I had joked about, of close to an infinite number of units of space multiplied by time all viewed at a single glance. My understanding had nothing to do with words, the lesson was contained in the sum total of the vision that appeared before my eyes one scene after another. What's more, the mythology and history of our village-as-nation-as-universe, in which, as I now saw, everything was visible at the same time, co-existing at the same time, that very mythology and history was in and of itself a manifestation of the *Man who deconstructs* grown to giant proportions. It was for that reason that roaming through every darkest corner of our forest beholding my vision as I walked amounted to re-creating the *Man who deconstructs* from the fragments into which he had broken apart. . . ."

Recalling my friend H's observation, I noticed once again that I had written nothing about birth and death. I was speaking only of the *Man who deconstructs,* a corpse dismembered but still pristine, undecayed. Yet the dreams from my childhood that were the basis of the image were directly related to birth and death. The glass beads that floated among the dark trees in the depth of the forest, illuminated from the inside by a glowing light, contained every human being from the past, present, and future of our village-nation=small universe. I myself was inside a cocoon like a chrysalis in a state of suspended animation. Those who were to be born into the real world of our village-nation=small universe had only to leave their cocoons and descend into the valley, drifting down like gliders. At the time of death, gliders again, they would return to their cocoons in the forest. And in the fullness of time they would leave the cocoon for the valley again and yet again as rebirth occurs. And the sum total of the people who belong to the complete history of our village-nation=small universe, the sum total of the cocoons of glass beads in the forest, is the *Man who deconstructs*. The youth=myself who tried to cover every inch of ground in our forest was attempting by that fever-addled act to bring him back to life. And once he revived, every last man, woman, and child of the past, present, and future of our village-nation=small universe, all subsumed in him, were to enter a new stage. A premonition of that grand achievement was always present in my recurrent dream as fierce longing accompanied by terror. In *The Contemporary Game,* the youth=myself has the following to say about the experiment that brought him as close as possible to achieving his goal but left him short of its actual attainment. It also happens to be the conclusion of the novel:

> Sister! The reason I was sobbing and screaming after the firemen in the rescue squad had pinned me down was that I was being forced to abandon the job of re-creating the physical body of the *Man who deconstructs*. I was giving up then and there the project that had been given to me as my personal trial. I was meant to make my way

through all the units of space x time in the mythology and the history of our village-nation=small universe, and by dint of that effort I was to re-create the body of the *Man who deconstructs* that had come apart, the bones, the muscles, the skin, the eyes and teeth and even all the hair. I'd accomplished the better part of it! I was carried down into the valley wailing in agony at having had to give up attaining the goal that was my trial, and I have lived outside the forest ever since, ridiculed and reviled as the long-nosed forest goblin's fag. . . .

Now then, this vision with its source in the dreams of my childhood maps onto Kathleen Raine's analysis of Blake's verse and the famous watercolor in the Petworth Collection, *A Vision of the Last Judgment.* And here again are grounds for considering as I do that perhaps everything I have felt and thought in my life, including areas close to my subconscious, was foretold in Blake. (The disjoined body of the *Man who deconstructs* mirrors symbolism which Blake used frequently and which Raine analyzes with reference to the Osiris myth that Martha Crowley had asked me about, and also to the myths of Dionysus and Orpheus. It might also be said that the youth=myself who transcends the realm of life and death to wander in the night forest is a variation of Blake's image of "the lost child, the discovered child".)

Referring to the river of humans flowing upward toward a radiant Christ on his throne and descending toward Hell in *A Vision of the Last Judgment,* Raine asserts that Blake is not depicting individuals but rather "a cluster of cells circulating through the vital force of universal life." She adds that the painting is Blake's version of Swedenborg's "great man," "divine humanity" in his case, or "Christ=imagination," that is, the one God in all things and all things in one God. In her view, *A Vision of the Last Judgment* with its close to numberless humans rendered in minute detail, represents, in its entirety, the one Jesus as imagination itself.

She refers the reader to the following passage:

> This world of Imagination is the World of Eternity it is the Divine bosom into which we shall all go after the death of the vegetated body. This world [of Imagination] is Infinite & Eternal whereas the world of Generation or Vegetation is Finite & [for a small moment] Temporal. There Exist in that Eternal World the Permanent Realities of Every Thing which we see reflected in this Vegetable Glass of Nature.
>
> All Things are comprehended in their Eternal Forms in the Divine body of the Saviour the True Vine of Eternity. The Human Imagination who appeared to Me as Coming to Judgment among his Saints & throwing off the Temporal that the Eternal might be established. Around him were seen the Images of Existence according to a certain order suited to my Imaginative Eye.

Raine sees the concept of "divine humanity" as the communal existence that also appears in *The Four Zoas;* she identifies verses in which Jesus manifests "the entirety of the world family as a single human being," and views *A Vision of the Last Judgment* as the ultimate expression in painting of Blake's spiritual universe, that is, of Jesus as a universe consisting of a single human being. When I hold up against Raine's analysis what I felt and thought about the numberless clusters of glass beads in the forest—I could call them cells just as well—and about the *Man who deconstructs* as the sum total of those clusters of beads from the model of a molecule, many things become clear. If there was something lacking in my vision, it was simply the notion that the day the body of the *Man who deconstructs,* of the savior, of Jesus, was returned to its original state was in fact the day of "the Last Judgment."

In one of Blake's most beautiful paintings, the pen and watercolor work titled *The Sea of Time and Space,* Raine sees the esoteric symbolism of the "cave of the nymphs." In what may be considered a neo-Platonic category, birth into the actual world meant for Blake a process of becoming mortal that began with a fall from eternal life and an entry into flesh of this world to be generated and to vegetate. In *The Book of Thel,* the souls on high hear the anguish of those who have left eternal life and become dwellers in the temporary world below, and wonder why they had to descend to earth. The vision of humans whose mortal bodies are being woven for them on a loom in the cave that connects heaven and earth is ubiquitous in Blake's verse. The following stanza put me in mind of Eeyore's deformed head as an infant, and there was a time when I was terrified my wife might discover it:

> *Thou Mother of my Mortal part,*
> *With cruelty dids't mould my Heart.*
> *And with false self-deceiving tears,*
> *Dids't bind my Nostrils Eyes & Ears.*

The verse I read just after entering college that was such a shock to me before I even knew it was Blake—*That Man should Labour & sorrow & learn & forget, & return / To the dark valley whence he came to begin his labours anew*—these lines were a grievous lament for the souls who must fall to earth repeatedly from the cave where their mortal bodies are woven. As a young man, I had been transported by these lines straight to the valley in the forest where I had been born and raised, and it seemed to me that the progress of my own life was being prophesied in them; my childhood reveries with that forest as their stage had the same roots as the cave where the nymphs wove mortal bodies for eternal souls. Until the moment of salvation arrived decisively—in Blake's symbolism, until the time of "the Final Judgment," and in the symbolism of my dreams and my novel, until the *Man who deconstructs* is resurrected—the souls of all people would reside in the glowing glass beads among the trees in the forest and must time and time again fall into the valley woven into their mortal bodies.

Eeyore's move to the dormitory was only two days away. Busy all day with household chores, my wife was staying up until late at night labeling the things he was required to take with him. When she had apportioned his epilepsy medicine in powder form into daily doses wrapped in individual papers and had inscribed the date on each dose, she had to put his name on an astonishing variety and number of articles. And each label had to be sewn on: bedding and quilt, two sheets, pajamas (1 pair), pillow, a cloth for bundling the pillow and pajamas. Undershirts (3), underpants (4 pairs), shirts and trousers for everyday wear (2 each), uniform and uniform shirts (2), training pants, training shirt, shorts (1 each), handkerchiefs (5), socks (5 pairs), hangers (3), umbrella (1), slippers for the room, slippers for the halls, everyday canvas shoes (1 pair each), toothbrush, tooth powder, cup, soap, soap case, comb, plastic container, 1 large and 1 small washbasin, shampoo, washcloth, and bath towel (1 each). My wife tilted her head back as she squinted down through her reading glasses at her sewing needle. It was not the first time I had seen her in this pose, but my feelings as I watched now were new and unexpected. I am told frequently that I am somehow childish for my age. If my behavior has to do with my relationship with Eeyore, who retains the spirit of a preschool child, then the same effect should have been at work on my wife. And though she did take pleasure in the amusing quirks of Eeyore's speech and laughed aloud at them, I had always perceived in her a certain youthfulness of her own that predated Eeyore's birth and was essentially unchanged. When he went away to the dormitory would she turn into a woman who behaved as though the passage of time had left her girlishness behind, quiet and rarely laughing? I wondered the same thing about myself. Just then, without slowing the nimble needle in her hand, my wife said, as though she were thinking the same thing, "When Saku came home from his club meeting today you know what he said first thing? That we wouldn't laugh as much when Eeyore moved to the dormitory. He didn't mean that Eeyore did funny things that made us laugh, he said it was because Eeyore kept us cheerful so we were able to laugh at trivial things."

I nodded my agreement with Eeyore's brother's explanation. If the atmosphere in our family was normally like a festival, it was because Eeyore was the festival clown and high priest.

"And yet when you were traveling in Europe," my wife continued, "he had us all walking on eggshells and we felt afraid to laugh in front of him."

"I received a New Year's greeting from a Japanese student in Germany today, and he wrote that a writer I met in Hamburg was worried about Eeyore. Apparently, the student translated a short story of mine about Eeyore and showed it to the writer, and he said that his heart went out to Eeyore more than to you or me. This is a man who has special feelings about violence based on his own experience, so what he says has some weight. His name is Eppendorfer."

With this giant of a man who was going bald but retained a youthful beauty around his eyes and mouth, I had ventured down into nuclear shelters in front of the Hamburg Central Station and in the entertainment district known as Reeperbahn. I had also participated in a symposium with Hamburg intellectuals that he chaired. This is how I introduced him in a pamphlet I wrote about my travels through Europe meeting people in the antinuclear and peace movements:

"There is something out of the ordinary I must explain about this writer who turned forty this year. It has to do with his approach to establishing a connection between nuclear violence on a global scale and the violence that resides in an individual. Eppendorfer is a writer who lives and works in Hamburg; but according to the autobiographical novel that may be his best work, *The Leather Man,* when he was a youth he murdered his girlfriend because she resembled his mother too closely. Subsequently, he spent ten years in prison. Currently he edits a magazine for homosexuals and works as a writer."

"Eppendorfer is asking how we can control violence," I said to my wife, "but he's coming from genuine sympathy for people who fall prey to violence or who can't deny the presence of violence in themselves. This is a man who was driven by sexual impulses to murder someone when he was about Eeyore's age. Maybe the latent violence in Eeyore reminded him of himself." The needle in my wife's fingers stopped moving and she turned around to look at me without removing her reading glasses. I could feel interrogation on the way and felt myself wincing in advance.

"Maybe that's because you've described Eeyore in your novels in a way that leads in that direction. I don't think you distorted what you wrote on purpose. When I read what you had written, I imagined you were describing just what you saw and that shocked you so when you came back from Europe. It's just that the rest of us didn't see him in quite that way when he was behaving so badly while you were gone."

My wife must have been referring to my description of what I had seen in Eeyore's eyes that first night, the beast in rut. "From the way you reacted, I was afraid something awful was happening that we'd never recover from. We had a terrible time with him while you were gone, but the worst part was the day you came home."

"I can see how you might have felt that way . . ." My wife's resentment, appearing now after a yearlong reprieve, had shaken me. "I said that Eppendorfer was seeing himself as a young man in Eeyore, but when I got back from Europe I may have been projecting Eppendorfer's crime onto Eeyore."

Something else at work beneath the surface had also affected how things had appeared to me, an experience I had had in Europe that I couldn't tell my wife. I watched her in silence as she went back to work on the labels, knitting her brow behind her reading glasses, seemingly lost in her own thoughts. Presently I withdrew and carried my glass of bedtime whisky upstairs to the room that was both my study and bedroom. Stopping at the door to my son's room, which was always partly open, I peered in at the bed where two days from now he would no longer be sleeping. His large head and the bowed arch of his nose visible in the pale light from the hall, he lay on his back looking straight up at the ceiling. The correctness of his posture despite his hulking body reminded me of my friend H lying on his deathbed. A sense of unredeemable loss assailed me. As I stood there, descending into a vast helplessness, Eeyore spoke to me in a gentle voice without turning his head or moving a muscle in his body: *"Can't you sleep, Papa? I wonder if you'll sleep when I'm not here? I expect you to cheer up and sleep!"*

There was another incident in Europe. We arrived in Vienna and joined a group of Japanese exchange students and some Austrians who were involved in the antinuclear movement. From Vienna we moved on to Hamburg, then took a night train south to Freiburg near the Swiss border to meet with activists and young politicians from the "alternative" party. From there our itinerary took us to Basel to speak with Swiss activists and then through Frankfurt and to our final destination, Berlin.

I enjoyed and was stimulated by the fever pitch at which the TV crew operated, driving themselves unsparingly according to the peculiar logic of their profession. Since we covered all this ground in just one week, our days began early in the morning and ended with dinner in the middle of the night. But our hectic schedule left me little time for feeling low.

In the medieval university town of Freiburg on the edge of the Black Forest, overlooking the Rhine from the slopes of the Schwarzwald, we had lunch at a ski lodge on the outskirts of the town. As I gazed out at the fir and beech woods in the noonday sun I saw the specter of a vast forest being consumed by a raging nuclear fire, such was my state of mind from confronting the reality of nuclear armament day and night. When I awoke in the middle of the night, I read some Blake in the Keynes edition I had bought on the road and felt as if I were clinging to the verse.

Our first night in Berlin, we attended a meeting of a group of students at Berlin Freedom University who had formed a movement to create a nuclear-free zone in Europe; the group had connections to the movement in East Berlin. The urban sophistication and composure of their arguments were an interesting contrast to the passionate gathering in Freiburg. Late that night, we ate what must have been an example of genuine Korean food intended for the Korean laborers in Germany, cold noodles served without broth and smeared with hot mustard, and, having once again confirmed that dinner as a group was an essential part of the process of a day's work together, I returned to my hotel.

It was already past two in the morning when the telephone at my bedside rang. With the curious combination of fluency and awkwardness that occurs when a Japanese who has been living in a foreign country attempts to speak her mother tongue, a middle-aged woman introduced herself. The instant I heard the voice I knew who the speaker was though I hadn't seen her in twenty years, and I could feel her reviving in my memory exactly as she had been the first time I had met her in our college days. Her father was a Korean who had taken a Japanese surname when his country had been annexed, then had graduated from Tokyo Imperial University and married a Japanese woman, and, on the occasion of Japan's defeat in 1945, had reclaimed his Korean surname, Ri. From the two elements used in writing the Chinese character for the surname Ri, "tree" and "child," I had derived the nickname "Ki-ko" for his daughter, who was now implying by her attitude on the phone that our connection, though no longer close, did at least require that we meet once when we found ourselves in the same city. It occurred to me that my choice of a Korean restaurant immediately after arriving in Berlin may have had something to do with subconscious thoughts about her. "Maybe you're not thrilled by a call from me out of the blue, but this is, you know, Ki-ko. My last name is different from last time, but it's a German name that wouldn't mean anything to you anyhow. I heard you were coming to Berlin at the same time I found out that H had died of leukemia, it's so sad. Anyhow, let's get together tonight."

"Tonight feels pretty much over," I said, recognizing her insistence on unconventionality as unchanged from the past (had I known where she was phoning me from I might have agreed, but I was only aware in a vague way that she was somewhere in the city). "Tomorrow morning I have a meeting with the TV crew, and then we'll be in East Berlin for the rest of the day. The day after tomorrow we're joining the Berlin antinuclear teach-in at the Otto Braun Hall, and then we finish up that night with a reception at the Japanese legation—"

"You don't sound very friendly, but I won't take it personally. I'll try getting into the teach-in. And don't you be ogling the crowd from the stage looking for a middle-aged woman who reminds you of Ki-ko when she was young! About the time you get back from dinner with the minister or whoever, I'll get in touch. If you've been traveling with a TV crew I bet you haven't been able to go looking for friendly ladies—you should be happy I turned up!"

The way she spoke fit perfectly the image of her that I retained from close to thirty years ago, though we had met more recently just once, and at the same time, in the voice she was affecting to help her bridge the gap of time passed, I could hear something aged. When I hesitated for an instant, Ki-ko spoke to me in a different tone of voice and then hung up: "I bet your trip to East Berlin tomorrow will be canceled—it's the day before the teach-in, right, that's been publicized all over the place? Anyway, I'm looking forward to the day after tomorrow."

Ki-ko's rooming house, near the Hongo campus of Tokyo University, had been enlarged repeatedly since it had been built before the war, and by the time she lived there it was filled with dark halls that ascended and descended at angles like passageways on a ship. There seemed to be no limit to the number of boarders it could house: I was constantly encountering new faces in the vestibule, which was cavernous in contrast to the rest of the cramped space, and around the main stairway. The mutual friend who was my connection to H was a student named I, now a Balzac scholar, who lived in a pentagonal room that was our gathering place. H's lover, a beautiful girl who was a classmate, shared a room in the same boardinghouse with several other girls from school. As a result of a simple misunderstanding between them—looking back, I can see that this sort of thing had frequently created turning points in H's life—she had rushed into the arms of a graduate student who was already producing superior work as a poet. (After H's funeral, a woman who had roomed with his erstwhile lover and who happens to be the wife of someone who was ahead of us in the department of French literature remarked, putting me in mind just now of the quaint phrase "rushed into his arms," that her friend had "jumped to the wrong conclusion" when she broke up with H: "The graduate student's room was on the same floor, and from that night on she just never came back!") Not that any of this affected me at the time; the only interest I took in my friends' love affairs was I's relationship to a high school girl whom he was grooming to pass the entrance exams to Tokyo University of the Arts. Partly because I alone lived in a different rooming house and partly because they treated me as the youngster of the group, though I spent time with H and the others in his three-way ménage, I was excluded from the romantic aspect of their lives.

Then a young girl moved into an isolated room like a lookout tower. She had grown up in Berlin, where her Korean father and Japanese mother still worked for a German construction company, and had returned to Tokyo in order to attend a Japanese university. Having graduated from a boarding school, she spoke adequate German and English, but her capacity to understand complex Japanese sentences was limited. The offer of a job tutoring her in reading Japanese made its way to me. As it happened, H's father was an executive in a Japanese construction company that was involved in a joint venture with the company in Berlin, and he had asked his son to look after the girl. It was H who had moved her into the rooming house from the apartment that the company had provided its foreign employees, insisting she would have no chance in such a place to experience Japanese student life firsthand. At the time, he was caught up in his three-way relationship and must have lacked the emotional leeway to assume the responsibility of a tutoring job.

I was twenty and Ki-ko was two years younger. Meeting her, I was impressed by her cheery drollness and by the curious degree to which she seemed physically off-balance, from her features to her body to the awkward way she sat on the floor of her room that made it clear this was her first experience of living on tatami mats (ten years later, when she had left her German husband and family in Europe and was living in Tokyo alone, the disjointed look of her late teens had transformed into an appearance and bearing I am tempted to call regal). Her hair, heaped above her head, was outlandishly abundant, and her features—crescent-moon eyebrows that recalled the princess in an historical drama, big bright eyes, a round nose, and a pert little mouth with thick lips—were set at odd angles one to the other in a large face with prominent cheekbones. The wry smile she wore may have been a reflection of her self-consciousness about her looks. Her body was large and ungainly, her legs in particular, which appeared far too substantial to belong to an Asian body and which she concealed beneath a thick skirt that reached to her heels and that she hugged to her chest. During our lessons she kept her long arms locked around her knees to balance herself on the tatami floor, otherwise she would have fallen backward. Her voice, which I had recognized the minute I heard it on the telephone in Berlin, made her sound like a small child, nasal and wheedling, but her subject matter and logic were thoroughly realistic.

If I felt there was something comical about Ki-ko, I'm sure she felt the same way about me. Years later, H revealed that Ki-ko had stipulated that he choose his most amusing friend to be her tutor, and I know she was pleased by the funny nickname I gave her. In view of H's very proper upbringing, his behavior strikes me as strange as I recall it now, but he had said to me, provocatively I thought, or possibly mockingly, that Ki-ko had grown up in a land that was sexually unrestrained and consequently that she was liberated to a degree that was unimaginable by our own Japanese standards. I did not shift responsibility to H at the time nor do I intend to now, but I will say that my subsequent behavior, not surprisingly for a young man with no experience, was profoundly influenced by the innuendo in what he had told me: I began tutoring Ki-ko in April when the new term began and stopped a year later when she was admitted to International Christian University, and for that entire year, except when she was having her period, we met every day for the exclusive purpose of having sex.

That summer vacation I went home to the forest in Shikoku, and Ki-ko traveled to Hokkaido to stay with relatives from whom she had been estranged ever since her mother had married a Korean. I had proposed that we live apart for those forty days and consider where each of us was going in our lives. Early in the fall, when I returned to Tokyo and stopped in at the boardinghouse with the Gallimard editions of Sartre that I had read in the valley in a pack on my back, a handsome young man wearing Ki-ko's sweater who appeared to be from Southeast Asia was watching the room for her, sitting on the tatami uncomfortably just as she did, his back against a rolled-up futon mattress. I went to I's room with my head spinning and unpacked my Sartre books one at a time and expounded on them and listened to his comments until I felt calm enough to return to my own rooming house. All that fall and into the winter I continued to surprise myself with the intensity of my own youthful suffering.

Through the information pipeline between Ki-ko and H, which remained open—his actual relationship to her was never clear: toward women with a certain kind of quirkiness he displayed a combination of intense devotion and thoroughgoing indifference that seemed to coexist without contradiction; since his death, I have encountered any number of women who profess to miss him keenly although their connection to him is a mystery—I was able to learn that Ki-ko had separated from the exchange student from Singapore and not long after had married a communications engineer who had been sent from Germany to train in Japan and had hired her as his interpreter, and that she had dropped out of college and returned with him to Europe.

Shortly after Eeyore was born with a deformed head, when I was deep in despair and bewilderment, Ki-ko had abruptly contacted me, as always, through H, and I had visited her in her room at the International House of Japan in Tokyo. My wife was still in the hospital. I have already mentioned that Ki-ko had turned into a gorgeous woman since I had seen her last, a transformation that was unexpected yet easily traced back to her appearance as a girl. And the treatment I received from her that day—I would have to call it sexual therapy—was a consolation to me. It also filled me from start to finish with a feeling of sinfulness so raw I might have been copulating with my sister, and churned to life in me something grotesque that resembled, in the poet Homei's words, "a desperate savageness." These feelings enabled me to understand, looking back, that I had been moved when I was twenty-one to propose that we spend the summer apart thinking about our own lives because my relationship with Ki-ko, whom I felt was younger than myself in those days, had also felt incestuous to me, as though I had been sleeping with my younger sister. This revival, nearly ten years later, of a sexual connection to Ki-ko was the basis for the scene in *A Personal Matter* when the hero has sex with a classmate who wrote her thesis on Blake. I understood perfectly well the importance of the haven Ki-ko had selflessly offered me, but I was just as egocentric at twenty-nine as I had been in my early twenties, and while I saw the scar across her right wrist I did not ask her about it—the fact that she was left-handed had intensified the ungainliness of her large body when she was a girl of eighteen or nineteen—did not inquire, that is, about what had happened during the nearly ten years she had spent in Europe. She was in Tokyo for two weeks, and, when she returned to Germany, the anguish I had experienced ten years earlier all that fall and into the winter struck me once again an unexpected blow. Scrawling these memories on the page as fast as my pen can move I am assailed by the feeling that I have yet to confront squarely the spoiled, indulgent cruelty of my younger years.

The teach-in proceeded according to schedule. During a break to adjust the time in the satellite broadcast that was beaming live to Japan, the group advocating the nuclear-free zone whom I had met just after arriving in Berlin approached me at the podium to reproach me gently for failing to appear in support of the antinuclear activists in East Berlin. Expecting that we would be meeting a group of clerics from various churches, they had even distributed copies of the English translation of my book of essays, *Hiroshima Notes*. I was moved to learn that the people I was supposed to have met intended to pray for the health of my handicapped son.

With a wisdom about the world that was the obverse of her eccentricity, Ki-ko had predicted correctly that a change in the TV crew's schedule would result in my trip to East Berlin being canceled. She had now installed herself in what would have been the best seat in the house at a concert, directly in front of the main stage, and was sitting there as majestically as always. With the exception of a small number of resident Japanese who had read about the event in the newsletter of the Japanese embassy, the audience filling the hall consisted of activists in the peace and antinuclear movements from all over West Germany. Many of them also belonged to the so-called alternative movement, which included the advocates of planned simplicity as an approach to conserving our natural resources. Sitting in that crowd with a mink coat draped around her shoulders,

Ki-ko was, to say the least, conspicuous, but not quite alone: one of the panelists on the stage, the theologian daughter of Ruprecht Heineman, West Berlin's only president to have visited Hiroshima, was also wearing a mink coat. The blond, blue-eyed daughter of the former president and Ki-ko with her jet- black hair heaped on her head as before appeared to confront each other from above and below the dais like two soaring mountain peaks. Clearly, Ki-ko had become a middle-aged woman, yet despite the striking appearance that was the result of hard work, I was aware of the same droll surprise at herself she had never been able to conceal as a girl of eighteen or nineteen. When our eyes met, she acknowledged me with an antique gesture that predated our generation. There was something like darkness in her glance, and as she tilted her head forward the upper portion of her face from her brow to her nose appeared to be shadowed by gloom. Later in the evening, as the teach-in intensified, I ceased to be aware of her. Afterward, there were farewells to be exchanged with my fellow panelists and discussions with the Japanese in the audience who came up to point out mistakes the German interpreter had made. I was aware, as of a battleship making its way into port, of Ki-ko's presence slowly approaching, but when I had a minute to look up and scan the auditorium she was nowhere to be seen.

It was close to midnight when I got back to my hotel room after dinner at the Japanese legation in Berlin, and the phone rang almost at once. It was Ki-ko calling to propose that we meet right away. She explained that she had been staying in a room on the top floor of my hotel for three days. She had been phoning every ten minutes to see if I had returned, yet it was at least an hour until she opened the door I had left unlocked without knocking and, looking calm and composed, stepped into the room. She was wearing a Korean dress I remembered having seen, of dazzling pale green silk, that reached to her ankles, and, on her bare chest just below her throat, a chrysanthemum. I realized once again that other than crocuses and forsythia I had not seen a single flower during my stay in Europe.

I had been lying on the bed with my shoes on, reading, and as I sat up, Ki-ko sat down on the empty bed across from me, and for a moment we just looked at each other appraisingly. Then I stood up and went to the refrigerator for little bottles of whisky and glasses, and Ki-ko, who already had alcohol on her breath, gave me her critique of the interpretor's German translation. It was her feeling that the real and current threat of nuclear attack that had been the point of my remarks had been somewhat blurred, and that the Soviet threat as outlined by Ishihara, the novelist who was also an LDP member of the Diet, had been glossed over out of consideration for the Soviets. "In other words, the arguments that got through to the German audience were less tense and confrontational than you intended. I guess that's part of the balancing act that professional interpreters do—"

As she spoke, just as when she had visited my rooming house as a young woman, Ki-ko picked up the books on my nightstand and examined them carefully—Blake, *The Golden Age of Russian Theater,* and a Penguin collection of Orwell essays. When I handed her a glass she was browsing in the Orwell, and, sitting down on the bed again with both her drink and the book gripped in her left hand, she said the following in the haughty tone of a female teacher:

"When H was here to research extremist groups he told me about your son. He must be almost an adult? Have you thought about what you're going to do when he goes *must?* He'll be a handful!"

I must have turned white with anger; as I sat there unable to say a word, my tongue paralyzed, Ki-ko's large face contorted stupidly with fear and sadness as if it were being slapped by each one of her cosmetic efforts. It was then that I saw for the first time the darkness of her mottled skin beneath the thick makeup.

"You're suggesting that my son will go *must* like an elephant or a camel but it won't do to shoot him, is that it? You're quoting from 'Shooting an Elephant.' Well here's another one of Orwell's words: 'I thought you were a more *decent* human being!'"

We sat in silence, looking down at our drinks. Presently Ki-ko placed her glass on the floor with a clumsy, somehow girlish movement of her left hand, then stood up, cleared her throat of phlegm with a groan, and said sourly, "Let's call it a night—I seem to have made a mistake that's not really like me. I'll show you around Berlin tomorrow." I could see the pitch-darkness into which I was about to plummet right before my eyes, but my tongue seemed paralyzed once again and I didn't even look up as she left the room.

The next day, dispiritedly, Ki-ko and I did some odd sightseeing in Berlin. Partly because the schedule had changed again and I was leaving for Frankfurt at three that afternoon, there was only time for each of us to choose one place to visit. Having seen while I was in college a photograph of a yellow electric eel that was supposed to be there still, I chose the aquarium on Budapest Strasse. The eel turned out to be a disappointment and so did the rest of the fish, but the plant life that had been installed dramatically to re-create their habitats was worth seeing. Ki-ko displayed no interest in the fish or the plants, and, unwilling to climb the stairs, had a lengthy conversation with an aging guard on the first floor.

Ki-ko's choice was a porn film, something she had become even more curious about since her German husband had refused to take her. We found an X-rated theater within walking distance of the aquarium, in the basement of one of the shops that lined the Kurfurstendamm in the middle of the entertainment district. When you bought your ticket you were also given a

miniature bottle of whisky. Negotiating with the young man at
the counter in fluent German that was emphatically upper class,
Ki-ko also received two small bottles of gin and a can of beer
for each of us; as we sat down in the theater she took a swig of
the beer and filled the can back up with the gin. I did the same,
but we didn't stay long enough to empty an entire bottle. Back
up on the street, Ki-ko said she wanted to shop for some ingredients for Korean food and we headed east along the Ku-damm
toward a department store that contained the most varied food
gallery in Berlin. We spoke only a few words along the way, but
our conversation was painful to me. I began with a comment
on the film: "The lead girl had so much sex it was cruel; but that
was a funny scene when she cooled her genitals with an ice-bag."
"When we were just children we had sex repeatedly," Ki-ko
replied. "So much it was cruel, as you'd say—worse than cruel,
if you ask me. . . ." Ki-ko also critiqued my remarks at the teach-
in: "You were saying a nuclear war won't happen in the near
future because it hasn't ever happened yet, am I right? Unfor-
tunately, I don't agree. I think the world has already been destroyed any number of times. I think a small number of people
survived, and they rebuilt this miserable world we live in now.
But what didn't survive was the lesson to be learned, that's my
conclusion after living in Europe for years. I think the destruction of Germany in World War Two—look over there, that's
what's left of the Kaiser Wilhelm Memorial Church!—was
equivalent to the apocalypse. I wonder if the same gang isn't
planning to use nuclear weapons to destroy the world and then
rebuild it again? A nuclear bomb shelter is a reality—we built
one at home."

"If it's possible," I said, "to rebuild the world."

"Even if they couldn't rebuild it, I think they'd insist
that was okay, too—these are people who believe in 'the last
judgment.'"

"That's not how Blake viewed the last judgment," I started to say, but I had no heart for continuing a debate with Ki-ko.

It was time to shake hands good-bye, and in the dry, German atmosphere beneath a cloudy sky, as she extended her left arm in a gesture familiar from years before, the face that Ki-ko turned directly toward me for the first time that day, while it retained its dignity and radiance, was clearly the face of a Korean woman nearing the end of middle age. When I returned alone to my hotel, the young men on our TV crew were piling gear into a mountain of cases just outside the front entrance— I expect they must have seen a Japanese man who was also nearing the end of middle age and who appeared to be consumed with grief. I had begun writing my series of stories about the symbiosis between Blake's Prophecies and my handicapped son by linking the grief of an aging writer and my son's unacted animal impulses. Here in Europe, could I deny that it was in me that both grief and animal impulses had been lodged? And wasn't that the reason I had been so shaken to discover the same sentiments in Eeyore when I returned to Japan?

By the time I woke up, my son had already left for the dormitory. That Monday with Eeyore gone, the space inside the house seemed vast and unfamiliar; even more unexpectedly, I felt as though I had more time on my hands than I knew how to fill. I wandered around the house looking for my wife. I wanted to talk to her about my feeling of being suspended helplessly in a thirty-hour day, but it was as though the house's interior had been enlarged and I had difficulty finding her. I felt apprehensive. Apparently my wife was also feeling at loose ends: in our winter-withered garden, she was clipping berry-covered vines out of the shrubbery to decorate a wreath of dried flowers.

I took refuge in Blake, lingering over minute details and losing my way in them. As I pored over the last prophecy, *Jerusalem,* reading Erdman's annotated text and studying a facsimile of Blake's own illuminations, I discovered a direct connection to my sort of poem about the rain tree. I didn't make the discovery entirely on my own; I was led to it by the music of my friend and mentor, the composer T. The first week Eeyore was away at the dormitory, a group of the best young musicians in the country performed an entire evening of T's works. The hall was in Yokohama; my wife and I had not been outside of Tokyo alone together since Eeyore had been born, and just stepping onto the train felt like a sort of renewal. My wife's buoyant mood was apparent in her unusual talkativeness even on the train. She told me about an elderly woman who had approached her after the ceremony when Eeyore had moved into the dormitory and said, "That school term when my child was in the dormitory was like the first vacation I ever had, and my last—"

"Does this feel like a vacation?" I responded.

"It does, because living with Eeyore is like living for two people," my wife answered in the bright voice of someone luxuriating on a vacation.

But as the train crossed the Tama River we saw the expanse of water reflecting the unnatural color of the snowy sky and fell silent. I felt something powerful rise from the surface of the water to churn the darkness inside me. Before the concert, T appeared at the foot of the stage to introduce his suite in three parts for guitar and alto flute titled *To the Sea;* and when he mentioned, speaking about the section called "Cape Cod," the darkness of the scenery along the coast of Nantucket, I thought I felt my wife's body shudder as she sat next to me. She shuddered again during the performance, which made me think that the dark surface of the Tama must have evoked something in her as well.

T's new piece for piano, "Rain Tree Sketches," was performed by the female pianist A, who had recently softened the unique scientific precision of her style with something richer and more mellow. The piece was a lucid and persistent restatement of the rain tree theme T had already used in his chamber music, but, short as it was, it was more than simply a restatement—T's "rain tree" as musical metaphor had grown more luxuriant, extending further its leafy branches. As for myself, I felt ashamed to think that I had already uprooted my own rain tree metaphor, but also somehow encouraged.

The feeling stayed with me through the intermission. The second half of the concert began with a percussion solo titled "Munari by Munari"; the score consisted of aphorisms and symbols T had written on a folded-paper creation by Munari, the Italian designer. The piece was an improvisation in his musical idiom by the speculative percussionist Yamashita. It was as if T's music from the first half of the concert were still reverberating, yet it was more than revival, it was new music in the process of creation. It was as if the percussionist were performing T's spirit and physical body, living in the present but moving toward the future.

The continuing music led me to a discovery. It was as though I had reencountered something dear and familiar to me that I had been missing keenly: Oh yes!, I seemed to say to myself, Blake's "tree of life" is precisely the "rain tree" I described having seen in a dark garden in Hawaii! Like the rain tree, its trunk soars upward darkly like a wall obscuring everything before it, and the colossal slab of its roots is identical.

At the beginning of the first story in my rain tree series, I described my encounter with the rain tree in the following way. With the clamor of a party at my back, I was peering out at a darkness with a rank smell:

That the darkness in front of me was mostly filled by a
single, giant tree was to be inferred from the layered mass
of roots faintly reflecting light and radiating outward in
this direction. Gradually, I perceived that this black mass
like an enclosure of boards was glowing palely with a
grayish-blue luster of its own. This centuries-old tree with
its welter of well-developed roots above the ground rose
into the darkness obscuring the sky above and the sea
below the cliff.

When I got home from the concert, I opened the facsimile
edition of *Jerusalem* to Plate 76 and wondered how I could have
failed to see until now that it was unmistakably the rain tree I
have described here. Jesus crucified on "the tree of life." Standing at the base of the tree with his arms spread, the giant Albion,
in whom all mankind is redeemed and embodied, directs his
reverent gaze upward at Jesus. Albion radiates youth; Jesus
appears to be approaching old age. This scene is intended as an
illustration of the confident, beautiful dialogue between Jesus
and Albion near the end of *Jerusalem*:

> *Jesus replied Fear not Albion unless I die thou canst not live*
> *But if I die I shall arise again & thou with me*
> *This is friendship & Brotherhood without it Man is Not*
>
> *So Jesus spoke! The Covering Cherub coming on in darkness*
> *Overshadowed them & Jesus and Thus do Men in Eternity*
> *One for another to put off by forgiveness, every sin.*

In this way, reading Blake, I happened on *The Tree of Life,*
an illustration that resembled my own image of the rain tree.
And reading in the text of *Jerusalem* the lengthy dialogue between Jesus nailed to the tree and the youthful Albion, I made

my way to the verses above. I realize it may sound far-fetched—
and it is an odd thing to write in light of what I myself had said
to H on his deathbed, that I did not believe in Christianity and
had no knowledge of it—but I did feel in the presence of something like grace (I overcome my hesitation to use the word by
telling myself that it was only through the agency of T's music
that grace became possible). Nevertheless, it is, or feels like, grace
that encourages me forward in the direction of the "forgiveness
of sin" that is at the heart of Jesus' thought in his dialogue with
Albion. Looking at Plate 76, I recited Blake's verse aloud to
myself repeatedly. And presently I became aware that "Beyond
the Rain Tree" was resonating harmonically with Blake's lines.

> *Toward the rain tree*
> *And through it to the world beyond*
> *Our spirits merged, consubstantial,*
> *Yet selves as free as they can be*
> *We return. . . .*

Born into this world on earth, Eeyore had gained precious
little through the power of reason, nor could it be said that he
had labored to build anything in particular in the real world.
But according to Blake the power of reason served only to lead
man into illusion; this world itself was the product of illusion.
And while Eeyore dwelled in this world, the power of his soul
had not been corrupted by experience: in Eeyore, the power of
innocence had been preserved. Eventually, Eeyore and I would
proceed toward the rain tree, and move through it, united as one
yet souls as free as they could be, to return to the world beyond.
And who, speaking for Eeyore or for me, was to say that this
was a meaningless process of life and death?
    I returned in my mind once again to my conversation with
H in his hospital room about the "forgiveness of sin." Though I

was still largely ignorant about Blake at the time, I had brought up his name, as though something were leading me in his direction. Had I known more about Blake, I might have responded to H's remark that believing in the "forgiveness of sin" made life easier by sending him the pages of the illustrated edition detached from their binding so he could rest them on his chest one plate at a time; useless now, the thought filled me with regret. It was in any event just another expression of a presentiment I had deep down, that I would be reading an unbound facsimile edition of *Jerusalem* on my own deathbed.

Late Saturday afternoon, with his brother and sister already home and awaiting him, Eeyore returned for his first weekend. It was immediately clear that even one week of dormitory life had made a difference in his behavior: there was no front gate clattering open, no sound of shoes being dragged down the walk, and no noisy entrance into the front hall. I was lying on the sofa reading Blake, as usual, and when I happened to look up Eeyore was coming through the door into the room with a large bag of dirty laundry on his shoulder. As I was lifting myself off the couch he quickly seized my left foot angled up at the ceiling and said, shaking it up and down in lieu of a handshake, "*Nice foot, excellent foot, was everything all right? Have you been well?*"

Lying on my back unable to move I burst out laughing, and so did Eeyore's brother and sister on their way downstairs from their rooms, and so did my wife in the kitchen. There was no question that Eeyore's behavior, not intentional but natural, brought levity to our family. But just now he was clearly exhausted, and gave no sign of responding to my wife's questions about life in the dormitory. Instead, he sat down in front of the hi-fi speakers with his rear end directly on the floor and appeared to be perplexed about which record to play first. His face had lost weight to a point where his profile was angular, and there was even an air of quiet wisdom around his double-lidded eyes. Instead of selecting a record on his own, he presently tuned the radio to *Classical Requests* on NHK FM. Until dinner was ready, as though his parched body and soul were gulping the water of the music, he sat there in silence, listening to the radio. Apparently, the challenge of playing the cassettes he had taken with him to the dormitory had proved too much for him.

He did stand at one point and go into the kitchen, and my wife told him to pour himself some juice from the refrigerator. Instead of obeying her as he normally would have done, he merely supplied the following information and returned to the radio, as though unwilling to miss a minute of the "short-tune request corner" at the end of the program. *"They said we couldn't have tea at the dormitory but there was tea. It was barley tea!"*

My wife and I and Eeyore's brother and sister waited until the radio program was ending to take our places at the dinner table, where Eeyore's favorite meal had been laid out, roast veal in cream sauce with spaghetti and potato salad. Though he had turned off the radio, Eeyore remained seated, removing records from the cabinet and replacing them. I called out to him, "Eeyore, dinner's ready. Come sit down." But Eeyore's eyes never moved from the record player, and then the muscles in his broad, manly shoulders tensed and he said, as though announcing a considered decision: *"Eeyore won't be coming. Since Eeyore isn't here anymore, altogether, he won't be coming over there!"*

I could feel my wife watching me as I looked down at the table; the sense of loss assaulting me was so virulent I didn't think I could handle her gaze. What had happened just now? Had it actually happened, and would it go on happening? A need to stamp my feet was building in me, and though I managed to keep tears from my eyes I was unable to stop myself from flushing from my cheeks to my ears. "Eeyore, no way! You've come home so of course you're here!" His younger sister's voice was soothing, but Eeyore remained silent. Eeyore's younger brother followed his sister by the beat or two it had taken him to examine his own thought: "He'll be twenty in June, maybe he doesn't want to be called Eeyore anymore. I bet he wants to be called by his real name—that's what they must be using at the dorm!"

An irrepressible man of action once he has taken a logical stand, Eeyore's brother crossed the room and said, squatting at his brother's side, "Hikari, let's eat. Mom's made all your favorites!" *"That should be fine. Thank you."* In contrast to his adolescent brother's cracking voice, Eeyore replied in the limpid voice of a young boy. The relief of the moment had something comical about it, like a joint abruptly dislocating, and it set my wife and Eeyore's sister to laughing aloud again.

Shoulder to shoulder despite the large difference in their height and girth, the two brothers came to the dining table. So this is it, I thought to myself as I watched them begin to attack their food, still feeling the shock of loss I had received a minute before: no more calling him Eeyore? The time was ripe, I supposed. My son, the time has surely come for us to cease calling you by your infant name and to begin calling you Hikari! You have arrived at that age. Before long, you, my son Hikari, and your younger brother, Sakurao, will stand before us as young men. Lines from Blake's preface to *Milton,* verses I had frequently recited to myself, seemed to rise up in me: "Rouse up O Young Men of the New Age! Set your foreheads against the ignorant Hirelings! For we have Hirelings in the Camp, the Court & the University: who would if they could, for ever depress Mental & prolong Corporeal War." With Blake as my guide, I beheld a phantasm of my sons as young men of a new age, a baleful, atomic age, which would require them the more urgently to set their foreheads against the ignorant Hirelings, and I could assuredly feel myself at their side, reborn as another young man. Presently, when old age approached and the time had come to endure the agony of death, I would hear the words proclaimed by the voice from The Tree of Life in encouragement to all Humankind as though they were spoken to me and to me alone: *Fear not Albion unless I die thou canst not live / But If I die I shall arise again & Thou With me.*

Afterword

The Imagination is not a State:
it is the Human Existence itself.

—WILLIAM BLAKE

Small wonder that Kenzaburo Oe chose William Blake as his ally in *Rouse Up O Young Men of the New Age!* Blake was a fervent champion of the imagination's power to transfigure reality, and transfiguration was what Oe set out to achieve. His method is similar to Blake's own: he deploys his imagination against the reality of his severely handicapped son. The father-narrator who is his alter ego is not a disinterested observer; on the contrary, he is an imagination warrior who deforms in order to transform and liberate himself from the circumstances he perceives even as he describes them.

Accordingly, *Rouse Up O Young Men of the New Age!* is fiction. To be sure, Oe has grounded his chronicle in real-life incidents, and uses actual details to convey a picture of life at home with Eeyore that is comic and grotesque and poignant and, perhaps above all, confounding to his caretakers, Oe himself and his wife and two younger children, who live in the shadow of Eeyore's sprawling presence. In its candor, this account is also the bravest installment in the idiot-son narratives that are central to Oe's work. Here for the first time he broaches the taboo subject of sexual desire in his retarded son, a child in a man's body with a penis that springs from its confining diaper like "the eight-headed serpent Yamata no Orochi baring its fangs to strike." In a dream, the narrator encounters a malign, reptilian version of Eeyore with his penis bloodied. But he uses the freedom bestowed on him by this imagined moment to divert the implications of the scene away from Eeyore to himself:

> But the malevolence of that image, no less than my bizarre scream, had its origin in me and no one else. This had nothing to do with my son. On the contrary, I felt like turning to myself and saying, "I see! So these are the twisted thoughts that occur at the outer limits of your consciousness when you consider the issue of your son's sexuality now that he's nineteen!"

Elsewhere, Oe levels a similarly unsparing eye on his own motives and behavior. In the kidnapping episode that is an elaboration of an incident that actually occurred, Oe criticizes his own righteousness with devastating accuracy in the student activist's diatribe:

> And ten years from now will your thinking have changed one bit? That's what's so irritating about you—you're like molasses! And what grounds do you have for thinking you're fine just the way you are and will never have to

change? We tried thinking about that from your point of view, and we concluded that your grounds are your handicapped child. . . . Your whole life revolves around your child, you've designed it that way, and your judgment is based on your experience, so outsiders can criticize you until they're blue in the face. Can you deny that?

There is no question that *Rouse Up O Young Men of the New Age!* is grounded in the reality of Oe's experience with his son. But even when the narrator is communicating "actual" moments from his life, he is transforming them in his imagination. Consider the episode in chapter 6 when he recalls his own father's humiliation at the hands of the local police chief. The prefectural governor has stopped at the village on tour in the last year of the war, and his father has been instructed to demonstrate the machine that is used to compress tree bark into bales. When he hesitates—because the press requires two men to operate and his partner is away at war—the police chief barks at him "'You there!'" in a voice that has never been used in the valley before, "not even with the livestock." Later, the youthful narrator deforms the images in his memory of the episode and reassembles them into a vision of social equality in which the humiliation that his father suffered could not have occurred:

The day the governor toured among his constituents and the police chief had lashed my father with his tongue and driven him to make a spectacle of his labor, what if, in that instant, the emperor's proclamation of the war's end had blared from a radio across the entire valley? Then my intrepid father in his cotton smock would have raised his hatchet high in his right hand and ordered the police chief and the governor to take their places at the crank handles and to begin the crunching and clanking. And three or

> so places back in the line, His Majesty the Emperor would
> have been removing his white gloves as he waited his turn
> to go to work. . . .

Imagining an ideal world does not make it so: listening to
a radio broadcast for "junior citizens" just after the war, the narrator realizes that "the social order with the emperor at its apex
had not turned upside down entirely, at least not to the extent
that His Majesty could now be forced to labor at a bark press."

Nonetheless, as Blake demonstrated time and again, the
moral man is obliged to oppose the reality of cruelty or injus-
tice with a redeeming vision. When Eeyore prevents his father
from taking the phone and expresses his own outrage at the student who kidnapped him—an act of defiance that lies far beyond the capacity of the actual Hikari!—his mother worries that
his agitation will provoke a seizure, and Eeyore, in his desire to
calm and console her, asserts an impossibility: "*He was a bad
person. But you don't have to worry, Mama. I won't be angry anymore. There's no bad person anymore. Absolutely!*" Listening at his
son's side, the narrator validates him: "Every man has the right
to his own illusions even if they are nothing more than that, and
the right to express them powerfully." And having echoed a
lesson learned from Blake, he quotes the poet exulting at an illusion of his own (that the French Revolution would make its
way to England): *And the fair Moon rejoices in the clear & cloudless
night; / For Empire is no more, and now the Lion & Wolf shall cease.*

In the original edition of *Rouse Up O Young Men of the New
Age!* the lines of dialogue spoken by "Eeyore" are set in boldface type that leaps from the page. I recently asked Oe what
effect he had intended to achieve with this. "My son's vision is
very poor," he replied, "and I wanted to make it easier for him

to read his own dialogue." I was surprised to see that he was in earnest, for no one knows better than Oe himself that Hikari does not read his father's books. Then I realized it was Eeyore he had in mind.

The principal focus of Oe's effort in *Rouse Up O Young Men of the New Age!* to redeem reality from itself is his handicapped son, Hikari. Born on September 19, 1963, with severe brain damage, Hikari was an enigma as a child, neither laughing nor crying, raptly focused on his own interior world. When he was thirteen, he began to compose short pieces for piano and flute or violin, which allowed him to express feelings for the first time in his life of joy and sadness (Hikari is the only idiot savant in medical history with perfect pitch who is able to compose in his head without first improvising on an instrument). But he remained, and remains today, at thirty-eight, much the same enigmatic presence he was as a child, responding to inquiries from the world outside himself, when he responds at all, with half-sentences that point tantalizingly toward a thought or feeling and then trail off.

Eeyore—or Mori or Jin as he is variously known—was born and raised in Oe's imagination. He, too, is severely retarded, but he transcends his limitations in ways that Hikari is unable to do: most dramatically, he is able to express himself in words, conveying wit and tenderness and compassion and his own brand of reductive wisdom about the world as he experiences it. It is this wisdom that enables him to help his father find his way in a manner that recalls Blake's "lost child."

The premise of *Rouse Up O Young Men of the New Age!* is that the father-narrator is at work on a guidebook to life for the benefit of his severely handicapped son. In fact, it is the idiot son who turns out to be the teacher. The lessons he delivers are about discovering the promise of renewal in a cruel and apparently unredeemable world. At the end of chapter 3, for example, on

the way home from Eeyore's narrow escape from drowning in
the diving tank emblematically known as the "dark pool," the
father is overwhelmed by his chagrin at having failed to act
decisively in the moment of his son's crisis, and Eeyore shows
him a way out of his despair:

> "Eeyore, what's wrong? Are you still feeling bad?"
> "*No! I'm all better,*" he replied emphatically. "*I sank. From
> now on I'm going to swim. I'm ready to swim now!*"

This is more than consolation: Eeyore's eagerness to succeed
where he has failed and his unassailable certainty of success are
an inspiration to his father. In a similar moment of revelation
in chapter 2, it is Eeyore who gives his father the perspective he
needs to live with the fact that the lump that was surgically removed from his son's skull as an infant was a second brain:

> I sat vacantly, unable to resolve my feelings, and Eeyore's
> cheerful surprise at learning the truth, his exultation, pro-
> vided me with a hint. What reason did I have not to be
> as encouraged as he was by this new knowledge? My son
> had come into the world burdened with two brains, but he
> had survived surgery and the aftereffects—doing his best
> though it was extremely painful—and he was standing
> on his own two feet.

In the second half of the book, Eeyore's relationship to his
father undergoes a change. He has already been transformed
from a menace into a source of consolation and a mentor; now,
as if he has stepped into Blake's vision of Albion, the Everyman
in whom all mankind is redeemed, he seems to hold out the
promise of redemption, very much as if he were his father's savior. In the beatific dream in which Eeyore appears as a radiant

youth, the narrator is given to understand that his son has the power to reveal to him the hidden meaning of his life. And on Christmas Eve, as Eeyore leads the handicapped children in a final chorus from inside Gulliver's papier-mâché foot, his father believes that connecting to his son will give him the courage he will need to combat his own destiny:

> Until now, it had been my goal to provide definitions of things and people for Eeyore's sake; but at this moment it was Eeyore, presenting me with a stanza from Blake's *Milton* as a lucid vision, who was creating a definition for his father:

> *Then first I saw him in the Zenith as a falling star,*
> *Descending perpendicular, swift as the swallow or swift;*
> *And on my left foot falling on the tarsus, enter'd there*

> This vision went on, however, to unfurl an urgent, baleful image of a black cloud redounding from my right foot to cover Europe, my contemporary world. And as if in hopes of finding courage to confront that ominous image, I lifted my own voice and truly began to sing.

In the concluding chapter, as in a grand fugue, Oe achieves an ecstatic resolution of the two incompatible domains that are the subject of his chronicle, the historical reality in which Hikari resides and the pure land of the imagination, a land of possibility and promise, represented by Eeyore. But first he must discover access for himself and his father-narrator to the faith that informs Blake's own visions. Earlier, the father has "superimposed" the figure of his son on "the radiantly joyful figure of Albion, that most good and beautiful form of humankind itself." Now he steps inside the faith he needs by superimposing his "rain tree" on Blake's "tree of life":

In this way, reading Blake, I happened on *The Tree of Life,* an illustration that resembled my own image of the rain tree. . . . I realize it may sound far-fetched—and it is an odd thing to write in light of what I myself had said to H on his deathbed, that I did not believe in Christianity and had no knowledge of it—but I did feel in the presence of something like grace (I overcome my hesitation to use the word by telling myself that it was only through the agency of T's music that grace became possible). Nevertheless, it is, or feels like, grace that encourages me forward in the direction of the "forgiveness of sin" that is at the heart of Jesus' thought in his dialogue with Albion.

In the culminating scene of the book, the idiot son rejects the name "Eeyore" and declines to join his family at the dinner table until his brother addresses him as Hikari. Watching his sons approach the table, the narrator's thoughts turn to Blake's preface to *Milton:*

> With Blake as my guide, I beheld a phantasm of my sons as young men of a new age, a baleful, atomic age, which would require them the more urgently to set their foreheads against the ignorant Hirelings, and I could assuredly feel myself at their side, reborn as another young man. Presently, when old age approached and the time had come to endure the agony of death, I would hear the words proclaimed by the voice from The Tree of Life in encouragement to all Humankind as though they were spoken to me and to me alone: *Fear not Albion unless I die thou canst not live / But If I die I shall arise again & Thou With me.*

Hikari means "light." When Eeyore steps into the radiance that is his birthright, he liberates his father into an ecstatic vi-

sion of renewal and redemption that enfolds not only the fic-
tive father and son but Oe and Hikari and his brother as well,
and which indeed extends to all Mankind. Once and for all, tri-
umphantly, the superior power of the imagination over grim
reality has been proclaimed and demonstrated. *And the fair Moon
rejoices in the clear & cloudless night; / For Empire is no more, and
now the Lion & Wolf shall cease.*

John Nathan
Montecito, California
June 21, 2001